CW00867115

THE HIDDEN DUCHESS

SPINSTERS OF THE NORTH

BOOK I

ISABELLA THORNE

Mikita Associates

COPYRIGHT

The Hidden Duchess

All rights reserved

This is a work of fiction. Names, characters, places and incidents are the products of the author's imagination and are used fictitiously. Any resemblance to actual persons, living or dead, events, or locales is entirely coincidental.

No part of this publication maybe reproduced, stores, or transmitted in any form or by any means, electronic, mechanical, photocopying, recording, scanning, or otherwise without written permission from the publisher.

The Hidden Duchess © 2022 by Isabella Thorne
Cover Art by Mary Lepiane

202 Mikita Associates Publishing
Published in the United States of America.

www.isabellathorne.com

CHAPTER 1

The wind raged against the latticed windowpanes of Miss Caroline Grave's darkened bedchamber. It rattled the windows, not unlike the masked assailant in the worn novella currently hidden beneath Miss Caroline's down filled quilt. The man pounded on the door, determined to take hostage the heroine of the book. Caroline stared out at the rain. Such imaginings were the only type of adventure that she was ever likely to have herself. She sat up and craned her neck toward a flicker of light that had appeared on the opposite side of the glass. Down below, someone had arrived. Miss Caroline listened, but could not make out voices.

A visitor? In this storm? At this hour? She wondered, but the chill of the room kept her from investigating. It would not be proper for a lady to roam the manor at night, in her bedclothes no less. Rather, she pulled the soft blankets up to her chin and told herself that Archibald, her father's butler, could redirect the travelers who had likely made a wrong turn in the downpour. More likely, the old grump had left the mundane duty to the under-butler. Such an event was commonplace and really not worth even thinking on, but it was late for a traveler. Her father, Baron Wickham, had many friends and acquaintances with whom Caroline was not familiar. She was a child of his second marriage, a love match, and most of Father's friends and their grown children were older than herself and already married. Caroline was acquainted with most, but did not know them well.

Yet, her mind turned again to the pages squirrelled away beneath her quilt. Perhaps, because her mind was already on intrigue, she wondered about the late-night visitors. Her heart raced as she wondered if they might be bandits. Maybe the French had made shore and trudged all the way to Northwickshire with the sole purpose of taking Gravesend Manor. At that thought, she giggled. It was a ridiculous and fantastical notion. Such things never happened in the humdrum lives of countrified nobility. Not really. Oh, one might hear of a lady gone missing here or there, but it always turned out that she had made a break for

Gretna Green, had taken a detour to Bath to take the waters, or some other foolish nonsense. Nothing exciting ever happened to Miss Caroline or even any of her acquaintances. Life was nothing like the grand adventures the heroines had in her novels.

Marilee, her lady's maid, often scolded her for reading tales which gave her such flights of fancy. "If you crave an adventure, then ask your father to take you to London when next Lords is in session," she would say with a petulant sigh. Marilee loved London and the bustle of the city, but she also loved her mistress. They were, first and foremost, dearest friends after such long years as companions. Such affection did not keep the maid from reminding the irregular lady that Marilee's nimble-fingered talent was wasted so far from the appreciative glances of the *Ton*.

Caroline would grumble that she would never return to the dreaded town where her mother had died of a sudden fever at the conclusion of Caroline's first, and only, season six long years ago. They had made quite an affair of the trip, as they always had for excursions to town, but this time had been different. Caroline had at last come out and there were parties and splendor and even offers from two droll gentlemen. Had she chosen to accept, she might be married with children of her own by now, she thought, but that had not come to pass. None of her suitors were interesting in the least, and she could not imagine spending a lifetime by their side.

She was nearly an old maid now at four and twenty, but Miss Caroline had been born willful and could never have been persuaded to such a dismal suit. Besides, Mama had fortified her decision with a wink and a promise that the season next would be even better. This first had been a dip of the toes, a test of the waters, Mother had said. Caroline had been only eighteen, after all. It had meant to be the most magical time of her life, and yet it had become instead her darkest memory. Six years had passed since that first season. Caroline was a spinster now and still refused to be courted. She remained in the country with her father.

Marilee would cluck her tongue and tease that, if not for her lady's sake, then the maid herself would relish a handsome face to look upon every now and then. Even better if the gentleman came with a fetching pair of valets so she could make her own choice, Marilee teased. "Put down your pages and peer at the world," her friend had oft been heard to say. "The best years of your life are passing you by."

Caroline would chuckle as she turned her resolute nose back to her books. There were no men worth a stolen glance at Gravesend Manor, nor was there like to be in the foreseeable future. None compared to the heroes of her novels; men who were resolute and honorable, although often misunderstood. She longed to bring such a man out of his doldrums, and for her effort, he would love her forever, but she knew such fancies belong only in fairy stories. Real life rarely turned out so neat. Real life villains often won the day and good people died. Happily-ever-after was a childish myth. She sighed. Why on earth was she so melancholic?

Perhaps it was the detestable rain. She snuggled down in the covers and turned the page of her book, leaning closer to the candle for light. She squinted. It was getting too dark to see the page, even with the help of the lone candle. The fire had burned to embers. There was no help for her there. She could get up and stir the embers and perhaps coax a bit more light from the fire, but the bed was so comfy with her bedwarmer at her feet. She was loath to budge. She closed the book and sighed.

Miss Caroline was disenchanted with what had become of her life. She was an only child and her mother had assured long before her death she would be granted the freedom of independent wealth even after the barony would pass beyond her father's line. The baron would have done anything asked by his beloved wife. He had, in those days, been devoted to nothing more so than the baroness, his second wife and first love, and their precious daughter. So it happened that Miss Caroline's allowance was such that she had no pressing need of a husband, really no need at all, and therefore possessed a definitive lack of enthusiasm to continue the hunt for a suitable match. She simply enjoyed her Season until her mother died and her whole world collapsed.

After her mother's stately funeral, Caroline had retired to her father's seat in Northwickshire and decided to forego the whole matter. Her father had not pressed the issue. He perhaps forgot for a while that he even had a daughter. She might have withdrawn to the countryside, but he had withdrawn into himself. He rarely even traveled the short distance to the little hamlet of Northwick. The loss of his true love had shattered the man, so much so. that he could hardly bring himself to look upon his daughter, whose features were eerily similar to that which he had lost. Caroline had outright refused to move forward without her mother to share in those most bonding of moments between a woman and her child.

Furthermore, she would not subject herself to the cold resignation that she had learned had been the stuff of her father's first marriage. He had found his first match attractive, he had told her, but he had never loved the woman. Theirs had been a union of bitter necessity. Although Caroline had never truly learned all the details, as Father only said he was a foolish and careless youth. Marilee had gleaned from the servant's whispers that the pair had been caught in a compromising embrace, and although both parties protested, they had been obligated to wed. The marriage had lasted only two years, although not through any fault of either. The tragic union had ended in an even more tragic manner. Lady Anne, and her babe, had both died in childbirth. Such an event had made Caroline's beloved mother, as well as her own uneventful entrance into this world, all the more precious to the baron.

Miss Caroline shook her head. No, she had no interest in marriage for the sake of marriage. She would much rather live through the fantastical events of her imaginings than face the harsh reality that life would never be what it had ought to have been. Miss Caroline tried to put these thoughts from her mind, thoughts and memories that only seemed to surface in the darkest hours of night.

The light outside her window flickered and then faded away. Who had been wandering in the night was gone now. With a she rolled over and pulled the coverlet over her head. No more than a minute later, her breathing slowed, and she fell fast asleep.

CHAPTER 2

The following morning, Miss Caroline noted that the weather gave no sign of ceasing its deluge. Caroline allowed Marilee to button her into a cheerful yellow housedress while the pair mused that the color looked to be the only spot of sunshine in their entire day.

"I shall have to bask in your rays whenever our paths do cross," the maid giggled, pretending to shield her eyes with the back of her hand.

"Ah, but do be careful," Miss Caroline replied with a devilish grin, "for I've been known to leave a burn."

Marilee's mouth puckered to the side as if she were deep in thought. Then, she waved her hand with a quick motion that drew Caroline's eyes to the iron in her hand. "Is this to be a contest?" the maid drawled with an air of superiority.

"I certainly hope not!" Miss Caroline let out a squeal and leaned away from the hot iron. Her feigned fear soon gave way to a hearty laugh as she declared, "You are the clear victor! You are the sun, Marilee! The Sun!"

"Don't fret, my lady," Marilee basked in her triumph. She gave her mistress two pats upon her head to declare their peace. Caroline righted in her seat and prepared to have her locks clamped so that the pomade might hold the neat ringlets that were meant to frame her face for the duration of the day. Miss Caroline's fine blonde hair was naturally straight, and it was only through Marilee's practiced care that the stubborn locks would bend at all. "I would never mar such a pretty canvas. Besides," she shivered, "then I might be sent off to dress someone truly odious."

"Am I only mostly odious?" Caroline pondered.

"Only half," Marilee replied. Her wink bespoke the lie and the true depth of their affection.

"Ah, well," Caroline grinned. "Half is not so bad considering you have naught but my features to look upon each morning."

Marilee sighed with exaggerated longing, set the iron back in the bowl of coals, and leaned forward so her chin rested upon Caroline's shoulder. She gave her best version of pleading eyes. "If not a valet, I would settle for a fine footman." Their eyes met in the mirror. "Or perhaps even a young stable master. Oh, how I should ride!" She winked at Caroline.

"You are incorrigible!" Caroline blushed and swatted at her friend.

A knock at the door had the women turning. Marilee answered and the housekeeper, Mrs. Prats, stepped in. Mrs. Prats was a rotund woman with a round face and a round belly. She always had a smile for Caroline, and indeed, after mother had died, Mrs. Prats stepped seamlessly into the role, sheltering Caroline and the other girls of the household who were heartbroken with grief. She had been the housekeeper for as long as Caroline could remember, although Caroline did not ever remember a Mr. Prats.

"You're wanted in the drawing room, my lady," the housekeeper said with a nod much more formal than her usual winks and smiles. Her fading Scottish accent and maternal demeanor had always given Caroline the impression of a clucking hen collecting her chicks. Caroline counted herself lucky to be considered one of those chicks. Mrs. Prats and Marilee offered their love and friendship when Father had only become withdrawn with grief. The last six years would have been very different without Marilee and Mrs. Prats.

"Does Papa want me?" Miss Caroline said with narrowed eyes. "I saw him yesterday." She waved her hand as if the obligation had been met. Her father would ask for her in another day or two. They would sit for a silent tea service, and then Caroline would ask about the tenants, to which he would offer only monosyllabic replies. She would comment on the weather and some movement or tone or look would remind him of her mother. His face would draw closed with a stab of pain, and he would abruptly excuse himself until when next he could stomach her presence. Such was their usual discourse.

"Yes. My lord," Mrs. Prats nodded, "and his guest."

"Beg pardon?" Miss Caroline scoffed at the same time as Marilee snorted in disbelief.

"A carriage came by in the wee hours, it did," Mrs. Prats explained. "The byway's washed clear through with the spring rains and so the gentleman came here instead. Knows my lord. Carron said," Mrs. Pratt provided as explanation. Caroline nodded. Mr. Carron was the butler. He would know the truth of the matter.

Caroline and Marilee stood up straight with interest, one with feminine curiosity and the other with nothing more than surprise. Only now did Miss Caroline recall the light she had seen the previous night. Either she had forgotten, or simply thought it a dream. Either way, the memory had been entirely lost to her until this very moment.

"Who is it?" Caroline asked, thinking that it might have been someone she had made acquaintance with all those years ago.

"I'd have told you if I'd known," the housekeeper clucked. "I've been too preoccupied all morning getting his rooms ready to poke about such nonsense." She nodded. "He's a duke, I'll give you that much."

"A duke! Is he young?" Caroline asked.

Marilee clasped her hands to her heart and sighed at Miss Caroline's romantic assumptions.

"Is he married?" Caroline continued.

Her questions went unanswered because the house-keeper had already turned upon her heel and exited the room, muttering something that sounded suspiciously like ninnies and death of me under her breath, but truth be told, if he was a duke, he was old. They all were. Only in books were dukes young and handsome and dashing.

. . .

A QUARTER HOUR LATER, MISS CAROLINE WAS READY to enter the drawing room. Marilee had added some final touches to her appearance and pinched some color into her pale cheeks.

"What a tale that would be," Caroline had sighed. "The fated storm demands that a quiet, but attractive, duke hole up for a fortnight," for that was the amount of time they recalled that it usually took the byway to drain.

"Only to fall madly in love with the young mistress of the house," Marilee continued the story laughing. "Without the storm, they'd have never met and so they owe their wedded bliss to some Grecian weather god or pagan harvest ritual which brought about the torrential rains."

"My word, Marilee! Don't let the Vicar hear you say such things. Pagan indeed!"

"The Vicar is on the other side of the byway! With the inns!" Marilee had giggled. "And if the Duke of Bramblewood did not give the vicar an apoplexy over Christmastide, I'm sure my mere words will not move him."

Caroline shook her head but could not help but feel her pulse quicken as she had descended the staircase. With every step nearer to the drawing-room door her anticipation grew exponentially until she had to force herself to tread slowly and stifle a smile as she tapped on the door and waited her father's invitation to enter before she crossed the threshold.

The draperies were drawn against the wet chill, but she knew the room well: the massive old furniture and the somewhat faded carpet which Father had not replaced, not due to lack of coin, but simply because he did not wish to change anything. A roaring fire burned, but she did not need its light to see the man who stood next to her father. Despite her knowledge of reality, she could not have helped but be persuaded somewhere deep within that it would have been something if the visitor were indeed a young, unmarried duke. What kind of something, she wasn't sure. But something indeed; a fairy story, perhaps.

"Caroline," her father beckoned her with an outstretched hand. "Come meet the Duke of Manchester. His Grace, George Bennington, my daughter, Miss Caroline Graves." The surname had rung a distant bell of familiarity, but for the moment, she could not say why.

From behind her father's towering form stepped another, nearly as tall as the Baron himself. But where her father was wide but firm, this man was sagged and paunchy, as if he had willingly spent every day in his life in excess. The Baron's hair was thinner than it had been five years past, but still dark and flowing. The duke's, well, the duke had hardly any to spare. His face had fashioned upon it what she thought must be his polite attempt at a smile, but she found that in his irritation it was rather more of a sneer. His cheeks were reddened as if the two men had been having a most unpleasant discussion. The annoyance in her father's eyes told her that she had been a welcome intrusion.

This man was quite simply everything opposite that she and her maid had imagined, except, perhaps, his remarkable height. His watery blue eyes were disconcerting.

"Father," Caroline stepped forward with an elegant nod and then dipped into a formal curtsey. "Your Grace."

The introductions made; Caroline had been forced to pull her hand away when it seemed that the duke held on a bit longer than felt proper. His gaze was assessing, as if he were the sort of man who always looked to make a play with his connections. In a way, she supposed that was true of all men, especially those of consequence and perhaps, most women as well.

"To think," the duke mused as if the topic were perfectly usual, "My sister gave birth to a disfigured whelp that killed her and yet you still managed to produce this. Life is not fair."

Bennington, she recalled now. Lady Anne Bennington, her father's first wife. This, she noted, was the belated woman's brother. Caroline had not known much about the woman's family. Not that any remained, and certainly not their status. It was no wonder Lady Anne had been disowned. Very likely her family had had higher aspirations for her than a baron.

"I have long heard whispers of your beauty, Lady Graves," the duke continued, "but I see now that the rumors fall short. You are... most delicious." He gestured at her, at all of her, with appreciation. It was as if she were a confection standing before them for examination and not a living being with agency of her own.

Miss Caroline shivered and then ground her teeth together, but gave no other indication that she had even heard the base comment. She had never encouraged the fascination with her physical features. In fact, since her mother had passed, she had made a concerted effort to downplay her innate beauty. Although there was little she could do about her grey eyes, which were by far her most startling feature. She shivered with disgust at the way the older gentleman's features had altered from disdain for her father to nearly salivating at the sight of her. She had been trained better, however, and her father's warning hand upon her arm told her that holding her tongue had been the right thing. The duke might have taken the gesture as mere fatherly affection, but she knew otherwise. Her father hadn't touched her in years and the rigid way his fingers pressed into her skin warned that this man was not to be trifled with. She knew that. He was, after all, a duke.

If the duke was to be stranded with them, and her father was clearly unnerved by the prospect, she would need to do all that she could to ensure civil interactions. Best to face the horns of the bull and be done with it, she decided.

"Your sister?" Caroline asked with feigned ignorance.

"Yes," the duke narrowed his eyes on her before they flicked sharply to her father. "The baron's first wife. Or has he not spoken of her at all?" A neat trap, Miss Caroline thought, but she would not be caught. She verbally stepped around it.

"He has, indeed," she replied with a gentle grin. "I have been told that she was very beautiful and that her death was mourned by all here at Gravesend Manor."

"According to custom," the duke nodded, clearly finding no fault with her reply and yet, it seemed, still determined to needle her father. "Although I doubt with anything but relief. A daughter," he blew out a sharp puff of air. "Had Anne birthed a son, however…" He let the words and their implication hang in the air.

"I did everything…" her father began to spit out, but Caroline took one more half step forward and intersected the men.

"Allow me to assure you otherwise, Your Grace." She looked up at her father with an honest smile this time, recalling her childhood. There was a bitter pang at the loss of what they had once shared, but she squelched it before it could bear witness on her face. "He was a most devoted father and husband," she said pointedly, "although I was of the lesser sex and was not an heir." Her cheery tone made it impossible for the duke to make another dig before she continued.

She offered a smile and redirected the conversation by asking the duke about the byway and how he had come to be such a welcomed guest in their quiet home. He may have a long-standing issue to take with her father, but habit and breeding had him donning his etiquette cap when it came to conversing with a lady. It was with a breath of relief that the tension in the room eased, and the gentlemen began talking of more practical things.

It was no wonder they had been near fisticuffs before she had come into the room, she thought. If this were the brother of the nearly ruined Lady Anne, and he somehow blamed the Baron for the woman's death all those years ago, then it was no wonder at all. Although her father had done his duty through marriage, it was always the lady's honor that bears the shame. A gentleman's indiscretions are easily overlooked. A man might bow to a lustful moment, but a woman must not. Not ever. Redemption, Caroline had learned, was rarely for the female. No, the sins of the female lived in infamy, much like that first sin of Eve.

She sat with her father and his guest for an hour before her father asked, "Did you not say you had better finish your painting today before the last of the blossoms fall and you lose your scene?" Caroline blinked at him.

"Off you go," her father said.

Caroline's mouth popped open, but she used the movement to reply.

"I did," she lied with an assured nod. She hated painting. She had never had any skill for painting or drawing. She preferred the out of doors, and riding her beautiful mare, Bella. Her major feminine accomplishments lay firmly in the musical arts of pianoforte and harpsichord. She could even sing passably. More than passably if she were to be honest. Yet, her father could not have asked her to practice those talents without the odd chance of the duke asking for an impromptu concert. It was clear she was meant to be shooed away. She would speak to Father about the reason at a later time. Now, she stood to leave and bid farewell to the gentlemen.

As Caroline made her way up the stairs to do heavens only knew what, for the next several hours under the illusion of artistic enrapture, she could not help but wonder what in the devil was going on in her father's mind. She certainly had no desire to spend an excessive amount of time with the duke, but he was their guest. As Lady of the house, she ought to be making an effort to at least keep him from coming to blows with the Baron. Had she not already proven that she could maneuver the conversation with ease? Furthermore, she was already cooped up in the Manor due to the torrents of rain that still came down out of doors, she did not need to be further relegated to a silent and hidden afternoon. There was her book, but she had already read it twice, and she did not appreciate being relegated to the sidelines.

She stomped the last two steps, just for good measure. She was far enough away that the gentlemen would not have heard, but Marilee certainly would. True to form, the maid's head popped out into the hall from Caroline's dressing room, where she had been doing the mending.

"Don't you dare scuff those slippers," Marilee hissed. Then her face shifted into a conspiratorial grin. She looked one way down the hall and then the other. "Well, come on." She swung the door open for Caroline to join her within. "Tell me everything."

CHAPTER 3

Caroline was summoned to her father's study thirty minutes prior to the time that she would have usually come down to join the gentlemen in the dining hall. She had expected to find the baron and his guest sharing brandy before the evening meal, but was surprised to find her father alone, pacing before the wide window that overlooked the lawn.

"Father?" She asked as she struck her knuckles along the frame of the doorway to announce her presence.

"Come," he said with a sense of urgency that immediately piqued her interest. "Close the door behind you." She did as he instructed and then crossed the room to join him at the window. In silence, she waited for an explanation. "Bennington won't be long dressing for dinner, so we haven't much time," her father muttered. Then, with piercing grey eyes, the only feature she had inherited from him, he turned to her. "You must not catch his attention, do you understand?"

Her brows furrowed. She did not. She certainly had given no indication that she wanted the duke's attention, had merely fulfilled her expected proprieties. Good heavens, he was more than twice her age! Even though he was a duke, she had no intention of marrying an old man. She had no intention of marrying at all.

Her father sighed and ran a hand down his long face. "He has already taken far too much interest in your beauty," the Baron explained with a grimace. She knew he must be thinking of her mother. "You must be careful. Your unwillingness to bend in fear of him will only drive him further. He is cunning and, given the opportunity, will view that as a challenge." Her father fixed her with a serious stare. "He is…" Father dithered a bit, which was unlike him. He usually said what he meant, and Caroline got much of her brash attitude from him.

"Is what?" Caroline persisted.

Father sucked in a breath. "Perhaps, he is a bit of a rake."

"At his age?" Miss Caroline challenged, thinking that such passions cooled with age.

"His age is of no consequence. Caroline, take care that you do not catch his eye. Best if he were to forget you are even here. As difficult as it is, be nondescript. Forgettable."

"I shall keep my tongue," she promised, but this did not seem to satisfy. It seemed that what she had thought was helpful to her father's plight this afternoon had been cause for concern. Perhaps he had not wished to mend bridges, she realized. Perhaps he had meant to bore the duke with brevity so that he would wish nothing more than to be on his way. She shivered at the thought that the gentleman would ever attempt to win her affections. She could think of no world where she would find him appealing. Some ladies might stoop so low as to make a play for his title, but not Caroline. Besides, from their conversation this afternoon she was well aware that the duke had been a widower for nigh on two decades. If he had not taken a wife by now, then certainly even she did not possess enough charm to turn his head, even if she had desired it. Which she did not. Title or no, if Caroline wanted to marry, she would not choose a man nearer to her father's age than her own.

"That is not enough," Her father continued. He went on to explain that she could neither be too demure, nor too disinterested. She could not be overly friendly, nor cross. She ought not to show her accomplishments or offer any shared interests.

"What am I to be, then?" she laughed. Certainly, her father was overreacting. Cunning though the duke may be, he had no reason to even look twice at her. Not to mention that it was clear that a rift existed between the two men. Caroline could not see how the duke would not simply bide his time, waiting for the road to be open and then hasten his retreat as soon as the byway was cleared.

"You are to be nothing," Father explained. "Make yourself scarce, dull, not worth a second thought. And wear something loose that does not cling to your figure. He must not see you."

Surely Father was over reacting. "I can assure you that there is no reason to think that His Grace would ever--"

Father cut her off. "He would," Father whispered. "He would if only to…"

She put her hand upon his arm, confusion twisting her features. For a father who had hardly deigned to look at her these past years, she could not understand the sudden concern that wracked his features. Even if the duke attempted to woo her, she would simply turn him away. The matter was as straightforward as that. As for an indiscretion, she would not even consider it. She would never be so silly as to be used as a method of revenge upon her father.

She smiled and put her hand on her father's forearm. "We may not always be close, Papa, but you are my father, and I love you."

He seemed completely undone by her declaration.

"I shall do as you say, Papa," she murmured. She stretched up on her toes and pressed a kiss to his cheek, surprised when he did not turn away. She then altered her voice, putting on her ruse and ending the conversation. "I'm not feeling well, anyway," she said with authority. "Perhaps you could have a tray sent to my room."

Her father was about to respond when the handle of the door turned and the duke let himself into the room. With a witness, it would be too late to cry off now when it was clear that she was not only well in health but had also dressed for the evening. Drat, she thought.

"Ah!" their intruder crooned. "I see that we have all gathered." He patted his rotund midsection and crooked his elbow at Caroline. "Shall we go in?"

CAROLINE HAD NOT BEEN ABLE TO WHEEDLE OUT OF that first dinner, although she made a point of finding herself unavailable for the following three. That did not stop the duke from hunting her down throughout the manor and even on the grounds. If she sat in the drawing room, he came to sit, calling for tea to keep her trapped. When she took her prized mare, Bella, out for a ride, he appeared atop a hillcrest astride his enormous black gelding. If she was in the library, he found himself in need of company and, "would she read aloud to him?" She dared not even play an instrument for fear that the sound would draw him out. The baron did his best to keep their guest distracted, but his own duties, and the frantic coordination of aide in the byway repair, required precious moments of his day. Besides, her father could not reveal that the duke's interest in his daughter bothered him, for that would only increase the gentleman's fervor. Caroline did not know why it was that the men could not come to agreeable terms, nor why she had any role to play in their feud. But as an innocent bystander, it was all that she could do, to not stoke the flames.

On the fourth day, the rain had ceased. When she had ventured out into the sun-filled gardens with her latest book in hand, she had allowed herself a breath of relief at the escape from the constant cloister of recent days. Her father had suggested a hunt comprised of the handful of nobles who were likewise isolated on this side of the crossing. Such an event would keep the gentlemen occupied for a large portion of the afternoon. While she would later be required to join the resulting feast, the presence of the hunting party and other guests would give Caroline ample opportunity to avoid the duke. The reprieve was short-lived and her heart sank when, with only one thrilling chapter left in the tale that she had been bent over for the bulk of the afternoon, she saw the duke ambling across the lawn toward her. She mumbled a curse most unbefitting of a lady before standing to greet him with an empty smile. Her book fell closed, losing her place. Drat. She was aching to know how the story in her novel ended. She did not even want to be civil to the duke right now.

"Your Grace," she said with a perfunctory curtsey. She glanced at her discarded book. Perhaps he would take the hint. He did not.

"Has the party returned so soon?" She made a point of craning her neck toward the stables, but saw no one else. A shiver of apprehension went through her. Not even Marilee was available to attend her.

He shook his head. "I'm afraid I had need to stay behind at the last moment," he drawled. "I had a letter that required my immediate attention." There was frustration in his tone. Whatever the correspondence, he was not happy about it.

"Perhaps you could still catch up to the hunt," she suggested. "They must be southwest of the house by now. If you cross the southern paddock, I am sure…"

"No," he grinned. His eyes narrowed, and she felt him assessing her, the fact that she was alone. "I cannot say that I am in the mood to hunt stag."

What was he in the mood to hunt? She shivered at the thought. Her. Could he mean that he would hunt her? Or perhaps something more sinister? There was a gleam in his eye that her limited acquaintance made difficult to interpret, but she trusted her father's words of caution.

"What a shame that you shall miss out on the triumph," she declared, taking a step toward the house. Perhaps she could call for an early tea which would bring the servants, but she did not want to spend so much time with him, even with the servants hovering. Her mind raced for an excuse to bolt that would do nothing to drive his predatory instincts. She had little reason or interest in bandying words with her father's guest.

"I shall have my victory," he laughed, deep and rich. The sound rattled her. It told her that he was used to having his way, expected nothing less. He took a step forward. "I always do." He made a flippant gesture with his hand. "Even when fate might twist all well-laid plans. There is always a solution if one persists."

"Oh?" she wondered. It was now clear that although her initial instincts had put her on edge, he was not speaking of her. His mind was elsewhere. It was likely, she deduced, that he was still ruminating over the correspondence that had kept him locked away for so many hours. She loosed a discreet breath of relief.

"Walk with me," he declared, without a hint of question in his voice. It was a command, and she obeyed, leaving her book on the bench and falling in step beside him. "There is nothing quite so effective, Miss Caroline," he said as he plucked a budding flower from a neighboring bush and pressed it into her hand, "as a show of strength to one's enemies. When one suffers a loss, a rally must be made and ground recovered."

"And have you enemies?" she asked. She wasn't daft enough to inquire after details as to whatever loss he may have suffered. She continued down the path, forcing him to keep pace or be left behind. A small quirk at the edge of his mouth was the only indication that he acknowledged her own, albeit small, feminine attempt at wresting control. Yes, she thought, she understood the complexities of social maneuvers just as well as he.

"Haven't we all?" he asked. When she assured him that she did not, he laughed outright. "Your father has enough to cover your lack, and I," he chuckled even deeper, "Well, I have twice the amount as he. Snakes in the grass, as it were. Though, while he prefers the quiet of the country, I pride myself on living in the thick of it and remaining always one step ahead."

"That seems a terrible way to pass one's days," she replied, "always wondering when some next fell moment should occur."

"You get used to it," he grumbled. Then he turned to her with a wry grin. "In fact, I would wager my entire fortune that you, Miss Caroline, would excel in such circumstances."

"Then you would soon be a pauper," she laughed, "for I have no stomach for intrigue and falsehood."

"No," he agreed. "I can see as much there. However, that is not what I meant and you well know it."

She raised her chin but said nothing, reminding herself that her entire goal these past days was to avoid his insight into her wit and will. Both aspects of her nature she feared would be most appealing to the duke. "You may not have a liking for it, but you have a skill for observation and a keen ability to play the role you deem necessary. Of that, there can be no doubt. You have done that much and more these past days with deft precision. Do you take me for a fool? You have given me little, or nothing, to hold interest, and yet the determination with which you withhold yourself is exactly that which has captured my attention. There is much more to Miss Caroline Graves than a mindless, unaccomplished bore, I think. The fact that you are a spinster by choice and not necessity spoke volumes even before my valet went digging."

She opened her eyes wide, surprised that he gave her a second thought.

"A cask of ale in a circle of men will loose even the tightest of tongues." His voice trailed off in thought, but his eyes remained firmly upon her. "A fascinating tool to whomever holds you in their arsenal."

"It is fortunate, then," she said with disinterest, although in truth her hackles were raised and bristling, "that I am not for sale."

"No?" he mused. "Who isn't? Your father won't be around forever. His title, these lands, will pass on to his nephew. Then what?"

"I have enough to live a comfortable life as I choose. My mother saw to it."

"Your mother," he said, and Caroline realized she should not have spoken of her mother. It brought to mind her father's first wife, his sister.

"Yes," he said sharply. "I remember her. You look like her. Beautiful as well as resourceful."

Caroline said nothing for a moment, stilled in the fear of the direction this conversation was taking. "Shall we have tea," she said, hastening towards the house.

He caught her arm, and her reaction was instantaneous, the reaction any young woman of quality might have when touched by a man, especially if that touch was unwanted. "Unhand me," she hissed, and his reaction was almost as automatic as her own. He released her but a moment later, his hand still rested upon her arm. "I have a better solution," he said leaning close. "Accept my offer." The acrid scent of stale cigar smoke permeated the man's breath and clothing.

Caroline felt at once that she would retch. "What offer is that?" she said playing dumb and hoping to gain a moment's time. There was nothing, absolutely nothing, which could entice her to marry the Duke of Manchester. Even if he weren't the most loathsome creature she had ever met, even if her own father had not warned her against him, he had all but told her she was nothing more than a sword to be wielded at his whim. Or, at the very least, a solution to whatever upset he had just been dealt. Still, she could not insult him. He was a duke. The repercussions against her father could be great. A duke would have the ear of the throne, distant relation or no, and one did not incur the wrath of a duke or the throne lightly.

"If you'll excuse me, Your Grace," she said with a deep curtsy before extricating herself and making to step around him and race toward the manor. If only she might pretend, she had not heard. "I'm afraid I forgot…"

"You didn't forget a god's damned thing," he snarled and grabbed her forearm, none too gently this time. Anything light about his tone melted away to cold and steel. "I asked you to marry me and any lady in her right mind would know to accept."

"Then my mind must surely be addled!" she shot back. She wrenched her arm out of his grasp and stared at him with open fury. Be damned what her father had warned her, for the duke had seen through the play either way. "For I would not marry you for all the stars in the heavens." She felt at once that her words were quite the most extravagant thing she could have said and yet, she meant them to her very core.

The duke snarled at her, baring his teeth as if to say that he could not possibly care less about her opinion. Only his opinion mattered to him.

"I've lost an heir, Miss Caroline, the only one worth his salt. The other is a womanizer and worthless."

Caroline bit her lip to keep from shouting, then the apple does not fall far from the tree. Instead, she held her tongue.

"I tell you this now. I will have a wife and it will be you!" He spun on his heel and made for the stables. Even though Caroline watched him mount his steed and race off at full speed, she could not bring herself to move. Rather, she stood there trembling for several long moments before finally going indoors. A wife? No, she thought. He didn't want a wife. He wanted a brood mare and one that could hold her own against the bite of London. The loss of an heir could be devastating to a bloodline in uncertain times but that was not her problem to solve.

Manchester had a spare; she had heard him speak of both of his sons. The eldest may have passed, but the other remained alive and in good health for all she could tell. Sure, he might be a rake but that wasn't all that uncommon. He would simply have to marry. Then the Duke would have no issue ensuring the continuation of the line unless some other fell happening took place. The odds of the loss of both sons by separate means were unfortunate but unlikely. Why the duke held such fascination for having two in line at all times was beyond Caroline's comprehension. His wife had borne two sons, two male heirs without even the complication of a daughter. How many women throughout the ages had failed to provide such an assurance? True, one had died, but one remained. Was that not the sole purpose of having had the second? The duke's lineage would be considered well protected by any reasonable onlooker; an addition to the line would only be a drain on resources. Wouldn't the duke be better off just passing his lot to his son and be done with it? He seemed adamant in his conviction, but Caroline still felt his urgency to be flawed. It was not as if he had loved his eldest. Sure, he thought him the prime example of what a successor ought to be, but even so, neither son had seemed to hold much of the duke's affection so why should he now prefer one so much above the other? Could the younger really be that incompetent? She doubted it. Moreover, why should she care? Rather than dwell on the strange workings of the duke's mind and motivation, she went straight up to her rooms, locked her door and settled on her bed with her book. Inexplicably, she began to cry. Tears streamed down her face unbidden.

CHAPTER 4

Only once before had she felt such a certain, impending sense of uncontrollable doom. That had been the day her mother had died. Then, she had known, had felt, that nothing would ever be the same again. This moment was no different. She had seen it in the duke's eyes. He had made up his mind. She might have refused him, but he would stop at nothing to have his way. He was a duke. He was right. She would not refuse him. She could not. She could only hope that her father would second her refusal. He had to. He must. And hopefully, the duke would relent. Else, where could she run?

Miss Caroline was in no mood for a celebration when the hunting party returned. The wives of their neighbors, noblemen who had joined the hunt, those bound to this side of the flooding, appeared just before nightfall. The boar would be roasted through the night by the servants who had erected a spit out of doors. Tonight, they would feast on the overabundance of the cellar and larder to make room for the fresh meat. It had been a bountiful year, especially after the last spare years when the influenza had wracked the land.

Despite the cheerful banter of their guests, she had little to entice her into conversation. Her father's friends were all nearly twice her age and their children, whom she had interacted with often in earlier years were all married off or away on some visit or other. She was alone in a room full of people. Yet, as she must, she fulfilled her duty by appearing at her father's side while the massive meal was laid in the ornate dining hall. She knew that her father could sense that something was amiss, but she had no way to tell him what had transpired between herself and the duke while they were surrounded by boisterous guests excited to tell the story of the hunt.

After dinner, they withdrew to the music hall where one of her father's closest friends, Sir Adam Jennings, pulled out his lute, as he was like to do on such evenings, so that the ladies might dance. He implored Miss Caroline to pluck the pianoforte at his side, but she refused. The duke watched her with a wry grin.

He seemed to add another tally to the list of things she had hid from him, and he was not wrong in that assumption. Miss Caroline had always enjoyed watching others dance. She even joined the merriment on occasion when her father would allow it, but for the most part, he preferred not to see her laugh and spin as her mother had so loved to do. Part of her longed for that freedom. She missed the feeling of being lost in the movement. More so now on this night when the threat of being torn from her own little paradise hung heavily in the air. Tonight, however, she would remain an observer for her mind was elsewhere.

She had long thought that this would be her life. The simplicity of the country surrounded by people that she knew and loved. Quiet, serenity, and joy without artifice or malice. There was something perfect about life here in Northwickshire. Something that she never wanted to change. Something that she had been certain never would.

She had no recollection of how long she stared at the joyful dancers. It was only when her father's hand settled upon her shoulder that she was startled back into the present. She had not even noticed that he had gotten up from the chair beside her. Nor had she any idea how long he had been gone. She glanced over at Sir Jennings who at some point had switched from a lively jig to the best rendition of a cotillion he could manage without other musicians. How many songs had been played between, she wondered? It seemed that she had been lost in her own thoughts for hours.

"A word," her father said with a nod toward the hall. Miss Caroline's heart leapt into her throat. He was looking at her, truly looking, with eyes full of hurt and sadness. His hand upon her shoulder, so unfamiliar and yet the memory of how he had used to comfort her with such a gesture when she had been a small girl made the moment all that more real.

"What is it, Father?" she asked with concern.

"Not here," he murmured. His eyes flickered to something behind her and she turned just enough to see the Duke of Manchester drinking heartily straight from a pitcher that he had pilfered from a passing servant. Miss Caroline felt ill. The duke looked far too celebratory for her liking. It was unseemly. He clapped a companion on the shoulder, clanged their drinks together, and threw back the last of the ale.

"Father..." she began.

"Not here," the baron repeated. His tone brooked no argument. She could see from the set of his jaw and the pitying way he looked down upon her that he had already made up his mind and determined that she would not like it. That could only mean one thing. Miss Caroline did not care what the duke had said to sway her father. She would fight tooth and nail to change his mind. It was, after all, a decision which would change her life.

Miss Caroline set her shoulders and steeled her iron will. She would speak to her father in private and they were both well aware that she was not like to hide the barbs on her tongue in closed quarters so well as she did under the watchful eyes of others.

Her father took a deep breath and stepped in front of her to lead the way.

So, it was to be a battle of wills, she thought. She bit her lip and kept her mouth closed with some effort.

"I won't do it," she snapped as soon as the door to the study had closed behind her. "I won't marry him. There is nothing that you can say to alter my decision."

"We haven't any choice," the baron murmured as he ran his hand down his face.

"I have every choice," she spat. "Mother made sure that I would always have the choice."

"Do you think so little of me?" he murmured. "We both, your mother and I, thought to give you the freedom to follow your heart. Something that I understand dearly now that I am unable to do so."

"Then why would you force this upon me now?" she asked. How could he have such a change of heart if it was not due to the fact that he had ceased to love her ever since her mother had died?

"The duke is old," he let out an exasperated breath, grasping at straws. "It isn't as if it will be forever."

"No," she let out a breath of disgust. "It could be a year or twenty, but even a day would be too much."

"Darling," he reached to brush a hand over her cheek but she backed away.

"Don't touch me," she spat. "Don't you dare pretend that you care after all these years. What did he give you? What am I worth?" Disgust laced her words, and she looked directly into her father's eyes before landing the final blow. "Or, are you simply so appalled by my presence that you've taken the first opportunity to send me away?"

The hurt in her father's eyes was evident. It was as if he was seeing her clearly for the first time since her mother's passing, seeing the hurt that he had caused her when he had only been thinking about his own pain.

"We have been brought to the point non plus," he repeated.

"You say 'we' as if this has anything to do with you. It doesn't. I am the one who will have to live with him. You can forget all about me. Forget that you even have a daughter. You would like it better that way."

"Never!" he said vehemently.

She glared at her father, tears in her eyes. Glared at him with every ounce of anger that was roiling through her body. Anger and fear she realized but clamped down on the later before it could smother her. "You won't be the one shipped off to become a tenant for life. You are selling me off like a slave. Mother would have protected me.

Her father's face crumpled as if her words had struck true, and she was glad of it. "I am sorry I look so much like her," she added as he drew himself up, took a deep breath and began to speak.

"You are aware that my first marriage was the result of an indiscretion, blasted calf-love, but there is more to that story than even the whispers could have told you."

He sank into his chair defeated, and for a moment she remembered that she loved her father, but she would not give in. She could not.

"You think I do not know the plight of women," he muttered. He cleared his throat and grimaced, as if saying these words aloud made him sick to his stomach. "She was my friend," he said distractedly. "Once the duke and I were friends too," he said sadly. "She said that another man, a lieutenant, had taken her... against her will. She begged me, to offer for her. Pleaded with me to defend her honor."

"Who?" Caroline demanded.

"Anastasia. Anne, my first wife. She was the duke's sister."

Of course, Caroline remembered now, but she could not understand what this had to do with her. There was an indiscretion. They married and now she was dead.

"I did offer for her," her father continued. "But I could not allow such injustice to stand. I sent a formal summons." Father looked across the room as if he could see into history.

"Dueling papers?" Caroline had asked with disbelief.

He shrugged. "I was a fair shot. Besides, I thought the lieutenant would back down, or we would both fire in the air and honor would be served."

She stared at her father. She couldn't imagine him in a duel. He certainly had never mentioned it. Not this

44

quiet, broken man. Still, in the defense of a lady's honor…

"I sent the terms," Father continued. "She would have been twice ruined and this time irrevocably. He was a base-born bastard, and she was so determined that her father never find out." He released a sardonic huff.

"What happened?" Caroline asked with bated breath.

"He died." Her father's voice was a bare whisper. "One shot, and he died. I was aiming over his shoulder but the bullet grazed his neck." Her father was silent, lost in the memory. His words, when he spoke again, were disjointed. "There was so much blood. He was dead in moments."

Caroline put her hand upon her father's arm to try to draw him away from the memories that had glazed his eyes. "You avenged her," she murmured. "There is no shame to be had in that."

"No," he groaned covering his face with his hands.

"The lieutenant *chose* to meet you," Caroline said softly, trying to exonerate her father from his guilt. She knelt in front of him, her hands on his knees.

"I killed an innocent man." Her father's voice was tortured. She had never seen him so beside himself.

Caroline felt her blood run cold, but she could say nothing, only waited for her father to continue.

"He hadn't taken her against her will," he revealed. "It was she who seduced him."

"Oh, Father," she said softly.

"I didn't find out until after we were wed, when she was so triumphant that he had perished."

"Power," he said. "That he would think he could force her into marriage…" He trailed off.

"She had to have the upper hand. She used me to have the upper hand. It's the reason that I was so cold to her in our years together, that hatred that grew and grew and made her brother want to punish me for the love that I refused to give her." He shook his head then, thinking of the past that would not be amended. "I could not love her. Not when she had tricked me into that. Not when she had used me to her own ends; put innocent blood on my hands." He grasped Caroline's own hands now with urgency.

"I tried to explain to Bennington. To make him see, but he wouldn't. He refused to believe anything contrary about his sister.

Even now, he thinks I made up this story to keep you from him. That I would go to any lengths.

"And I would, but this was the truth. He would not hear me. It had only ever been, in his eyes, I alone that had brought her to shame. Never, never could it be something of her own doing. She was and continues to be his baby sister, sainted in his eyes. Especially now that she is dead."

"I don't understand," Caroline said with a shake of her head. "Why would she want you to kill a man? Humiliate him perhaps, but to kill him? Why?"

"She was…" he hesitated obviously unwilling to broach this topic with his daughter. "I'd had no idea. I thought…" Her father paused, his words barely above a whisper. It was like he was speaking only for himself, and likely he was. This was not a topic shared with an unmarried daughter. "I thought I was her only love, but I was not. She hid it well. I found out that she'd been dallying with him for months, maybe longer. He was infatuated, intoxicated. I suppose, we all were. We were blinded by her beauty. She could shine down any other female in the room with the slightest glance. She played so innocent." He stopped to think. "Perhaps that is why her brother could never think poorly of her."

Still not able to see why Lady Anne's dalliances would require the death of her lover when she had already been protected by the engagement to a baron, Caroline waited in silence for her father to go on.

"The lieutenant perhaps was not so innocent. He too wanted power. He wanted to marry up. She would not have him. He threatened to go to her father; tell him that he had despoiled her. Demanded payment for his silence," the Baron revealed. "The knowledge would ruin her fully, free me of the obligation, remove all of her prospects. She'd been so sly that she had never once given a thought to the fact that her indiscretions might come home to light. To be outed twice in so many months would have been her undoing."

"So, she had fooled you into handling the problem." Caroline stated.

Her father nodded with solemn regret. "She had to silence him." He shrugged. "One way or another. I was only the instrument."

Caroline thought for a long while and then blurted, "but there's no proof. It's been ages and you've not been charged with his murder. The duel is long over. Why should this all matter now?"

"Because Bennington has proof," the Baron corrected. "He has the letter, my formal challenge. I thought the lieutenant would have burned the thing, like any gentleman with an ounce of honor. Who knows what sort of scrubs the duke may have working for him, but he said it did not take him long after his sister's passing to find what he called retribution." Caroline still did not understand why this would all come to light at this moment, and not decades prior when he first discovered the letter. He could have punished her father long ago. She said as much and he continued. "George is conniving. He plots and moves the world around him like pieces on a chess board. He said a conviction was not enough. The gallows would be too swift. He wanted pain, the unending kind, and he is well aware that he will achieve it now that he has set his cap to you, my daughter in exchange for his sister."

Miss Caroline could hardly breathe. She could not wrap her thoughts around the knowledge that her father had participated in a duel. More than that, since most duels ended with little more than a show of honor, that he had killed a man. Murder. A death in a duel, for honor or no, was illegal and still punishable to the full extent of murder in certain instances. Certainly, the duke would take advantage of this fact.

Her father nodded, knowing that she could now see their predicament. "And so, if you don't marry him… I will hang. A baron cannot nay say a duke." He gazed at her with sorrow and love in his eyes. A love that she had not seen light of in years. He was sorry that he could not protect them from this. "I would gladly give my life for you if that were to be the end of it, but if I am branded a criminal, all I have will be taken away, posthumously. Everything I own forfeited. Your income, having been settled after my crime, confiscated. I shall die and you will be destitute; put out to the streets, and left to starve or suffer worse fates."

Caroline felt the world shift beneath her. A single tear ran down her cheek. She turned her head when her father moved to wipe it away. There was nothing for it. She would have to marry the monster who was blackmailing her father. She squared her shoulders, swiped at the tear, and nodded. "I understand," she said softly.

"I am sorry," her father murmured. "I am so so sorry, Caroline."

"I think I want to be alone now," she whispered, and without another word, her father left the room, closing the door softly behind him.

CHAPTER 5

C aroline allowed herself to be loaded into the carriage no sooner than she and her new husband had passed through the church doors and out into the open air; loaded, like nothing more than the trunks and hatboxes strapped behind and above the carriage. She was a thing, a showpiece, a possession and she had blatantly refused to participate in the congratulatory breakfast that would have been expected to follow the ceremony. She had not spoken a single word to the duke. She felt frozen, like a block of ice. She was a stone statue of herself devoid of emotion, or so she told herself. Perhaps it would hurt less if she could keep the façade.

A fortnight was all that it had taken for the duke to receive the special license and throw this farce of a marriage together. Sped along by his royal connections, she had neither the time nor the opportunity to extricate herself from the bargain. She had declined to participate in the planning, little good it did her. She had even refused to order or choose a special gown, instead opting for the oldest thing she could find in her closet. It was still fine by any standard, a deep burgundy that had not suited the spring season, but that was all the defiance she could muster. Her father recognized the gesture for what it was with a sad frown. As a true lady, Caroline did not own anything that could not have been considered presentable in public. Anything that she no longer cared to wear had always been given to Marilee to alter to her own, much shorter, measurements. Caroline would have asked to borrow one of her friend's repurposed gowns had they not now threatened to hang scandalously above her ankle. She had always prided herself that Marilee was dressed as fine as any lady, if slightly behind in the current fashions, but for once she wished that she had kept one, just one gown to age and crumple in the back of the wardrobe. She would have worn that garment.

Best of all, or worst depending on one's perspective, Caroline had refused to even speak to her father or the duke since the evening that she had been informed of their engagement. She had not come out of her room, not even for meals. She had not accepted the gifts or notes that had been sent from both gentlemen in the attempts of incurring her favor. The gifts had been left in the hall and the notes thrown promptly in the fire, unread. She felt that if she should open her mouth, she would break. She did not speak, lest she might burst into tears.

Finally, she had refused to allow any witnesses beyond the bare minimum. She was attended only by her father, Marilee, and the unavoidable addition of the local rector's wife.

The woman was a bane. Her husband had tripped all over himself when given the chance to sanctify a union blessed by the King himself. Mrs. Adelman had not stopped prattling all morning about how Caroline would be forever honored by the connection and what a blessing it was. Caroline wanted to slap the woman silly.

"A blessing?" Caroline had hissed to Marilee while they sat in the carriage waiting to be joined by the duke. "A wedding so hasty will only lead to speculation that I am with child!"

"When the appropriate time has passed and there is no babe, the gossipmongers shall be put to rest," Marilee said.

The thought of children and the act to get them made the bile rise in Caroline's throat. "If His Grace," she said with disgust, "has any say in it then there should be very little time wasted." The thought brought her pause. The idea of being bedded by the duke was repulsive. Their brief kiss in the church had made her stomach roll. His breath was rotten. The odor of his body was pungent as if no amount of bathing could wash the taint from his skin. Even his lingering looks left an oily feeling upon her. She had no desire to feel his actual touch, but she would have no choice. As his wife, she would belong to him. She supposed, if she looked at his features from very far away he may have been passable in his youth, although it was clear he was no Adonis, but his looks did not dissuade her. It was the ugliness of his character. Still, her bitter aversion had sprung Marilee into action and thus their plan had been hatched. At least, they could delay the act.

By forcing the carriage to make an immediate departure for the long trip to Heatherton Hall, the Duke's Manchester estate, the women hoped to delay the dreaded consummation for a few days. The horses could be changed out to keep the pace for a day or two, but it was inevitable that at some point on the long journey they would be forced to take a room at an inn. Thus began the next twist in their ploy. Miss Caroline was to claim severe illness, a result of the harrowing journey, as she was unused to travel these many years.

Marilee had somehow procured a small vial of tartar emetic without suspicion. Caroline did not ask for explanations. The tiniest pinch in her drink would be enough to empty the contents of Caroline's stomach but not enough to make the effects linger. They knew that such a display could not be disputed by the duke and he would leave her to her feigned rest and recovery for the duration of their travels. Another pinch here and there would maintain the ruse. Once they reached Heatherton Hall, it would become more difficult. Busy as he must be, there was no chance of the duke leaving to attend his business without fulfilling his husbandly duties first. Marilee guessed that they could prolong the illness for a week at most after their arrival.

A false, or true if it so happened, claim of her cycle would buy them another week. Beyond that, they did not know. All the vials and cycles in the world could do nothing to keep her husband from her bedchamber indefinitely. It was a fool's hope that they could procure the proof that was being used to blackmail her father and claim the marriage unofficial in such a short time, but it was the only plan they had. Marilee would be her witness and perhaps, with some stroke of luck, this could be undone.

If they failed in their mission, Caroline knew that it would be impossible to delay the act forever, but she would buy as much time as she could even if it meant stooping to deception. After that, she could only pray that she was quickly fertile so that he would leave her be for months on end. The last thing that she wanted was for him to make a continual effort. After all, all he really wanted was another heir. Caroline would pray for a son. She would produce the child and wash her hands of the duke.

She doubted that he would allow her much influence over the child as it would be his intention to form his son in his own image. Being an only child, Caroline had always wanted a family to love. Although she had resigned herself to spinsterhood, a part of her always wished for children. Now that wish was dashed. With Caroline actively undoing the duke's efforts, she was very likely to be separated from her own offspring. Such thoughts were against everything she had been taught it meant to be a wife or mother. She did not care; she could not care; she loathed her husband.

. . .

THE DUKE WAITED UNTIL THE SECOND DAY TO SPEAK to her. The first she had spent with her nose resolutely buried in her book while he slept noisily with his head thrown back and mouth hanging wide open. Drool collected in the corner of his mouth. Caroline turned to stare out the window. Marriage, it seemed, was exhausting. Marilee had rubbed her fingers together, miming pinching some of the poisonous crystals into his open maw, but the light in her eyes revealed that she was only teasing. There would certainly be questions if the duke should fall ill or even die in the company of his new wife, and even her melancholia could not make her consider such a heinous act.

Caroline shook her head and returned to her pages. Thank the Lord she would still have Marilee, she thought. The truth was, that no matter the dire nature of their situation neither woman would ever stoop to harm the man. True, Miss Caroline was willing to ingest a small amount of the poison herself, less than even a physician might prescribe, but causing herself temporary discomfort was a means worth the end. She was not harming anyone but herself. Luckily, she did not try because presently her nemesis awoke.

"That's a prime bit of blood you have out there," he said with a jerk of his chin to the wall at her back. Tied behind the carriage was Bella, who made a nickering fuss every few miles as if keenly aware of her lady's displeasure. "I know just the stud to pair her with to the result of invaluable offspring."

"Is that all you think about?" Caroline snapped.

"Making the most of my... assets?" he asked with humor, "or... procreation?"

"Both," she replied, refusing to allow the blush he had assumed would rise to her feminine cheeks. She wasn't missish to be shocked by the topic. Her father's stallion had covered the mares at the barony, and although she was not supposed to know about such things, Father was not terribly attentive and she was always curious. As long as she could relegate the thought to Bella and some unnamed stallion, she could keep her composure. She looked out of the window, pointedly ignoring the duke. A lady was only like to blush when such things were said in intimacy, and she refused to think on it. The duke may be attempting to flirt with her although she was nothing but revolted.

"They are one and the same," he drawled. His eyes upon her breasts told Caroline that they were no longer talking about horses.

"You still have a son," she spat as she pulled her pelisse closed. "A grown son." Her disbelief that he would so easily disregard his own blood was evident.

Marilee's breath grew deathly still at Miss Caroline's side and her eyes flicked back and forth between the pair as they faced off. She wondered what his son would think of her and his father's attempt to replace him. Of course, that was not how the succession worked. The eldest living son would inherit the dukedom. She said as much.

"My preferred heir is dead," he said with cold calculation. "I have a spare who is neither settled nor adept at managing all that my position requires. He may inherit the dukedom, but he will not inherit the coin, nor any of the unentailed properties. He is a spendthrift."

"One might say that the fault lies on your shoulders for not preparing both equally," she jabbed.

"I had no need to prepare Edward. With Robert at the helm, it would have been a considerable waste of effort to even bother. The other was raised to want for nothing, to take his leisure and hold his place." She expected his sneer to hold malice but instead found that he was enjoying their spat. The lust in his rheumy eyes nearly made her change the topic, but she needed him to continue. If she were heading straight toward this family with all their foibles, then she needed to know the powers at play and where she, or her future children, might fit into them. "Robert was infallible," he continued, "primed for his role... until he abandoned it."

"Death is not abandonment," she hissed with shock at the father's unfeeling revelation.

"Edward should have gone to war, not Robert," the duke grunted.

She wondered idly if Robert had gone to war to escape his despicable father.

"Maybe then Edward would have learned a thing or two. Even as marquess, Robert had all the makings of a duke. He was driven, organized, efficient, respected by our tenants and prudent in his companionships. I like to think he was a fine model of his father," he boasted and it was all that she could do not to cringe at the thought that there had once been two men as beastly as he. "Edward is none of those things. Charming, yes, but not a leader with any foresight." He waved a hand in the air as if the younger of his two sons was nothing more than a social entertainment. "My son," she realized he was referring to the elder again, "was engaged to be wed to the most beautiful lady of her season, a true diamond of the first water. What a grand Duchess she would have been. But, no. Five years!" He shouted so suddenly that both Caroline and Marilee jumped. "Five years he had been gone and she waiting. Do you know how many heirs I could have had by now if he had stayed?"

More than ever, she thought this Robert had gone to war to escape his father's clutches. If only she could be so lucky.

"If you want to be cross with anyone for your situation," he said, "let it be Robert. He volunteered. I did not have to lose my son to the wretched French! If he had done his duty to his family instead of gallivanting off to become an admiral and fulfill some duty to the crown that was completely unnecessary then I might not have had to call on your father's shame. I might have done so just for the pleasure of it, true, but, blast it, Robert has left me in the lurch yet again."

"Edward might still produce an heir," she said softly. "Perhaps a grandson will be more to your liking." She suspected that his sons were somewhere around her own age. They could not be more than five or ten years her elder. Certainly, if the duke still thought himself spry enough to produce offspring, then his son should be more than capable.

"Have you ever heard the phrase, faber est suae quisque fortunae?" he asked, suddenly lost in introspection.

She thought for a minute, the Latin rusted in her mind. "It means something like, every man is the maker of his own fortune."

"A bluestocking!" he mused. "What have I married?"

She wanted to offer a retort that he could take her back, but of course, he could not. The words were spoken. She was married now.

"My education did not lack," she stated in a flat tone.

"These words I live by," he revealed. "It is the reason for all of my successes. I do not leave it to others to act. I can hope Edward produces a viable heir. Yet, what if I live out my years trusting that he will do so and he produces only daughters," he scoffed, "or, worse yet, a son, like himself, with no ambition and only debauchery?"

She gaped at him. He did not see taking a woman young enough to be his daughter as debauchery. She supposed he was not the only duke that felt this way. A shiver went up her spine.

"Now you see," he laughed, thinking she agreed when the reality was that she was dumbfounded by his sheer obsession. "I must take precautions to ensure my bloodline. Take them into my own hands so that there can be no doubt."

"And what might Edward think of this?" she asked. "What might he say that you plan to usurp his inheritance? Furthermore, how is he not to think of me as anything less than an enemy? A child of mine would be a threat to his future."

"Not at all," the duke laughed. "Edward has no capacity for the daily requirements of my position. At best he would steer my investments off course out of sheer stupidity, at worst he would sink the entire ship!" She could not conceive that he had so little faith in his own son. She felt bad for this Lord Edward who had been deemed unworthy before he had even been given a chance to prove his mettle. "No, when we arrive and I reveal our union, he will capitulate."

"If he does not," she said softly.

"I will deal with him," he said gruffly, making Caroline wonder to what extremes might he be willing to go. "We shall train your son up to replace Robert. With you by my side, and that of our offspring," he grinned, "there is no doubt in my mind that we cannot create a masterpiece. Your son can manage the estate when the time comes and Edward can keep the title and glory. I shall give Edward a generous allowance. He will be glad he does not have to work for it."

Caroline thought that was ridiculous. Of course, she had heard of such arrangements where a lord might pass some of his obligations onto his brothers, but it was obscene to think of marrying, of having a child simply to achieve that end.

The duke snapped his fingers as if he had just had a brilliant thought. He looked at her, assessing the skills that he had already determined she possessed.

"You'll like Edward," he grinned. "He's a pleasant fellow. And he shall certainly like you. He has an eye for pretty things." She stared at him. "When the time comes and I pass from this world, I see no reason why you two couldn't simply…" he rolled his hand in a circle between them, "continue. If you wished. That would truly solidify the line."

"You are foul," she hissed. "If passing me along to your son was a consideration then why didn't you just bind me to him to begin with?"

"As I said," he chuckled at her outrage, clearly taking it as a signifier that he had won their standoff, "I control my own destiny. Besides, I am in perfect health, why should I not enjoy you for myself when I intend to have many long years ahead?" Maybe he had won, she thought, as she crossed her arms in front of her and shifted so that she could look out the window and no longer see even a sliver of his form in her peripheral vision. The man was a fiend, and she prayed to be free of him.

CHAPTER 6

The following evening, the duke was irate that they had not reached a stopping place before nightfall. A pair of carts piled high with straw had collided leaving their contents strewn across the narrow roadway and making it impassable. One of the drivers had offered an alternate route to the nearby town when the duke had raged at the inconvenience. It would take several hours to clear the mess and right and repair the carts. Not to mention that one of the horses was nowhere to be found. Miss Caroline had offered to allow Bella to help right the wagons, but the duke had refused.

"It's only two miles further to go around," he grumbled. "I cannot be bothered with such a menial task. Honestly, they should make the hands take the longer route and leave the main road open for those who have not the time to spare."

Caroline had issued her rebuttal, but had been over-ruled with a firm demand to haul yourself back into that carriage at once! A farmer, busy as they were, should have use of the shorter route, she had argued. Gentle folk on an already lengthy journey had nothing but time to spare while the poor men forking hay from the roadway were already well behind in their sched-ules. Besides, she thought, arriving late at the inn would likely make for a swift dinner and easy claim of exhaustion. She would not even have need of the tonic this evening, she predicted. Surely the duke would head straight to his own chamber to sleep away his frustrations.

They were both still seething at the exchange an hour later when the carriage slowed to a halt. The duke pulled back the curtain to peer out into the darkness and, when they could see nothing by the faint light of the moon, he banged his crop, which had been lain across the seat beside him for just such a purpose, on the roof of the carriage.

"What is the meaning of this!" he shouted to the driver. "Chauncey, roll on!"

A shot rang through the air and there was a distinct thump as a body fell to the ground.

Marilee opened her mouth to scream, but Caroline covered the maid's mouth with her hand and warned her with her eyes to remain silent.

"Out of the rig you nabob and meet my barking irons!" The voice was gruff and calm. Caroline felt her stomach rise to her throat. This was no drunkard or desperate fool. No, she thought, this was an unflinching highwayman.

"I am no cit!" the duke declared as he flung the door open in full defense of his pride. He puffed out his chest. "I am Duke of Manchester, fourth cousin once to His Majesty George William Frederick, and you will leave at once or suffer the King's vengeance."

Caroline and Marilee dared not move lest the carriage sway and announce their presence. They sat, gripping each other's shoulders tightly in solidarity. Caroline hoped that the duke's peacocking worked and caused the highwayman to take flight. The title alone ought to be enough to scare them off. She heard their two remaining attendants climb down from the back of the carriage, the click of their own pistols bringing her a moment of relief.

"Excellent," the highwayman chortled. "And you're surrounded."

No less than a dozen shots rang out in quick succession. Caroline could not tell which had come from their own men and which from the robbers but the last few gasps of dying men sounded and then silence fell.

"You handle the ribbons," that same gruff voice commanded and Caroline nearly gagged with fear. "Pull it to the side. Take anything of value. And fiend seize it put his Grace's plump arse back in the rig." The title had been cast off with mockery rather than fear or respect.

There was no hiding. There could be no sneaking out the other door and making a mad dash for the woods. Caroline took a steadying breath. Ladies had some value in ransom, she told herself. It was true that the highwaymen had just killed a full member of the gentry and she and Marilee were witness to that crime, but they were only women. She hoped they could be overlooked as witnesses. She prayed that if she swore to their silence, perhaps her father would be able to buy their lives. He would pay any amount, she knew. At very least he could pull from her own substantial wealth even if it drained her dry.

Her gaze landed on Marilee who was trembling in her seat. The knowledge that servants of a highway attack were oft left dead at the side of the road, or never found at all, was written well on her face.

Caroline grabbed Marilee's shoulders and turned her to face her lady. She modeled slow breathing until her friend began to mimic the gesture. Caroline drove swift fingers into Marilee's hair, removing pins from the cap that was all that signified she was a lady's maid and not a lady herself. Caroline sent up a prayer of thanksgiving that Marilee was wearing one of her old gowns today.

"You're a lady," she whispered with shaking breath. "My cousin. Kate. Do you remember her?" Caroline said as she quickly braided her maid's hair.

Marilee nodded while Caroline shoved the cap deep into the crevice of the seat.

Caroline knew that Lady Katherine was currently in Rome with her family while her brother took part in the Grand Tour. There would be no verifying that she was anywhere else in England and so Marilee could assume her cousin's identity for a short while. She only hoped that Marilee recalled enough facts about her cousin to play the part convincingly.

"My lady…" Marilee began, her voice barely audible in their attempts to prolong their concealment.

Caroline grasped her friend's shoulders and gave her a firm shake. "Call me Caroline. You are a lady," she repeated with fervor. "You cannot falter."

Marilee squared her shoulders and straightened her back. The slight adjustment did help her to look the part.

"What if we…" Her eyes darted to the door and the noises outside growing ever closer as the highwaymen shifted the bodies of the duke and his men to the side of the road. "What if they…"

Caroline did not want to think about it. She could not consider any alternative but their survival.

"We will not die this day," she promised. She took Marilee's hand into her own. "Papa will buy us both. I will make sure of it."

Just then the door was wrenched open and a bedraggled man smelling of camphor barked in surprise.

"Oy!" he called over his shoulder. "We're in a hobble here."

The man dragged Caroline and Marilee out of the carriage with such force that Marilee's frock ripped straight through to reveal her chemise and Caroline had lost one of her half-boots entirely. She had forgotten that she had loosened the laces for comfort during the ride.

The leader, a towering man with most of his face covered by a dirty scrap of fabric, let out a string of obscenities.

"This wasn't what we discussed," the one holding their arms in grips so firm the women would surely bruise said with a ring of panic.

The leader swore again, pacing. "Be silent while I think!" he shouted.

"My father will pay for us," Caroline offered. "He's a baron. He'll pay any ransom for my cousin and I."

The leader was staring down at the duke's dead body. Caroline refused to look, did not want to see him lifeless and bloodied. Had her prayers brought this upon them? She squelched a sob. She hadn't wanted to be married to the duke, but neither had she wanted this.

Finally, the man whirled on them.

"Is one of you, his mistress?" he demanded. His beady eyes searched their faces. "Do you carry his child?"

Caroline had to think fast. She knew there was only one answer that would get them out of this. Would a pregnancy force the men to show them mercy? Would the lie of a duke's child be a safety net for the two women?

She watched as he glanced down at the duke once more, disgust written all over his face. He kicked the limp form.

"Do you carry this gundigut's seed?" No, she thought. Aligning herself with the duke was the wrong route. Besides, she did not think she was a good enough actress to pretend she had any dealings with the man, and perhaps that was the safer route anyway. After all, they had killed the gentleman without hesitation.

"No!" she said, letting her face show offense at the suggestion. "He is merely chaperoning us from one location to the next as a favor to my father, the Baron Wickham," she lied. "I hardly know him!" That, at least, was the truth.

Marilee's eyes were firmly on the ground, but her back was as straight as the most regal lady at court, refusing to reveal the slightest betrayal of her lady's tale. Good, Caroline thought, she would second whatever web Caroline wove, but it was clear the deception was in Caroline's hands.

"We should take them to her," another voice suggested from behind them. Caroline shivered at the way the man had said her with a mixture of both fear and respect. She was not sure that she wanted to meet this mysterious female, but she supposed anything was better than death.

"Two ransoms will make anything in this haul look like pauper's pickin's," one highwayman said greedily.

Caroline nodded in agreement. "My father is very wealthy."

"And we haven't seen your faces," Marilee added. "We won't say anything. Just, please…"

"No one can know but us," the leader snarled, turning to the circle of men who had drawn close. "It's our ransom, our reward. If anyone asks, as far as we knew, they weren't even here. We'll split the coin among ourselves without the gentleman knowing."

"The duke was out by himself as expected," one of the vagrants added. "Whatever happened to them wasn't our problem."

"We get the ransom and this time," the leader's eyes crinkled with what must have been a smug grin, "it lines our pockets."

Caroline never thought she would be thankful for greed, but she raised her eyes briefly heavenward in a silent prayer. At least their lives had been spared for the moment. Who knew what the future would bring, but with life, there was hope.

. . .

IT WAS A TWO-DAY JOURNEY WITHOUT THE USE OF main roads to wherever it was that they were being taken. The carriage had been stripped of all livery and the highwaymen had decided to sell it as soon as they arrived at their destination so that it might not be traced back to them. The initial plan had been to leave the vehicle on the side of the road but instead Caroline and Marilee rode in silence inside. The decision had been made since it would not have done to put two ladies on horses, even one as fine as Bella, in the middle of a band of unkempt, masked men. Caroline had wished that they had put her on the mare. She was a fine horsewoman and could easily have outrun the lot of them. But, she would never have left Marilee even if she had been given the opportunity, and Bella would not have been able to carry a double load as fast or far as they would require. Instead, they had been bound, gagged, and for occasional long hours drugged with something that made them sleepy and compliant.

With every passing mile she wondered what their fate would be.

The men had fought about sending a ransom letter from the nearest town.

"We have to wait for things to settle," their leader had said. Now that they had decided to keep the women alive the men were careful not to use names and to keep their faces covered in the females' presence. "We can't risk any of this being tied to us, especially not the duke. Every watchman in England will be searching for them for at least a month. When it calms down, and there is less interest, that is when we make our demands."

"What are we supposed to do with two ladies for a fortnight?" one of his cronies had asked with incredulity.

"We'll take them to her house," he had replied. Again, that ominous reference. "She can keep them with her birds until we are ready."

Birds? Caroline thought with a sudden rush of dread. Her eyes met Marilee's, and she knew that her maid was thinking the same thing. They were being taken to a brothel.

CHAPTER 7

They arrived in the dead of night. Caroline was unloaded from the carriage with a musty felted bag over her head. Her wrists were bound behind her back and a forceful hand kept shoving her along until they had entered a house, passed down a long hallway, and she was shoved down onto a plush bench while the door clicked shut on the other side of the room. The room smelled of perfume and cigar smoke. Marilee's whimper and then the clumsy pressure of her shoulder at Caroline's side revealed that her friend had been brought along as well. There was music playing at the front of the house and a series of moans and noises on the other side of the wall that Miss Caroline refused to identify. An unfamiliar, sickly-sweet scent, opium she guessed, permeated the place.

This was a whorehouse to be sure.

A short while later the door opened and slammed with such force that Caroline flinched.

"Lawks! What were you thinking?" a female voice exclaimed in a harsh whisper. "What if one of my patrons had seen?"

"We brought them in through the back," the raspy-voiced leader explained, "like the others."

Others, Caroline wondered? So, they had not been the first women kidnapped?

"The others weren't highborn ladies!" she hissed. "No one would be looking for them."

"We thought you could keep them here until things settle down," one of the men said. "Then we'll say we found them, lost in the woods or something."

"I can't keep them here!" The woman shrieked. She was pacing now. "My rooms are full. My girls are working. The last thing I need is some bold young lordling wandering in and finding this! You know the gentleman would have our heads if he found out. Get them out, now."

"We got nowhere to take them," the leader spoke again. This time, Caroline heard panic in his voice. He had truly thought that this woman would help them. It was clear that she had taken poor indentured females before, had no qualms about that. Please, Caroline sent up a fervent prayer, please don't let them discover that Marilee is a maid! For the time being, her friend's best protection was the illusion of her status.

A soft huff, the clink of glass and the glug glug of a bottle being emptied into the glass was all that could be heard for several long moments. Nails tapped against the drink as if the woman were thinking. More pacing, and then the glass was thumped down on a table. Empty.

"They'll have to be split up," she declared. "Each will go to a different house through my… connections."

"No!" Caroline cried.

The woman's footsteps led right up to their bench and Caroline felt a swift, booted kick to her shins.

"You will keep your mouth shut, Missy, if you know what's good for you. You'll both work as maids," the woman hissed. "Your income will come to me for the benevolence of permitting you to live. If you speak a word of this to anyone, identify yourself; try to escape… I'll have the other killed before you can say m'lady. If you do as I say, without incident, then I will release you to your families for the appropriate fee. If even the slightest rumor surfaces before or after that time, I will send my hounds to hunt you down and finish what these dimwits should have done from the off." Caroline had a very distinct feeling that the Madam's hounds were not mere hunting dogs, but cold-blooded assassins. "Do I make myself clear?" She said, one claw-like fingernail under Caroline's chin.

Caroline nodded, the nail digging into her skin, and she guessed that Marilee did the same beside her.

Another pair of kicks had both the captives gasping with pain. "That won't do. How do you address your superiors?"

"Yes, ma'am," Marilee said quickly.

"Yes, ma'am," Caroline parroted. The subservience felt foreign on her tongue but Caroline willed herself to get used to it. Fulfilling this role would come easier for Marilee than pretending to be a lady had. For Caroline, she was going to have to retrain every instinct that had been drilled into her since birth.

She would do it. She would do whatever it took to keep them both alive. She could not risk Marilee's life by defiance.

A soft boot slipped under the hem of Caroline's skirt, this time from her side. Hidden beneath the piles of fabric, Marilee pressed her foot ever so slightly down upon Caroline's toes. Escape if you can, even if it means my death, the gesture said. Marilee would always put her lady first. The knowledge that once they were separated, it would be more difficult to get Caroline's father to understand that the second captive was not some random impersonator of Lady Katherine, but someone important within his household who also needed to be rescued, hung between them. If he revealed, before Caroline could speak with him, that Lady Kate was on holiday and that the second female could not possibly be she, then Marilee was doomed. Caroline lifted her toes in return and applied upward pressure. She would do what she could, but in her heart, she knew that she must be very careful not to risk her dearest friend's demise.

CAROLINE HAD BEEN GIVEN A SIMPLE, DARK DRESS and a cream apron with a yellowish stain on the front. Caroline could not tell if the dress was a worn black or a very dark brown. It was well-made and sturdy, but far too large for her thin frame. She was told she could take it in if she ever had a spare moment. The Madam, a buxom woman with fiery red hair and a bosom pushed so high she might have been able to rest her chin on it, had laughed at that.

"You'll be far too busy to even think," she had been told. "I've arranged for a position as a maid of all work in a house where I have many eyes." The look she had leveled upon Miss Caroline threatened untold punishments if one of those eyes reported that anything was amiss.

Marilee had been taken away a half hour before. She had been dressed and given a similar speech, before she left. Caroline only knew that she had been placed as a laundress.

"It's tinted with red ochre," the Madam said when she caught Caroline looking at her vibrant locks and trying to determine if they were natural or not. "If you'd rather stay here, we can try it on yours…"

Caroline choked in shock at the suggestion that she might wish to remain in the brothel and firmly declined. Again, the Madam had laughed, the garish sound going through to Caroline's bones.

Her own hair had been brushed out and tied in a neat chignon at the base of her neck. A mobcap was snapped over top before Caroline was bodily spun to look at herself in the mirror. She was unrecognizable. Caroline had never stopped to consider how one's clothing could alter one's entire appearance. Gone was the highborn, independent lady. Gone was her poise and the elegant, feminine shape that her gowns had done well to accentuate. The glossy shimmer of her beautiful blonde tresses, of which she had always received ample compliments, was hidden beneath ruffles of the hideous cap.

"Don't make me regret not killing you," the sensual voice whispered into Caroline's ear. Her tone, smooth and friendly, belied the wicked words.

With that, Caroline had been thrust back out into the midnight alley, loaded into the back of a grimy milk cart, and hauled off toward whatever new horrors might await.

SHE HAD ARRIVED, AGAIN, IN THE DEAD OF NIGHT. The housekeeper, a fractious Mrs. Reilly, had greeted her at the door with a sharp, "get inside before you let in the cold!"

Caroline could not tell if the woman was naturally irritable, put off by being awakened in the middle of the night to fill an empty position of employ, or was disturbed and angry about the risks of her involvement in this treachery. The first two options, Caroline mused, might mean that Mrs. Reilly was an innocent bystander who had no knowledge of her real identity. The last, would mean she was a ruthless and dangerous criminal who had taken advantage of her position in a noble house to aid in the trafficking of impoverished women. Caroline could not make a determination and it was far too dangerous to ask. It would be best to bide her time.

"I've been short a girl for two weeks," Mrs. Reilly had said as she turned on her heel and made for a narrow staircase at the back of the house. Caroline stared after the woman, in shock that she had simply walked away from a lady mid-conversation. For a moment she had forgotten that she was meant to play a lowly maid. "Well, have you grown roots?" the housekeeper had turned at the base of the stairs and called out. Too late Caroline realized that she had been expected to follow. "I'd better not catch you standing around like that when there is work to be done," Mrs. Reilly had continued as they climbed up and up and up. The staircase was so narrow that Caroline was not sure how the plump woman managed to squeeze herself through. "If I find you dawdling, I'll take the switch to you myself."

"Yes, Ma'am," Caroline whispered in response. She was too afraid to say anything else that might be interpreted as insubordinate. Mrs. Reilly's grunt of approval was the only response.

"You'll sleep on the palette in Lizzy's room," the housekeeper said as she opened a door to what amounted to nothing more than a broom closet in Caroline's mind. Inside was a single bed with a dark form curled up in the center. On the floor, was a lumpy looking straw palette with what appeared to be a scratchy wool blanket. She had never fully appreciated the indulgent down mattress and layers upon layers of soft blankets that had covered her bed at Gravesend Manor. Caroline grimaced but schooled her features before the older woman could take note. It would have to do. *Just until the ransom is offered and father can purchase my freedom.* "Now," Mrs. Reilly pulled a letter out of her pocket and squinted at the words by the light of the lone candle that had been lit in the servant's hall, "Emily Baker, is it?"

Caroline swallowed and gave one curt nod.

"You have two hours to rest. I need you up and lighting fires before the rest of the house wakes. Rise at five and you shall thrive, I've always said." The woman had said the rhyme in a sing-song voice as if proud of the common adage. Caroline had heard it used before but had certainly never awoken at five in the morning in her lifetime. "None of the family is in residence and there are no guests at the moment so you can forego the bedrooms." Caroline could hardly stand on her feet after the emotional toll of the past few days. How could she possibly be expected to wake in a mere two hours? "Afterward, come find me.

I want this house in tip-top shape by the time the house is to be used by the family."

Caroline nodded once more.

"Good," Mrs. Reilly dusted her hands off as if she were ridding herself of a nuisance. Without another word she disappeared down the hall. Caroline was left standing in the open doorway to the servant's quarter, the straw mat not looking so terrible now that she had let her exhaustion take hold. She sank down onto the palette, not bothering to remove her clothes or her shoes, not even to pull the coarse wool blanket over her weary form, and she slept.

CHAPTER 8

T he next morning, Caroline was roused by the previously sleeping Lizzy, but they had no time to talk.

Caroline had just finished lighting the last fire when she started to see signs of the other members of staff moving about. She was glad that her first assignment had occurred before anyone else had awoken because it had taken her nearly a quarter hour to figure out how to use the fire striker. She had witnessed hundreds of fires being lit in her lifetime, but had never truly understood how difficult a task it could be.

By midday, she was dead on her feet. Her fingers ached and her dress had been ruined by soot, further complicated when she had spilled a jar of leather grease down her front. Mrs. Reilly, who had already had more than enough of Caroline's failures at that point, had thrown her hands in the air and demanded of the heavens why she was being tested so. Once the head housekeeper had gathered her wits, she had taken Caroline to the linen closet, instructed her to disrobe, threw the soiled dress in a bin, and tossed her a new one. Then, she had handed over a neatly folded pile that contained two more uniforms and three aprons and threatened that the next one she ruined she would pay for with extra chamber pot duty. Caroline was much more careful after that.

Lunch was a blissful reprieve and although the meal was bland, consisting of a large piece of crusty bread, a hunk of cheese, and a bowl of spare vegetable soup, she could not even find it within herself to care. She downed two cups of the weakest tea that she had ever tasted. Black, no cream or sugar to be added. She vowed that if she ever returned to the luxury of her previous life that she would push her nose into every corner of her own household's dealings to make sure that her own servants had better care than this. She did not think that her father treated theirs badly. They had certainly all seemed happy and Marilee had never complained, but now she needed to be absolutely certain.

She had been instructed to dust the parlor from floor to ceiling and, "if I find one speck upon inspection then you can forget about supper."

Caroline had taken the threat to heart and been dusting for two hours when she decided to open the long draperies so that the incoming light would reveal any hidden surfaces that she might have missed. She flung them wide and gasped.

Hyde Park sat only a stone's throw away, across the cobbled lane. She dug back into her memories for the layout of London's most fashionable areas. It had been so long. Park Lane, the words suddenly sprang to mind. She was on Park Lane in the center of London! Her father's townhouse was on Grosvenor. If she could just manage to get to it, she would be saved! Even though her father was not there, servants kept the townhouse. They would send word to her father.

Her heart sank. She could not leave. Not only would it put Marilee in direct danger but there was not a single chance that she would ever be allowed to venture out of the house. Perhaps she could convince one of the runners to get a letter out, she thought. But determining who, if anyone at all, was trustworthy in this house was going to be a task in itself. Still, she was emboldened by her proximity to safety. She knew her father's townhouse was closed until Lords, but there had to be at least one or two of the staff manning the house.

She dusted with new vigor, even passing Mrs. Reilly's inspection with aplomb.

"It's a good thing you are finally taking your duties to heart," the housekeeper said. "I've just had a note from His Grace that he is to stay at Heatherton Hall for a fortnight before returning to us with a new bride! Who would have guessed? His Grace, married!"

The room spun and Caroline felt so suddenly as if the floor had fallen from beneath her that she had to grab on to a nearby table to keep from fainting.

"His Grace?" she said breathily. Heatherton Hall? She felt ill. Heatherton hall… where she had been heading just a few days prior.

"Lord Bennington," Mrs. Reilly said as if she had expected the matter to have been obvious. "The Duke of Manchester."

Caroline recalled that the duke had sent a letter from her father's house just before they had begun their journey. He had said he was to inform his son of his nuptials and to tell the staff to prepare a jolly feast for their reception. She had not dwelled on it at the time, only thinking that the last thing she would want to do was celebrate.

They did not even know, she realized. They did not even know that their master was dead, that she, the new duchess, for all they might guess, was likewise deceased. They did not yet know that the carriage had never arrived at Heatherton Hall. They didn't know that their lady, Caroline herself, was standing in the very house where she had been meant to become mistress. The thugs could not have known to avoid such a thing because she had claimed no association to the duke. She had merely said that he was escorting her to her own location. Lud, she thought, she was a prisoner in what amounted to be her own home.

She almost blurted all of the facts to Mrs. Reilly, almost claimed her position and demanded to be set free from her bondage. But she stopped when she realized that the older lady was staring at her as if she had lost her senses. Either the housekeeper truly had no idea that the men that had brought Caroline to this house had been involved in the duke's murder or she was an excellent actress.

"Are you alright, Emily?" she asked with a hand to her mouth, stifling a laugh. "You must be shocked to have been placed in such a noble house. I assure you;

you'll get used to it. In any case, you will not have the occasion to be seen by the family."

Caroline held her tongue. Of course, she could not spew that information out as if it were to be believed. The housekeeper would think Caroline an unstable liar and have her sent straight back to the rookery. Mrs. Reilly, even if she was involved in filtering kidnapped ladies through her staff, could have no idea that her new maid was of gentle birth. Had she not heard the madam and the highwaymen swear, seal the bargain with their blood, that they would only say that she had been plucked from the gutters. No one would believe her, even if Mrs. Reilly could be trusted, and there was no guarantee of that. Caroline had to think! In the meantime, she would keep her mouth shut.

Of course, Mrs. Reilly would think that such a step up would be an overwhelming improvement to one from the lowly beginnings that she suspected.

Caroline made a paltry excuse about the dust having gotten to her as she did her best to collect herself. It would not be safe to have Mrs. Reilly, or anyone in the house, suspect who she really was. If she were discovered, they might arrange to have her killed. She did not know who to trust, therefore, she could trust no one. Even being unaware of the greater facts did not make them innocent overall.

"Go splash some cool water on your face and then prepare the bed in Lord Edward's room." Mrs. Reilly declared. "He should arrive before long and I should think that he will wish to celebrate. His older brother's ship was sunk by the French last month and he must have been very distraught because he hasn't ventured out from his apartment since the news." She smiled, clearly having motherly affection toward Lord Edward.

"It will be nice to have something for him to celebrate," Caroline said with what voice she could muster. Soon, Lord Edward would be mourning more than just his brother, the poor man. Strange that she felt some sympathy for him.

Mrs. Reilly leaned forward with a conspiratorial gleam in her eye. "His grace will throw parties for a month to show off his new pet," she whispered. "He wrote that she's young and will need to be introduced all throughout London so that she can make the proper connections. If you ask me, I pity the girl."

Caroline did not know how to respond to that so she merely nodded. "I should go," she said.

"Yes," Mrs. Reilly chirped, "lots to do!"

Caroline hurried out into the hall and immediately collided with someone who had been moving to pass through the doorway from the opposite direction.

"Lord Edward!" Mrs. Reilly exclaimed. Caroline had never heard the housekeeper sound so jovial.

Caroline looked up into the aristocratic face of an attractive blond male. He was wearing a thick riding cloak and his cheeks were flushed against the cool evening air. His half-grin was arresting and caused her to stumble backward. Mrs. Reilly gave a disapproving cough and Caroline recalled her place.

She bowed her head and dipped into a low curtsy. "My lord," she murmured.

He gave a nod of acknowledgement to each female before hanging his silver handled walking stick on a hook in the hall.

"I received your note that I was to return to receive important news," he said with a deep, languid tone. "What is it?"

"Your father's been wed," Mrs. Reilly said with a look in her eye that Caroline could not read. "I thought you should hear it in person."

Lord Edward's face paled.

"They left Northwickshire for Heatherton Hall straight after the ceremony," she added. "He received a special license and decided to surprise us all."

Lord Edward muttered a curse that no gentleman would have voiced before a lady, but Caroline remembered, he did not think her more than a maid of all work.

Caroline tried to read the emotions that played over his features but he was too quick to cover them with a blank expression. Worry. Anger. Annoyance. Hurt. Maybe even fear. He headed down the hall and into the study, slamming the door behind him. Caroline could not blame the man. The duke had said that his son would not care that his position might be lessened by their marriage, but she had not believed it and now she knew it was so. Even if Lord Edward had never aspired to be duke, it could only hurt his pride to know that his father had so little respect for him as to marry in secret for what could only be one reason. He had no idea that his father was dead, that the marriage was meaningless now. All he could know was that Caroline's own union had likely been a cut direct from this gentleman's own flesh and blood. Caroline was glad that she had not precipitously revealed her own identity.

"Off to the linens," Mrs. Reilly said, back to her usual abrupt self. She made to follow Lord Edward into the study. Perhaps the old woman thought that she could settle the gentleman. "You haven't time to wash your face now, girl. Get on, go! First door at the top of the stairs."

Caroline scurried off like a scolded puppy and went to prepare Lord Edward's rooms as she had been bid.

CHAPTER 9

A week flew by and Caroline became more adept at her regular chores. She still had issues whenever something new was attempted for the first time, like when she scoured the back hall with vinegar and had not known to mix the foul liquid into a bucket of water. The entire house had reeked to high heaven for two days and they had been forced to open the windows even though the weather was unseasonably cool. The staff had all resorted to walking around wearing cloaks even within the house. She thought that some were teasing her, but she still did not know who to trust. In addition, Caroline's delicate hands were reddened and cracked by the caustic liquid and Mrs. Reilly was incensed that she had used the entire bottle of vinegar and had not finished the cleaning.

Lord Edward had thought the mishap hilarious and had pestered the staff relentlessly to find out who had been responsible.

"Tell me you did it on purpose," he laughed one evening when she had brought a load of wood into the parlor. They had finally been able to close the windows, the smell only present in whiffs every now and then near the servants' entrance.

"I didn't," she had promised and shook her head at her own foolishness.

"Mrs. Reilly says that you have been sent from hell to test her." He grinned.

"She'd be justified in that thought," Caroline groaned. "I can't pretend to be bothered one way or another." Caroline still did not know whether or not to trust the head housekeeper, but she knew beyond doubt that the woman had cursed the day she had been saddled with Emily Baker and as a result had made Caroline's workload miserable on purpose. So far, she had decided not to trust any of the male servants outright, if only because all of the highwaymen had been male and not female. She liked her roommate, Lizzy, who worked in the kitchens but hardly spoke, and she was nearly certain that the fat chef would throttle her if she ever had one of her mishaps in his kitchen so she was almost confident that made him one of the Madam's cronies. The scullery maids were always digging for gossip so she could not confide in them. They would not keep her secret and the other maids went about their duties so quickly that Caroline had never had a chance to have a real conversation with any of them. They seemed not to have a comradery between them.

"You're bold, for a maid," Lord Edward observed.

Caroline cursed herself. She had been looking straight at him and speaking with as much wry confidence as she would have as Miss Caroline Graves, or moreover the Duchess of Manchester.

"My apologies," she murmured and turned to make a silent retreat like a dutiful maid.

He stepped in front of her before she could slip out of the room.

"You're new," he noted. "I don't remember you. I've been distracted of late but I'm certain that even a blind fool would have noticed a beauty like you."

Caroline could not believe it, but she blushed.

"I should have come around the house sooner," he teased. She wanted to school him, as she would if they were equals, but knew that it was better to keep her tongue tied and face demure. The gentleman was possibly flirting with her, a maid, and to make it all the more absurd she was technically his stepmother now. Men, she thought with a mental roll of her eyes.

He touched a stray lock of hair and for a moment, her heart beat rapidly. He was very handsome, and he knew it. A rake, she realized. A charming rake, but a rake nonetheless. Even with that knowledge she found herself thinking that if she had had to have been married into this blasted family, she would have much rather have had the son than the father. Lord Edward seemed the complete opposite of his conniving, foul father. In fact, she felt somewhat bad for him and his plight. He certainly had not had an easy upbringing, what with knowing his father disapproved of him and always living in the shadow of his brother's successes. Yes, she much preferred Lord Edward, she decided. That is, if she did not have a choice and had to marry a Bennington, she had amended. It did not really matter now, she laughed to herself. She was either now a widow or free of the contract entirely since the marriage had never been consummated. She only prayed that the knowledge of her father's actions had died with the duke. She suspected that they had, for the duke had seemed the sort of man to keep his aces close to his chest. All she had to do was survive until she could be ransomed and return to her quiet life in the country. The country which seemed not only miles away, but a lifetime away.

"It's nice to meet you, Miss…" He took her hand and bowed to her, playacting as he waited for her to provide her name and she automatically dipped into a curtsey as she might have done if they were introduced as equals at a ball.

He chuckled softly, and she realized her mistake. He thought she was playacting too. She froze in terror as he pulled the pins from her cap and her hair fell about her shoulders.

"Baker," she said hastily. "Miss Baker." Her hand went to the crown of her head, trying to gather the silken sheet of her hair.

"And your given name?" he asked. His eyes were hot upon her.

"If you'll excuse me, my lord," she curtsied again leaving the cap behind as she fled, "I believe that I am needed in the kitchen," she threw over her shoulder as she ran. His laughter followed her and for some reason she was reminded of his wretched father, the dead duke. Even though Emily was not her true name, she had not been able to bring herself to offer it. It seemed far too personal in Caroline's mind. She realized that she did not know much about the personal lives of maids but as a lady, there were only a handful of men that she had permitted to call her Caroline alone. With no title to tie down that formality, a single name seemed strangely intimate.

She heard his deep, masculine chuckle follow her from the room and for some reason it frightened her to her core.

Yes, she decided, he was charming to be sure, but more than that, dangerous.

NEWS OF THE DUKE OF MANCHESTER'S DEMISE rocked London the following morning. The bodies of the duke and his men had been found floating along Brackenbrush creek outside of a small farming village. How far they had drifted from the site of the murders Caroline could not glean from the random tidbits that she picked up as the servants all chattered in frenzied whispers.

It did not take long for it to come to light that no female forms had been found.

"Poor lady. They think that the Duchess might not have drifted downstream as far," A pert brunette named Mary had told the other servants at their afternoon tea, "perhaps her gown got caught on a branch. Perhaps she was swept even further if she was petite. Or, she might not have been with him at all. No one seems to know but the local constable is searching the river banks for ten leagues in either direction."

"Poor lady," said another. "No doubt she has been subjected to a fate worse than death."

Caroline could not add that was far more close to the truth than she would have liked. She shuddered remembering the whorehouse where she and Marilee had first been taken. Poor Marilee. Where was she now?

"To think," a young scullery maid chimed in, "She'd only been married for a handful of days at most. It's bad luck to be sure."

"Her bad luck began when she married the duke," Mrs. Reilly scoffed. "I've never heard of her. Probably an upstart marrying his Grace for title and coin." She harrumphed. "The one I pity is her maid. No one speaks of it, but there should have been two women at the least. A duchess does not travel alone."

Caroline wished nothing more than to defend her own honor, but there was no way to do so without sounding too smoky by half. Besides, she still did not know who in this room was in league with her captors and dared not risk a word getting back to the Madam. She opted for attentive silence.

"They must have been set upon by brigands," a young footman, named Charles, added. "I heard tell the duke was shot straight through the heart." He made a cross over his face. "And you all know Jerry. He might have been a bastard, and a mean 'ol drunkard, but he was a fine shot and a better brawler. He wouldn't have gone down easy. I suppose someone should carry word to his mum."

Caroline caught her breath. She had not thought of the coachman and his family. More than the duke had died that day.

The others all bowed their heads respectfully as well. Caroline was reminded that these people had known the duke and his men, likely quite well. None seemed overly upset about their master's demise. Few had cared for the man, she had learned. Still, it was a voracious piece of gossip that had them all in titters and making concerted attempts to get into the good graces of Lord Edward, no…Lord Manchester, their new duke.

A FEW HOURS LATER THE HOUSE RECEIVED A VISIT from one Lady Lydia Blackwell, who had come to pay her respects.

"That's Lord Robert's betrothed," Lizzy had whispered as she and Caroline had peered out from behind a tapestry at the beautiful lady who was shaking the damp from her cloak in the hall. "Or, she had been. She must have really loved him to have waited so long."

Lady Blackwell was unnervingly tall, nearly standing equal to the gentleman. She was willowy and so graceful that her height only enhanced her beauty. She had raven black hair and eyes the same color blue as her cerulean gown. She really was striking.

"Oh, Edward," Lady Lydia held out her hands and gave the only remaining Bennington a sad sigh as he approached her. One lone tear trickled down the impeccable smoothness of her cheek. "Your Grace," she amended. "My heart is broken. It's as if I've lost my own father. Who could have guessed we would lose him so soon after dear Robert's passing?" She wiped at her eyes and Lord Edward patted her on the shoulder.

"You've had more than your fill of tragedies these few months. With Robert lost," Edward said.

"I know that we weren't officially family yet," she whimpered, "but I had to come because no one else will understand what we've suffered. I don't know how you manage to keep soldiering on." She laid a comforting hand on his arm.

"One does what one must," Edward said. He gestured toward the parlor and the lady preceded him in.

"Poor lady," Lydia repeated the sentiment that had been used earlier that day. "I'm starting to think that women around the Benningtons are cursed."

"Are there more?" Caroline whispered to Lizzy.

Lizzy laughed as if even she thought her theory ridiculous but could not help herself. "The house is cursed," she revealed as if it were a well-known fact.

"How so?"

"Well," Lizzy ticked the list off her fingers. "They say that the duke's first wife died of the winter fever, but my mother; she works at Heatherton Hall," she sidetracked, "that's how I got a position here." She continued, "She thinks the Duchess poisoned herself. She had terrible bouts of melancholy and loathed the duke so much that she most often resided at Heatherton while the duke remained in London. The only thing that made her happy were her sons."

Caroline listened with bated breath.

"When they went to Eton, she had nothing left, and mother thinks she couldn't bear it any longer. He drove her to it, you know."

"The old duke?" Caroline whispered.

Lizzy nodded.

"That's horrible," Caroline exclaimed. It did not sound so unlike the future that she had thought awaited her. She thought that she would never have resorted to such depths, but there was no telling what horrors the duchess had endured in all her years married to the horrible man.

"You haven't met the duke," Lizzy replied before clapping her hand over her mouth for having said such a terrible thing about the deceased. Caroline had, in fact, met the late duke, but she was not ready to tell Lizzy that quite yet.

She asked the maid to continue.

"Well, Lord Robert was killed at sea... leaving his betrothed," Lizzy gestured toward the parlor, "who had waited for five long years to marry, heartbroken and alone. She's practically on the shelf now when at one time she had been the most eligible lady in London and in line to marry a marquess who would one day be duke." She ticked a third finger. "Next, the new Lady Bennington dies only days after her wedding in some horrible accident."

Caroline was nodding now, but none of this was new information to her. It was tragic, but it certainly did not mean that the house was cursed.

"Don't even get me started on the maids," Lizzy finished with a flourish.

"What about the maids?" Caroline asked. She felt all the way to her bones that this information was pivotal.

"They disappear," Lizzy shrugged. "All the time. In the middle of the night. Poof, they're gone! A few days later a new one appears. Then poof, she's gone too. You can't ask where they went. No one knows, or if they do, they aren't telling. I heard that the last girl who asked too many questions got sent to the Americas. It's a curse; I tell you."

Caroline gaped. Lizzy may be naïve, but she had just confirmed Caroline's worst fear. Women were being filtered in and out of this house like slaves. She still did not know how many people were involved, or if the duke and his sons had been aware of the criminal activity taking place under their own roof. Her late husband had certainly been capable of such treachery, she realized, and she did recall that her father had mentioned that the duke had unnamed, sordid contacts. He prided himself on taking advantage of people. Hadn't he taken advantage of her? Still, the highwaymen had not brought her directly to this house, but a brothel, leading her to wonder whether or not they had any direct connection to the Benningtons at all. She thought rather that it might be a network of households all across London working with the madam, which meant she could trust no one. However, if the duke had been involved, he would not have been killed by his own men, would he? For the moment it was all too muddled for Caroline to make sense of, but she knew that if she had any hope of escaping, she had to find out more.

"I hope you stay," Lizzy eventually said in a matter-of-fact tone. "I like you."

"I hope I stay too," Caroline added. She was not happy as a maid, but who knew what worse fate might be in store for her. At least here she was only a short distance from her father's townhouse. She only had to walk there on her day off, but when she asked when her day off would be, Mrs. Reilly laughed outright. "We shall see in a few months," she said. "Anyway, where would you go, girl? Do you have family in London? I was told the contrary."

Caroline bit her lip and shook her head. She could not say.

CHAPTER 10

Mrs. Reilly was in a tither over who would serve the tea and biscuits in the parlor. The footman who normally did the job had a cold and was sneezing most indecorously. The other male servants were out on various tasks, and the usual girl that Mrs. Reilly hoped to use had taken a temporary leave of absence and returned to her father's farm in Scotland with her brother, one of the aforementioned footmen. Caroline learned that the maid had been in love with the late duke's valet and was taking his death to heart. She wished that she could have comforted the girl and told her that her lover had died an honorable death protecting his lord and lady.

"I can do it," Caroline volunteered.

"You?" Mrs. Reilly said incredulously, but Caroline carried the tray with enough grace that Mrs. Reilly beamed and declared that she was, "pleased to see there is something you can do without a catastrophe." The housekeeper did not know that serving tea was one thing she was more than adept at. Still, it rankled that she hadn't gotten credit for being a fast learner. Sure, she had made more mistakes than she could count, but she never made the same mistake twice.

She entered the parlor on silent footsteps and set about arranging the tray at a table by the windowsill. Lord Edward and his guest were sitting in chairs opposite one another.

"You'll have to plan the funeral service," Lady Blackwell was saying. "I could help. I still have many of the contacts your father had sent me as we were arranging Robert's service." She sighed. "It could be a dual service for your father and your brother."

"Triple," Lord Edward corrected.

"Who?" Lady Blackwell wondered aloud.

"The duchess."

"He really married?" Lady Blackwell murmured with wonder. Caroline pretended to be busy arranging the spoons and napkins. She ought not to have been spying, but she needed to hear more. "To think that Robert's death drove him that far from sanity."

"Apparently," Lord Edward laughed sadly. "He could have married you if he had been that desperate, in Robert's stead." Caroline could tell that Lord Edward was teasing, but Lady Blackwell's cringe was visible. "We are both aware that he had more faith in you than he ever did in me," Edward added.

"I think even he knew better than to suggest such a thing," she replied.

"You were far too smart for him," Lord Edward agreed. "You would have been a nightmare as his duchess."

"That's why I was better off with Robert," she said in a soft tone.

"Of course, you were better off with me," a deep male voice said with what sounded like a smile from the doorway.

Lady Lydia screamed and Caroline, her back turned to the doorway and therefore having no warning, threw the teapot into the air and watched in horror as it came crashing and splashing down at her feet. She bent at once to begin soaking up the scalding liquid before it ruined the beautiful carpet. The shards of ceramic lay scattered around her. She would have to be careful not to cut herself when she collected them. The lords and lady did not even take note of her mess. Or if they did, they did not mention it. Servants were meant to be invisible and ignored. Of course dropping the tea set did not lend itself to inconspicuousness.

"ROBERT!" Lady Lydia gasped when she had finally collected herself. The gentleman had approached the lady, grasped her by the elbows as if to take her in his arms, but Lady Lydia had pulled away and stared up into the gentleman's face with unbridled horror. "You were dead," she said.

"My demise was grossly overstated," Robert replied.

"What happened? How… How are you here?" Lady Lydia stuttered.

Caroline could see nothing, but the back of the gentleman's overcoat, but from her position on the floor she had a clear view of the shock and terror on the faces of the other two occupants of the room. Without even seeing his face, she could discern that he struck likely the most imposing figure that London had seen in a decade. He was taller than both of them, his massive, but lean form dwarfing the pair like a beast who stalked the night. That must have been exactly what the horrified pair were thinking, Caroline mused, that he was a specter raised from the dead.

"I came as soon as I could," he explained. "I wasn't on that ship. I had taken another post but the paperwork for the transfer hadn't become official yet. When I realized that my death notice had been sent, I raced to Bath to meet father. There, I learned that he had gone north to Heatherton. When I got there, they said he had never arrived."

Caroline wanted to clarify that there were a lot of pieces missing from that story, but there was no way that the gentleman could have known about the byway being washed out and his father's delay.

"I took his usual route from Manchester to Bath in reverse hoping that we might cross paths and that I could tell him that I was alive and well."

"Good God, man," Lord Edward finally broke forth from his shock. He put one hand upon his brother's shoulder, slowly as if afraid that if he touched him, he would dissolve into mist. "Father is dead. We found out this morning."

"I know," Lord Robert informed them with a solemn sigh. No, not Lord Robert. His Grace, Caroline corrected herself mentally. First, she had been married to the duke. Then, they had all thought Lord Edward the new duke. And now it seemed that the real heir, Lord Robert, had arrived, and he was in fact the new Duke of Manchester. It was all so confusing. She knew she should leave the room. Any good maid would do so, but as Mrs. Reilly kept reminding her, she was a terrible maid. She stayed where she was kneeling among the shards of the teapot, unabashedly listening.

"I happened to pass through the town where they found the bodies," Lord Robert said. "They had identified him the day prior from the livery and sent the notice. I made a list of all of the usual belongings that he traveled with that would be recognizable. If any come up for public sale, we might be able to trace them to the culprits. It's not likely, however, only a fool's hope. I suspect they would be smart enough to smuggle their spoils to France or India where they would go unnoticed." He ran a hand through his already disheveled hair and Caroline noted that he was as dark as his brother was fair. "I confirmed the identification and thought that, perhaps, if I rode fast enough, I might be able to arrive before the letter and tell you myself. I was delayed when they informed me of a certificate of marriage that had been found with him and that there was still no sign of his wife. I took the time to compose a letter to the lady's father offering my condolences and informing him of the tragedy. From what I'm told it was pure ill-starred chance and there was nothing that could have been done to prevent it, not on that stretch of road."

Caroline was dumbfounded. The late duke, his father, had not been exaggerating when he had claimed that his eldest son was efficient and skilled at managing all manner of situations. The murder had only been made public for a few hours and already he had taken the matter well in hand.

Her heart ached for her father, for the letter that he must receive. He would believe it at first, she realized, that she was dead. He would mourn her and the cross words that had been their final parting. As time passed, the investigation drew to an end, and if no body was found he might, only then, begin to hope. The constable would finally permit her father to put out a reward for any information on her whereabouts and that is when the ransom would be presented. The brigands would not waste resources on a ransom when all signs pointed to her demise. That process was still weeks away, she realized, but she was satisfied that she was now even one step closer to being free of this horrible plight.

Caroline had nearly finished amassing the last pieces of the teapot in her gathered apron when Lady Lydia made her way over to the table beside where Caroline stood and picked up a biscuit from the tray. She fingered the food, crumbling the corner onto a napkin, but did not eat. Caroline wondered if the shock of seeing her lover appear when she had thought him dead had made the lady shy. It certainly must have been a shock.

"I'll bring more tea," Caroline said loud enough only for the lady to hear.

"There's no need," Lady Lydia replied. "I shall be going."

"Lydia," The new duke said in a patient and just barely pleading tone. "We should talk."

"Tomorrow," the lady said with a shaky breath. Her gazed remained on the biscuit and she refused to look toward the men. She set the food down uneaten on the napkin and exited the room without bidding farewell.

Strange, Caroline thought. She was certain the duke had expected his betrothed to be elated with the news of his good health, but perhaps grief and then sudden happiness were too potent of emotions for the lady to handle with grace. Caroline hoped her own father was able to react with a bit more aplomb when she was finally returned to him. The baron had not shown her affection in years, but she at least hoped for a smile. Lady Lydia had given nothing of the sort.

"I should go as well," Lord Edward's charismatic voice broke the heavy silence. He was stiff, as if trying to balance being happy that his brother had returned and a pervasive dislike that seemed to ripple between the gentlemen. They did not get on, she determined, likely never had, and she realized, with their father pitting them against one another it was no wonder.

She reminded herself that the elder, so like his father, must have been a brute for the jovial and charming Edward to have grown up alongside, but he did not seem so formidable to her. Large certainly, and capable. Still, what she knew of the man from his own father's stories told her that would have been enough to build an impenetrable wall between them. Hadn't Lord Robert come in and taken immediate control even after being gone for more than five years and recently presumed dead? And Edward, without a single word, had been demoted to lesser son once more. She wondered if the traits men often boasted as admirable for leadership were really just disguises for the monster within.

Lord Edward brushed past her, grabbing a biscuit and giving her a covert wink before he left. Caroline was left standing like an idiot with an apron full of broken ceramic and an ugly dress whose entire front was soaked in tea.

"Shall I get more tea?" she asked dumbly. She would have left in silence but the sag of the duke's shoulders after being abandoned by his betrothed and his brother made her want to say something to comfort him. He had made his entrance with such a cheerful tone. There was no doubt in her mind that he had been expecting a joyful reception.

He turned toward her, surprised to hear a maid speak in his presence, perhaps. Caroline gasped.

His face was similar to his father's in the basic masculine bone structure with a square jaw and firm brow, but it was more angular. His father had been paunchy. The younger man was anything but soft. This is what that face would have looked like if the duke had been thirty years younger as well as muscular and lean. His features, like his eyes, were hard. They bespoke the sight of many horrors. Horrors which he had not intention of sharing. He held them close.

None of those things were what had forced Caroline to swallow her gasp though. No, he would have been a shocking enough man on his own, not handsome exactly, never beautiful like his brother, but intriguing at least to look upon. He had a presence, a gruff brooding style, but commanding all the same. Still, that was not what drew her eye.

No, it was the jagged scar that ran down his face that would forever be the first thing that drew an onlooker's eye. It ran from his temple, down his cheek, over the strong curve of his chin, and continued down the side of his neck. Down all the way into the collar of his shirt and who knew how much further. She could not take her eyes from the disfigurement.

It was healed. Several months old at least and no longer puckered or discolored. But it looked angry, jagged, and wide. It must have been incredibly painful when it had first been received. It had missed his eye by a hair's breadth. She guessed that most people, upon seeing it for the first time, would be unable to control their shock and horror. Children might scream, bystanders would certainly stare, and he would very likely be gifted with one of two dreadful reactions. Pity or disgust.

Caroline thanked her lucky stars that she had been raised a lady and not a maid, for she had not flinched in the least. Her childhood governess would have been proud. She blinked once and stared him straight in the eyes ignoring the disfigurement. It was well out of line for who he thought she was, her lowly station, but she felt that he deserved this little show of strength when she doubted that he was often met without fear.

Like a punch to the gut, she understood Lady Lydia's reaction. The lady had likely been told about the injury in words but, having not laid eyes upon her promised for five years, she might not have under-stood the full extent of the damage. Her shock and horror had not been that he was alive, although that would have been part of it, so much as at the first glimpse of his visage.

Caroline noticed that the duke was staring at her, as if he were waiting for her delayed reaction and steeling himself to weather it.

"I'm sure, she'll get used to it," slipped out before the words could be stopped. She instantly regretted the speech. If she were Miss Caroline, and perhaps if she and the duke were well acquainted, she might be permitted to make such bald statements. A daughter of a baron could speak. Miss Emily Baker, a maid in his house, would have done better to keep her mouth shut.

His eyes narrowed, and he hit her with a look that would set the most seasoned soldier to quaking in his boots. And my, did she quake.

She opened her mouth to apologize, but he spoke before she could.

"Get out," he growled.

Caroline ran from the room, losing several pieces of pottery from her apron in her wake. She did not turn around to collect them.

CHAPTER 11

Caroline spent the rest of the day terrified that the duke was going to sack her. If she were fired, then what would happen? Where would she go? Would she be sent back to the rookery to do only heavens knew what? Would she be deemed too much trouble and finally disposed of? Worse, she thought with a twist of her gut, what would happen to Marilee? She had no idea where her friend was or what sort of conditions she had been placed in, other than that her supposed title was laundress. She could be anywhere and subject to any number of horrors. Caroline tried not to think on the matter too much else she would find herself spiraling into a pit of despair.

Worry after worry cascaded upon her. What if the maid was found out and no longer protected by her supposed nobility? Caroline could not begin to imagine the horrors that might occur if such a thing became known, not when it was already apparent that these vagrants were skilled at making females of lesser origins simply disappear.

When evening came and Caroline lay upon her uneven palette, she found that sleep evaded her. She could not stop worrying that she had stepped out of line and perhaps angered a very dangerous and very powerful man. If the new duke was anything like his father there would be hell to pay.

In the morning, Mrs. Reilly was still short with her, but no more than usual. The housekeeper did not seem to have any knowledge of the incident else Caroline was sure she would have gotten a tongue lashing, or worse. She shivered at the thought. She had never been beaten but would not put it past the woman to give her the first taste of the vulgar punishment. Perhaps the duke had said nothing. She was beneath his notice. Still, she decided that it was best if she avoided the duke outright. Best not to tempt fate, she thought.

She went about her duties with all the stealth of a servant who had been born to the task. On any occasion that she was asked to enter a room where the duke might have been present, she was able to pass the task off to one of the other maids in exchange for taking on their more cumbersome chores. It was exhausting but necessary and the other females were more than happy to take advantage of her offer without question.

She was glad of it because whispers through the house alleged that the duke had been surly and curt since his return. He and his brother had faced off in several sharp rows that had left the house on tenterhooks. The gentlemen were not in agreement with the duke's determination to avenge his father, his brother seeming to think that the money and effort being devoted a futile effort. They had no leads and no evidence. In a way, Caroline agreed with Lord Edward. She could not inform the brothers that the highwaymen had seemed to have come across them by sheer accident. They had not even been traveling the usual route after all. Beyond that, she had heard nothing during her capture of anything tying them to a specific group or purpose. The only thing that she knew was that they had connections at one of the many brothels in London's seedier areas. There were innumerable brothels in London, and Caroline could not even lead them to the right place. The madam had not been pleased with their actions and so Caroline had determined that as awful as the woman may be, she had not ordered the attack. It was most likely, as Lord Edward had professed, that the thugs had simply been in the habit of accosting carriages for no other purpose than to rob the occupants. Having come across a duke who had been determined to stand his ground, the situation had spun out of control. Still the elder brother had been determined to find the culprits and avenge his father. Accident or no he wanted the men responsible brought to justice. Caroline wanted the same although she could scarcely think how it might ever come to pass.

Caroline could not decide if the duke's efforts meant that she ought to trust him outright or if they were a signal of his true involvement in the underbellies of London's less desirable nature. If he were acting from a place of honor, then he could be trusted. On the other hand, if he had his own criminal network to defend it would make sense that one band of miscreants might wish revenge on another. She had heard tell that such groups were protective of their own people and territories. My she had become such a cynical thing, but there were far too many unknowns for Caroline to put herself, and Marilee, in the line of fire. She had to bide her time. It was better to be safe than play her hand too soon and lose all.

To make matters more difficult, the young duke visited Lady Lydia Blackwell daily, but she had yet to return to the house, and it seemed that the duke's mood was spiraling with every passing day that his betrothed expressed discomfort at the mere sight of him. Five years of letters, it had seemed, did not make up for the shock of what it meant to live with his disfigurement. He had returned home expecting a warm welcome, and was met nothing but misfortune from every angle. She could almost feel sorry for him. Almost.

Caroline had assured him that the lady would get used to it. Now, she was confident that even the sight of her in his presence would remind the gentleman that she had been sorely wrong. Consequently, she stayed out of his sight.

By the third day of evasion, it was not uncommon to be approached with a sly grin and a cheerful, "I'll handle the tea service if you iron the linens." Serving tea took no more than a quarter of the hour. Ironing all of the freshly laundered bed linens and clothing items for two Lords' rooms took two hours at best and that was if she didn't burn anything, or herself, with the hot irons.

She had just finished that exact task, her arms laden with a basket of neatly folded shirts, when her path crossed Lord Edward's in the hall.

"A beautiful face on a dreary day," Lord Edward had crooned with a glance out the window at the grey clouds. His back was rigid and from the way that he had been stomping down the hall he had just broke free from another spat. "Just the tonic I needed."

With the basket in her arms, she was unable to push by him and he stood in the middle of the hall as if he was fully aware that she would not.

"I have to get these to Melly," she murmured as if he knew who the new maid was that had arrived only the day before.

"She can wait," he grinned. "If she complains simply tell her that it was my doing and she can take up any issue with me."

Caroline loosed a breath and waited in demure silence. She kept her head down and gaze on the floor between them. Lord Edward stepped forward and hooked a finger beneath her chin, drawing her gaze upward to meet his own.

"How about a kiss to warm a man on this dreary day?" he suggested.

Bold! She must have shown that she had been startled by the request because he chuckled. He leaned forward as if to kiss her. A lady would have slapped him in the face, but Caroline was not entirely sure what a maid was supposed to do. She froze. His lips aimed for hers, but diverted purposefully at the last moment to land on her exposed neck just beneath her ear. What a cad, she thought! He had meant to shake her, was testing the stubborn will that he seemed to sense bubbled beneath the surface. He was toying with her, she realized.

He chuckled softly.

While Caroline was still setting about collecting herself, Lord Edward strolled away whistling a happy tune.

She decided that she could not stay in the house any longer. Between the moody duke and his devilish rake of a brother Caroline was definitely over her head.

She had to get a letter out. She had to get word to her father that she was alive and in London.

She was fairly certain that she would not be permitted to send a letter, at least not one addressed in her name, false or otherwise. Still, she doubted that the wicked members of the household knew who she really was, and therefore, she hoped that they would not recognize that mail should not at all be sent to Gravesend Manor in Northwickshire. She wished Father was in London, but she knew he was not. Lords did not open for another week, even if Father chose to attend. The letter would take several days in travel to reach him in Northwickshire, and then, of course, Father would have to travel to Town. The thought made her seethe with impatience.

She scrawled a quick note. Nothing too obvious, just I'm in London, father. Please, come to the house. She did not sign it. She knew that her father was acute enough to place that his daughter was in London at what he would assume was either her husband's town-home or his own. Anyone reading it could not have known that she had given away the specific location of her imprisonment. She folded the paper closed and left no indication of the sender. Then, she slipped the letter into the hallway basket that held several other outgoing letters from the staff.

With a deep breath and a solemn prayer, she went back to her work and awaited her rescue.

CHAPTER 12

That evening she was too nervous to gather with the rest of the servants as they waited for the house to quiet before they finished their evening chores in secret. Many had gone to bed, but a handful remained playing cards in the kitchen and Caroline found that the raucous noise was too much for her agitated state.

She knew that Lord Edward was in the parlor sharing a drink with two of his schoolmates from Eton. They were loud and promised to be up for several hours before she could slip in and put the room back to rights.

The duke had gone out; his valet had said as much as he had taken a bottle of dark amber drink and the hand of Mary out into the alley. James had it easy compared to other valets, he often boasted. The duke did not like him to wait up and help the gentleman prepare for bed. That made for early nights and a surplus of free time for a position that had meant to be around the clock. Lord Edward was the more demanding of the two, but James did not seem to mind working for that brother.

All this meant, Caroline realized, that the study was empty, and she had several hours to herself. She had been eyeing the bookshelf for weeks. She had noticed that the lowest shelf beside the fireplace was filled with no less than two dozen novellas. It had been an age since she could lose herself in a book. She sorely needed the relief. The books must have belonged to the duchess before her passing and so Caroline supposed, in a way, they were hers. She had been waiting for the right moment to leaf through their pages but now she thought with excitement that she might even be able to sit by the firelight and read more fully while she waited for Lord Edward to clear out of the parlor.

The room was filled with shadow except for the spaces nearest to the dying fire. It was just enough light for her to pick over the adjacent shelf without needing to light a lamp.

She opened the door further and peered in. Blessed silence, she thought. With a deep sigh she stepped inside and shut the door behind her. If anyone were to enter, she would hear the door first and simply claim that she had been preparing to check the flame for the evening.

Quiet steps on the soft carpet made her stealthy as a feline. She approached the shelf, crouched before it, and pulled a volume from the mahogany bookcase.

She had to hold it in front of the fire to read the title. It happened to be something that she had already read, she noted, and put it back where it belonged. She checked another. It was old and worn, as if it had been thumbed through a thousand times. If the duchess had enjoyed this tale enough to read it over and over, then Caroline would take that as a solid recommendation.

She settled herself in front of the fire and cracked open the aged binding.

"What are you doing?" an amused voice asked from the darkness.

Caroline gasped and scrambled to get to her feet but found herself tangled in the thick layers of dress. It was not graceful and when she had finally righted herself, she was gasping from sheer panic as well as the effort.

The duke, on the other hand, was laughing. A deep, vibrant sound that sounded far more natural than she had expected, as if he were given over to the act often.

"You don't bat an eye upon beholding my face but leap out of your britches doing what?" He chuckled and stood from where he had been seated in the far corner behind his desk to come take the book from her trembling hand. "Reading a romance?" he said. She wanted to remind him that women did not wear britches, but she understood his meaning and decided that it was best not to split hairs.

"I-I thought the room was empty," she stammered. It was not really an answer, but it was all that she could manage in the moment.

"You've been avoiding me," he said with a pointed lift of one brow. He offered the book back, and she snatched it, clasping it to her breast as if it were a shield between them. He expected her to put it back, she guessed. But first, she needed to apologize and explain.

"I didn't want you to fire me. I need this job," she lied. Well, it was a partial truth. "I was out of line other day and..."

"No. It is I who was out of line," he cut her off. "A gentleman should not raise his voice."

"I am only the help," she began.

"Especially to the help," he replied, "who have no recourse."

"You had a long day yourself," she soothed. "A thousand pardons, Your Grace."

He nodded. "I was cross and tired, but that was no reason to take out my spleen upon an innocent." He shook his head. "I had spent the previous days racing around the country trying to set my life back to rights only to feel as if it was all falling apart one ruthless stroke of fate at a time. It had nothing to do with you. I offer my apology." Caroline gaped at him. Had he, a duke, really just apologized to a maid? What was even more shocking was that it had not felt like he had done so out of obligation. He had sounded sincere.

She might have been surprised that he had such insight, but realized that his father had had unique skill for evaluating a situation as well, even if he used the knowledge for ill gains. She reminded herself that this man was trained to be dangerous, both on the battlefield and in the ballroom. This mishap might be something that he chose to use against her in the future. That or he wished to ingratiate her towards him so that she might become less of a problem.

"Please don't tell Mrs. Reilly that I was in here," she begged. "I'm supposed to wait with the other servants in the kitchen until everyone has gone to bed to finish my chores, but after a day of hard work it is just so loud. I was searching for a moment of silence." She realized just how much she missed the quiet of her former life. Everything had been moving so fast around her recently that she had not had a blessed moment to herself. For one sweet second, she had held it in her grasp. "I wasn't going to steal it," she said holding up the book. "Just read," she promised. "I won't do it again."

"I spend most evenings in here working or thinking until the early morning hours," he said as if that were an answer. "If you wait for me to retire before doing whatever it is that you must do, you'll never get any rest."

"It is your house," she replied. It was not as if she could order him to go to sleep. Such a thought was laughable really.

"Like you, I am more at home in the quiet," he continued. "This study has become somewhat of a sanctuary since my return. London is a lot louder than I remembered. I will be glad when the majority of the ton removes to Bath and Brighton."

Caroline knew exactly what he meant. It had been five years for him and six since she had last been to London. The city had seemed to double in size from what she remembered, or perhaps it had simply been so long that she had forgotten the constant chaos of it. Even though she had yet to venture outside of this house, she was well aware of the hundreds, maybe thousands of people that passed by on Park Lane each day. She had become used to the quiet of the country and she supposed that, when it was not engaged in battle, a ship at sea might have been peaceful as well.

"You are welcome to read here in the evenings until the others go to bed," he said when she had only nodded her understanding. "I promise not to spill your secret or release you from your position." He chuckled as if he found her concern amusing, "and I'm fairly quiet if you don't mind my company. I'd still like use of this room for my own purposes."

Caroline looked at him with wariness. Was this a trap? Or might it simply be a kind offer so long as she did not disturb his privacy?

She could not say and her hesitation must have been apparent because he stepped away and moved back to his corner. Without a word he lit the lamp on his desk and pulled a pile of papers to him. He placed one elbow on the desk, fisted his hand, and leaned the uninjured side of his chin upon it before starting to read.

It was as if he were trying to show her that this was all that he would be doing if she chose to join him. That she was welcome to do whatever she pleased so long as she left him to his ledgers.

Warning bells went off in Caroline's mind. He was being too kind, too gentle. She pictured his father, which was done without difficultly because they were very clearly relations, and reminded herself that the elder gentleman had been able to appear kind and accommodating too if it suited his purpose. Then, she recalled the way she had run from the room after he had shouted at her and she told herself that that beast must still be in there somewhere, waiting to take a swipe with his piercing claw.

Without a word, Caroline returned the book to the shelf and exited the study.

He did not make an effort to call her back or repeat the offer. He did not even look up as she closed the door softly behind her. She left him in the darkened study and was determined never to return.

WHEN CAROLINE FINALLY ENTERED THEIR LITTLE bedchamber, she found Lizzy sound asleep. Caroline slipped out of her dress, into her nightclothes, and lay down on the mat. She felt something poking her through the thin fabric and reached beneath her to see what it was. Her hand settled into a pile of torn paper that had been hidden beneath her woolen blanket so that only she might discover it.

Caroline carried the scraps to the hall where she might look at them in the light, but the knot in her stomach told her that she already knew what they were.

Her letter.

It had been torn and left so that there could be no mistaking that it had not been sent; that it would never be allowed to be sent; that she would never be permitted to have a letter leave this house no matter how neatly disguised.

Someone was reading the servants' mail, she realized, and she still had no idea who it might be.

CHAPTER 13

Lady Lydia paid her first visit to the duke two days later and Caroline supposed that her conversation with Lord Robert had made it safe enough at least to serve the tea. The other maids were disappointed, but Caroline had decided that she would rather face the gentleman than wash another chamber pot. One of the servants had been feeling ill these past few days and she simply would not do it.

Caroline felt sorry for the socialite who seemed to be trying so hard to force herself to fall into easy conversation with the duke. No matter Lady Lydia's best effort she stumbled every time that she happened to look at his face.

Whether the duke had noted his betrothed's stiffness or the way that her eyes lingered on his arms or his shoulders, anywhere but his face, he did not let on. Once, when Caroline was setting their cups and saucers down on the table between them, she saw the lady's eyes drift to his hands as if still searching for an actual piece of the duke, and not his clothing, that she still found appealing.

Lady Blackwell had gritted her teeth and turned to stare out the window instead. Her voice had been cheerful and her conversation light, but her stature was anything but.

Caroline had chanced at glance down at the duke's hands and noticed another long scar on the back of the hand nearest her that disappeared into the cuff of his jacket. Was there no part of him unscathed? What on earth had he been through? And how could Lady Blackwell look at such markings on the man that she loved and view them with aversion rather than an overwhelming urge to soothe away his pain? Was that not what love was? Caroline might not care for the duke, but even she could see that there was more to the gentleman than his scars. Certainly, Lady Lydia's longstanding affection could help her to look beyond the mar if a stranger were able to do so. Lady Blackwell at least had the memory of the man before the injury. Caroline felt an upwelling of righteous indignation on his behalf. She wanted to shake the lady until some sense rattled around in her empty brain.

Was there any inch of this man's body that wasn't mangled with hurt? She felt a blush rise to her neck at the inappropriate image that rose to mind, of the fact that to answer that question she would have to see a man, this man in particular, naked. Caroline pushed that thought aside, chalking it up to pure feminine innocence that would rise any time the suggestion of nudity was made. She was only embarrassed that the thought had occurred in the first place. It was uncouth to wonder about anything more than could be seen by the casual eye. It was likely that Lady Lydia had considered the very same thing and perhaps that was what had made her uncomfortable.

Caroline had straightened and caught the duke watching her. She would have bet her entire fortune on the fact that he had noted Lady Blackwell's reaction, noted that Caroline had seen it as well, and followed Caroline's gaze to the offending scar. Why did he have to be so observant? And how was he so casual about what had transpired? She felt a flush rise again. Oh Lord, she hoped that he had not seen the first. Hadn't seen it, and had not gleaned what kind of untoward thoughts might have had such a result. She told herself that he had not, but this time she would not bet her fortune on it.

. . .

Weeks passed and Caroline could not continue to avoid Lord Edward. She crossed paths with him when she was collecting his dinner plates from his room. She had thought that he had departed, but it seemed that he had returned to retrieve something and just in time to catch her unawares. She did not think he had followed her, did not deign him so low that he would be crass enough to take advantage of the knowledge that she would have to enter his bedchamber. But it seemed that she was wrong. She was finding, she noted with a wry twist of her gut, that she was wrong more oft than not these days. Oh, how she longed for her own life where she knew her place in the world. With her father, everything was easy and quiet, and others had to answer her questions rather than demanding answers from her or ignoring her as if she were nothing more than a dormouse.

"Ah, Emily, you have been avoiding me these past weeks," Lord Edward crooned, coming up behind her and lacing his hands around her waist. She could feel him pressed up against the entire length of her back and she balked. "Don't you worry in the least," he said, "I don't bite."

"But I do!" she exclaimed, turning in his arms and shoving him away.

He just laughed and proceeded to back her against the wall.

"You shall come to me eventually," he murmured against her neck. "They always do and you won't regret it. It isn't as if anyone need know. It's just you and I," his voice was smooth and held an appealing tone that she knew had worked for him in the past. Perhaps with an upstart or overly trusting soul, but never with a fine bred lady who had been trained to abhor just such circumstances. In Caroline's eyes, this behavior did much to sour her opinion of the gentleman. A tiny voice in the back of her mind did argue, however. What if he was meant to love you but he is fighting his own control because he thinks you to be too low for acceptance? She thought just as his hand settled upon her waist and made as if to inch its way northward toward her breast. No! This was not right. He had no right to her. It was an even more despicable act, considering as a maid, she was beholden to him as her employer.

"Get off me!" she hissed. Caroline was fearful because she dared not yell. Maids, no matter the situation, were not permitted to cause a scene especially if it involved the family of the house direct. She found herself thinking that she hated nothing more than the bindings of this station. Mayhap, she hated murder more, she acquiesced, but not by leaps or bounds. She swore that if she ever got back to her old life, she would tell every servant in her company to yell as loud as they wish if the ever had need. Honestly, this behavior was repulsive. Oughtn't a Lord to know better? Lord Robert—no the Duke of Manchester—knew better.

Lord Edward pulled away but not before his tongue snaked out and tasted the flesh at her neck. She froze in horror.

"Later," he promised. "You'll want me later."

"You are a monster," she snarled as she grabbed the tray and scurried from the room. The more that she thought on it the more repulsed she became. Others? So he made a habit of this behavior? It was second nature to him and nothing more than a game, an intrigue. Disgusting, vile creature. To think, she had thought Edward the better of the two men. Lord Robert might still be a monster in his own right, but he certainly was not the same sort as his brother. He may yet be worse. The elder may be the seller of women sort instead of their despoiler. How could one chose between bad and worse? She had to focus on the details that she could confirm at present.

She had sorely misread Lord Edward's character. Maybe she had been more inclined to like him because of his easy features and charming style. His nature in general seemed amiable and kind. It was only in these small hidden moments that anyone might suspect different. Perhaps she had pitied him for his plight as a second, underappreciated son, and because he did not have his father's dark visage. Now she was starting to think that his father had not been mistaken in his evaluation that his younger son did not have the makings of a duke. He did not even have the makings of a gentleman. The entire family was a bane, she decided. From sire to spawn they each seemed corrupt in one manner or another, no matter how well they might try to hide the truth, it would out.

Spring rolled into summer and Caroline found that she could not escape Lord Edward. This task was particularly bothersome since she was not allowed to leave the premises. She completed the same series of tasks every day so it was not difficult of him to learn her patterns. He was never as bold as that day in his bedchamber, but he did nothing to hide the lust in his eyes every time their paths crossed. He was hopeful, she realized, that she really would come to him.

If he were to come upon her at her lonesome, he would tuck a strand of hair beneath her cap, using the opportunity to slip a charm or the bud of a flower beneath its band as a gift she supposed. She had stopped wearing the cap and simply braided her hair.

He might trail his hand down her arm or lean in close to breathe in the scent of her. She took to ducking into the nearest room whenever she heard booted footsteps that might have a chance, slim or no, of being his.

When Lord Edward learned that she had spare hours while she waited for the final closing of the night, he began to send the butler to call her up from where she had gathered with the other servants in the kitchen, so that she might read to him since his eyes were tired or he had the beginnings of a megrim. She thought that he must have learned this technique from his father who had used the exact method. The pitying glances that she got from the other maids told her that they understood her predicament. She was only grateful that they did not assume that she was receptive to his attentions. Despite their silent support, they could do nothing to ease her burden. It seemed that the whole house was simply waiting for her to give him what he wished so that he might burn out whatever lust he had gathered and be on to the next maid who caught his fancy.

AFTER SEVERAL WEEKS OF THIS, CAROLINE COULD take no more. She had vowed that she would not return to the study and bother the duke, or fall into one of his schemes, but her evaluation told her that any of Lord Robert's schemes had to be better than Lord Edward's. One brother might look like his father but the other acted like him. The rotter had dropped a piece of an ice confection down the front of her dress in the hope of watching her squirm and reach in to fish it out.

She hadn't.

She had stared at him in cold fury, still as a statue, and let it melt.

"Your stubbornness is unshakable," he had mused with awe. Too late Caroline had realized that her response had only succeeded in making him want her more. She ought to have known, based on her father's warnings about the late duke, that such behavior would be viewed as a challenge to be bested.

So it was that she found herself slipping into the safety of the study just before the sound of boot heels came around the bend. Lord Edward would not dare enter this room. The brothers rarely sought each other out and when they did, it was only to exchange clipped tones and well-disguised insults. At first Caroline had sided with Lord Edward, thinking it right that he should punish his brother for being a authoritarian brute. Now, as time went on, she knew she'd had it wrong. The duke was disapproving of his brother and made no attempt to hide it. From what Caroline had now seen, he had every reason to withhold his endorsement.

The duke was sprawled out on one of the pair of velvet rolled-arm sofas that faced each other perpendicular to the hearth with his cravat undone. The windows were open to let in a breeze. He had one arm tucked behind his head and he was reading a pamphlet that was folded in half in the other. The piles of pamphlets on the floor beside him were either waiting to be read or had already been discarded.

If he noticed her arrival, he did nothing to indicate it.

The room was brighter than usual with the evening sun shining its last rays through the window. In addition, the lamp on the table behind his sofa had been lit so that the duke might not strain his eyesight.

Caroline padded in and headed for the aged book that had sat unread on the lower shelf since that first night. She retrieved her prize, checked again to see if he was watching her; he was not, lit the lamp behind her seat, and took her place on the settee opposite.

They sat in companionable silence for that first evening, and Caroline breathed a sigh of relief. For the first time in months, she felt safe.

CHAPTER 14

It became habit for Caroline to slip into the study for several hours each evening. Sometimes they were silent and sometimes they talked. They never spoke about anything significant. It was not as if Caroline could talk about her past or explain how she had come to be a maid in his house. The only thing that she could be honest about was her deep friendship with Marilee. She was able to speak openly, only adjusting the tales enough to allow him to assume the friendship of two maids, because no one knew that the other captive was anyone other than her cousin, Kate. If somehow her musings did get out, they would mean nothing to her enemies. At least, she hoped that they would not. She certainly could not tell the duke that she was being held against her will and was actually the woman he was devoting a good portion of his time and income to finding. For all she knew, he was aware of the house's inner workings. For all she knew, he wanted to find her for no other reason than to tie up loose ends. Perhaps his father had been killed by accident. It was possible. Lord Bennington was not supposed to have been on the road that evening. Not only had his trip been seriously delayed by the flooding of the byway in Northwick-shire, but the carriage had been forced to take an alternate route due to the overturned hay carts. But if the murder revealed the threads of a twisted plot in London involving highway robberies and the selling of indentured women, then whoever was in charge would do whatever it took to make sure that no evidence led back to the source. She was evidence... living, breathing evidence. If he did not realize that she was Miss Caroline Graves that might be the only thing keeping her alive. If he or anyone else discovered that she had the knowledge to lay bare the entire plot then she might as well pull the trigger herself. Besides, there was Marilee to think about. Even if the duke were somehow, miraculously, oblivious to the treachery under his roof, Marilee would be harmed if Caroline told anyone the truth, himself included. It was best to handle things on her own or wait for her father to pay the ransom. She had known that these things took time, but the waiting was excruciating.

The duke truly had been devoting a considerable amount of effort into finding his father's wife's body, she had learned. She encouraged the topic to come up more often than was prudent, if only to track the progress of the constables and try to predict the time-frame that the ransom would be declared. At this point, she wondered if they ever were going to call for a ransom. It had been months since the duke's murder and her father would still not be like to believe that she was alive. Everyone was firmly convinced that she was dead and any call for payment would be viewed as nothing more than an attempt to exhort money from a grieving father. Too often ransoms were paid only to find that thugs had never even been in possession of the person to be recovered. Only when every other avenue had been exhausted would anyone take the claim in earnest.

Caroline tried to keep her mind on those distrustful thoughts. It was too confusing to consider the alternative.

During her evenings in the study, she found out that Lord Robert was still looking for her father's murderer and his missing step-mother. He was nothing if not persistent, she thought. If Lord Robert were providing time and resources toward looking for a lady that he had never even met out of a mere sense of duty or familial obligation, then he was a better man than she had ever given him credit for. She hated to think that she might be misjudging him so poorly. So many times, she considered unburdening herself, but still she hesitated. It was better to be safe, however, than to be sorry.

"Do you ever do anything besides toil over your duties?" she had asked on the third evening when he had seemed more weary than usual.

"No," he had chuckled as if the matter were obvious. "What else would I do?"

"I cannot say. What do you find enjoyment in?" she had pressed.

"Work," he laughed.

"I do not mean satisfaction," she explained. "I mean enjoyment. Something that has no attainable end other than your own pleasure. For example, I read." She could not tell him that she also enjoyed music, that she was skilled on several instruments and liked nothing more than to lose herself for an afternoon in the workings of Johann Sebastian Bach or ride pell-mell across her father's country fields on her mare Bella. The thought of Bella brought a sudden deep sadness to her heart. She had no idea where the mare might be, and probably never would find her. She hoped that wherever the mare was, she would be well treated.

The duke was looking at her with a puzzled expression on his face. He was too observant by half. She shook off the thoughts. A maid would not possess such skills as a horsewoman or knowledge of music and she certainly would not have received regular lessons for the first sixteen years of their lives.

"I haven't had time for diversions," he admitted with a thoughtful frown. "My father was very rigid in my education. Focus was a necessity at all times. Edward has all of the interesting talents."

Caroline did not want to speak of Lord Edward and his many interests.

"What of the years following your education," she wondered aloud. "Did you never attempt something frivolous then?"

"One does not have time for frivolous endeavors on a ship." He said so with a matter-of-fact shrug that saddened her. "Even if I wanted to, I would not have had the opportunity to make a go of it. We spend long months at sea between moorings."

"Why did you go?" she asked softly.

"To serve my country," he answered, but she sensed there was more of a reason there. She still felt he left to get far from his overbearing father. "I suppose, I thought of all the young sons who were required to go to war. Why should I be exempt?"

Why indeed she thought.

"It is our duties to do our part…"

"You aren't on a ship, now, m'lord," she said. She was careful to use the slurred sound rather than the proper my lord that had rolled more naturally from her tongue in the early days of her capture. Now, she seemed to be a part of this world. Sometimes how easily she fit to the mold frightened her.

"No, I suppose that excuse won't hold water."

"Do you expect to return to the war front?" She had wondered this for some time. What would Lady Lydia think? Caroline did not expect that his betrothed would be willing to be left behind for long durations of their marriage. Perhaps that was a part of the reason that the lady was so reticent.

"No," he admitted with a sigh. "Those days are over and perhaps they should have been a long time ago. I have other duties now."

"Will you regret your retirement?" she asked. "Miss it…"

"The war? The bloodshed? Not a lick." His firm resolve bolstered the words with truth. "I shall miss my men and the ease between us but we can arrange our meetings when they take their leaves of duty. In truth, most of them have been wed in recent years and are settling into new lives themselves. I've been told that I should have buckled down and finished that task myself." He sighed heartily.

"Do you not want to marry Lady Lydia?" she asked when his tone had seemed less than enthusiastic. She bit her lip. That was certainly too forward, but he seemed not to notice her curiosity.

"I do. I'm sure I do," he repeated, perhaps more for himself. "Sometimes it feels like we hardly know each other anymore. We spent our childhoods together, knowing from our childhood years that we would be matched. Our fathers had made the arrangements, and it felt right."

"She is very beautiful."

He lifted his eyes to hers and looked at her. Suddenly, Caroline felt very self-conscious under his scrutiny. He studied her, his eyes roving over her skin like a physical touch.

"Beautiful," he repeated softly.

"I thought…" she stuttered and began again. "From the way that the servants talk you were both very much in love," she hoped that he did not note that she had made the reference in the past tense.

"We never had a raging, passionate romance like Lydia had wanted," he admitted standing and pacing across the room. "Even without that I do think that we make a fair pair. We are both driven with single-minded focus to our own ends. I doubt we will get in each other's business much," he added. "I only thought that with more time we could both be certain. Perhaps that was the reason that I never felt a pressing need move quickly. I wanted her to have the chance to find what she wanted for herself, if she wished. Then, after the… he gestured lamely towards his marred cheek. Caroline wondered when she had ceased to notice the flaw.

"Or maybe I wanted to give her time to find another. I thought she might break off the engagement."

"You are a duke," Caroline said.

"Yes," he said softly. He seemed to look down upon his ruined form, running a finger over the scar on his hand. "Life does not always seem to go to plan," he whispered.

Caroline did not speak, but he did not seem upset by Lady Lydia's coolness towards him. It sounded to her like Lord Robert had wanted his betrothed to find her passionate love elsewhere, as if that might free him of the expectations that his father had set for his life. She knew just how forceful his father could be when it came to getting his way. Perhaps he had hoped that she would change her mind and he would not be responsible for jilting the lady, or perhaps Caroline was filling her own head with wishful thoughts.

"Her letters were always so angry," he continued. His voice was soft and introspective, as if perhaps he had never voiced any of this aloud. "She would complain that I was avoiding it, putting it off, and wasting her time. Father's would say the same... I was shirking my duties. Perhaps they were both right..."

"You are your own man now," she said. "What will you do?" She realized that she wanted to know. He was free of his father's constraints but she could tell that he still felt the heavy burden of obligation to the lady after she had kept herself on the shelf for the sole purpose of marriage to him. Even though it was clear Lady Lydia could barely lay eyes on her betrothed, she did not sever the engagement.

"Now that my father is dead there is no further reason to delay. I will have to fill the shoes that I was born to." He explained, with no surprise to Caroline, that it had been well ingrained that the express roll of the duke was to provide an heir and continue the legacy.

"It is time that I take control of my father's holdings and the future of such responsibility. None of that can be managed from the wheel of a ship."

"It is not my place to say," she began, but his look reminded her that he had on more than one occasion given her permission to speak freely and she had certainly availed herself of that option. "I think you have done well in giving Lady Lydia time to make up her mind. She might not see that now, but I do think that she will come 'round." They agreed that the lady's icy demeanor had lessened as of late, albeit slowly. The duke was hopeful that the ease of their past could be established once more. Caroline thought that all that it might take for such a goal to be achieved was for the duke to be as forthcoming with his betrothed as he had been with his maid. Hadn't these few evenings in his company had a similar effect on Caroline? Hadn't they eased some of the distrust and fear that she had once felt in his presence? The more they talked and the more she grew to take comfort in his quiet tone and deep rumbling laughter, she was beginning to wonder why she had ever thought that he was corrupt at all. She found herself nearly ready to unburden herself and trust him, when the butler knocked on the door.

"I have a letter for you, your Grace," he said.

Caroline snatched up her dust cloth and fled from the room.

WHEN NEXT CAROLINE FOUND HERSELF SERVING LADY Lydia a tray of cucumber sandwiches, crispy bread, and a decadent bowl of blackberry preserves, it was all she could do not to put in a good word for the duke. The lady was alone in the parlor as she waited for the gentleman to return and partner her on a ride through Hyde Park. She knew that she ought to keep her mouth shut. She did not know Lady Lydia well enough to be in her confidence, but she did know the duke quite well.

"How wonderful that his Grace intends to give up his military contract," she had offered before she could stop herself. Caroline had continued to suspect that if Lady Lydia was unaware of this information, it might be a cause for her hesitance in giving her heart back over to the duke.

Lady Blackwell's cool eyes narrowed and her attention fell upon Caroline's face with a look of horror at having been spoken to.

"My apologies, m'lady." Caroline curtsied. "I only meant that it must be a relief for you, to know that he shall remain... safe." She hadn't known how to finish or even what she had meant to say. The look that she was being leveled with had made each word increasingly awkward.

Lady Blackwell's face morphed into an angelic grin. Caroline allowed herself to take a breath of relief. When the lady leaned forward and beckoned Caroline with the crook of her finger, Caroline bade.

"When I'm the duchess," she whispered. "If you ever again speak to me out of turn, I'll have you dismissed like that." She snapped her fingers. The friendly smile was gone and again her cool eyes stared straight through Caroline. An act. "Do I make myself clear?"

Caroline nodded, muttered her apology, and excused herself from the room just as Lord Edward was entering. His gaze followed Caroline so closely that she felt as if she had spiders crawling over her skin wherever he looked.

"Really, Ed?" Lady Lydia's disapproval rang loud against his chuckle.

"It's just a bit of fun," the male voice responded.

CHAPTER 15

The leaves were turning and the first frost had crusted the ground outside the window. In the study, Caroline and Lord Robert had thrown the curtains open and were standing shoulder to shoulder looking out at the golden leaves that drifted down around the London streetlamps. The bright colors had dimmed the grey of London's daytime activities and, looking out upon the emptiness of Hyde Park, as the trees stretched branches towards the heavens, Caroline thought that she could almost pretend that it was the rolling hills and dense forests of the countryside. Someday, when she felt safe again, she might ask her father to bring her to London again. She had not wanted to travel with Father in years, but she now found that she never wanted to feel trapped in one place ever again. With an ache in her heart, she wondered if there was any chance that she might be returned to her father in time for the holiday festivities.

The duke had returned from his ride alone and gone straight to his study. When she joined him several hours later, Caroline had sorrowfully admitted that she might have been the one to put Lady Blackwell in a fractious mood. He had assured her that, according to Lord Blackwell, the lady had been cross long before her meeting with Caroline, of which he had been well informed when she had requested Emily's dismissal. He had half-heartedly laughed off the encounter as if it were usual for Lady Blackwell to take her personal moods out on the help, or perhaps those around her in general. She had gotten into an argument with Lord Edward as well, he had clarified, although he was not sure about what. Only that Lady Lydia had told his brother that he was not welcome upon their ride and Edward had laughed and wished the duke luck in surviving the barbs of his betrothed's tongue.

Caroline wanted to dislike Lady Lydia, but she also knew that the female's behavior was not unusual. Not that it was an excuse, she thought, but many noble ladies felt the need to throw their weight against anything that was within their power to control. Servants and gentlemen were the two most common areas of exploit. Caroline had never gotten on with those that did such things, but she had certainly met her fair share of such women.

Before she could put a halt to the thought, Caroline's mind whispered that Lady Lydia was not deserving of the gentleman. She found herself biting the inside of her cheek to turn the thought away as well as chastise herself for having had it in the first place. She gave a sidelong glance to the man at her side. He was a good man, she decided, and yet, she could not bring herself to share her predicament with him. There was too much at stake; not only her own life, but Marilee's.

"This is my favorite time of year," the duke said in a soft voice beside her.

"Yes. It's almost beautiful," she agreed. Almost, she thought. It would be beautiful if she were looking at it as a free woman. It was slightly less so in her current state.

When he did not respond she looked up to find him staring down at her. His mouth was open as if he wanted to say something, perhaps tell her that she was beautiful, but he didn't and she was grateful. Such conversations were inappropriate between a Lord and his servant and she realized just how very different the duke was from his brother. He stood with his hands firmly behind his back. He didn't touch her.

Unbidden, she realized she wanted to be touched. Without a thought, she found herself reaching up to run the tips of her fingers over the scar at his cheek. She had been curious, that was all. She had never meant for the touch to be sensual, but when he closed his eyes to mask the pain behind his lids, her heart broke a little bit for him. She wondered if he were thinking about another lady and wishing that she would touch his hurt so freely.

"Are you going to ask me about it?" he whispered when her breath had caught and she had pulled away.

"No," she replied with a trembling breath.

"Why not?" he murmured. She realized that he may have taken her withdrawal as the usual response that his scars garnered and offered him a tentative smile to prove otherwise.

"You'll tell me if you wish it," she sighed and returned her gaze to the serene snowfall. "And I'm certain that you already get asked the question far more often than you like as it is."

"You aren't wrong," he said with a huff and a smile that broke with relief. "I want you to ask though. I'm not sure why."

"Then tell me." She said without looking toward him. She refused eye contact for two very important reasons. The first was that she wanted him to speak freely. She wanted him to tell his tale without the pressure of someone looking at the scars and imagining every detail of the horror. Secondly, she wanted to keep from him the knowledge that her heart had gone out to him. She would hate for him to misinterpret compassion for pity. She hated that he carried this burden; that others could not see the man beneath the scars. That she herself had once only seen a beast and now had come to regret it.

"Do you want the version I tell, or the whole story?"

"Both," she breathed. She drew patterns with her fingers in the fog that had gathered on the window panes as much to keep him distracted as to keep her own hands from reaching out to him. In the back of her mind, she realized now that some maid, probably herself would have to wipe those smears away, but she did not care. The motion soothed her. She realized now that, besides occasional kind conversations with Lizzy, he was her only friend in the house. Yes, they were friends well and true.

"When I'm asked what happened and I'm," he paused, "uncomfortable... I say that, years ago, when I was a second officer, our ship was boarded by pirates along the coast of France. We were outnumbered and fought fiercely until we were able to disengage and make our escape back to the safety of the rest of our fleet." A tidy story.

"Now the truth," she said, her finger drawing a mast and sail on the ship that had unconsciously appeared in her pattern.

"When our ship was boarded, the captain and first officer were killed immediately." Caroline's eyes snapped up to his face. Her shock must have been evident but not the kind he had come to expect, only worry on his behalf, so he continued. "The rest of us were so frantic, so young and inexperienced that over half of the crew was slaughtered. Seven of us were able to hold the captain's deck, and another nineteen held the bow. Fifty men manned the ladders and kept any of Frenchmen from descending. That would have sealed our fates if they had. They were French, but not naval," he clarified. "We were eventually able to throw off the riggings and prevent any more from boarding but as I was doing so, I found myself surrounded and out of reach of my companions. I was now the ranking officer, and I ordered them to drop the sheets rather than save me. We could save the ship and those who were still alive, or maybe just one man. Me." The unsaid words hung between them. He had ordered his crew to set sail knowing that it would mean his death, so that once they were well away, they could pick off the remaining attackers, trapped aboard their vessel, one by one.

Caroline felt her heart pounding in her throat. She could not find the will to look away. He was a hero and yet for every moment since he had been looked upon with horror and pity. He had been shamed, even by his own family, for his service. That, she realized, was why he had never left the royal navy. His own men would never look at his scars and see a broken man. They would see an Admiral worth following.

"I fought every last man around me until I could barely stand and I couldn't know how much of the blood was theirs or my own. We were a small ship, and fast, so once we broke free there was no catching us. It took every man that was capable to keep the ship limping along but we made it back to England. I don't remember much of the return journey if I'm being honest."

"You received honors," she stated. It was not a question.

"A few," he nodded. And yet she recalled that his father had still been furious at what he had referred to as his son's abandonment.

"Have you told this to Lady Blackwell?" Caroline could not imagine that the lady would ever stare at her betrothed with anything but awe if she had heard the full story.

"No," he admitted.

"Why ever not?" she cried. It was absurd. The base facts were the same, but they were two entirely diverging stories. She wondered how many others knew this version and had no doubt that beyond his men there were less than she could count on one hand. She was honored to count herself among the few.

"I thought it best to wait until she could look at me without flinching. It's not a topic that she prefers."

Caroline released an agonized groan. How could the world be so callous and cruel?

"I am sorry," she wanted to soothe the pain away, but it was not her place. She wanted to throw her arms around him and tell him that he was worthy of Lady Blackwell's love. She wasn't convinced that the lady was deserving of his, but Caroline told herself that did not matter. He had committed his life to Lady Blackwell, and she had no doubt that he had given the lady his everlasting devotion. If only the lady could see the value in that promise.

"I do not need your pity," he said, taking a step away from her as if he had been slapped.

"It is not pity," she assured. She stepped forward and again she placed her hand against his cheek, this time her full palm, to prove that she had no fear of his harrowing tale. Her hand retreated, and she stepped back before the heat in her cheeks, and admittedly her body, could rise.

"Then what is it?" He was hesitant, unaccustomed to any other response.

"I'm not sure…," she admitted. "Perhaps a mutual understanding."

"You'll have to explain," he huffed, but he sounded hopeful. Hopeful that she did not pity him. Hopeful that someone else might understand.

"When my mother died, everyone treated me like I was forever broken," she began. "Even my own father. He never looked at me the same after her death."

She explained, in cautious terms so as not to reveal too much about her true status, that people had pitied her. She told him how those she had known her whole life now treated her with kid gloves and whispered in her presence. She revealed that when she would go out into public other women would bemoan the fact that she was alone and offer to take her under their own protective wing. She hadn't wanted charity. She hadn't wanted to be coddled or told that her life would never be the same again. She had loved her mother, missed her dearly, but she had been told she was broken and so she had felt broken. She had since learned that she was not broken.

"It came to pass that I could not even bring myself to leave our home, for fear of such treatment," she said. "It was easier to stay locked away from the stares and the whispers and the hurt. I could not experience anything wonderful without being reminded how tragic it was that she was not there to share it with me. Whenever I went out, their looks and words made me relive my loss, like I couldn't escape it. And so, I stayed away." The truth of her words rang clear between them. Even Caroline had not realized the full depth of her feelings all these years until the words were spilling out of her. "I locked myself away because I was tired of being pitied. I think now, that I let them pity me because it was easier to hate them then to face starting over with a whole new life… without my mother."

A sob caught in her throat and she forced back the tears. She would not cry. The hurt was an old one. How did it still feel so fresh? Would there always be a gaping hole where her mother's love should be? She bit her lip and forced back the tears.

The duke looked down upon her with awe at her words, at her ability to put his feelings into her own words and experience, and released a shallow breath.

He closed the distance between them, placing his hands upon her slender waist, and leaned his forehead against her own. She had thought he might kiss her. More shocking, she had wanted him to kiss her. He was restraining himself, had so much restraint. She trembled in his hands, considering what might happen if she turned her face up to his. Was there any chance that Lord Robert knew the truth? Or perhaps some instinct inside of him was crying out for her love? Did he know that she was indeed his equal? No, that could not be. If he knew, he would not be holding her so with time held suspended between them.

She would only have to move a few inches and their mouths would be joined. But she remained frozen, sure that such a movement would startle him like a stag in the wood. Still, she wondered…

"Emily," he murmured. The name snapped Caroline out of her stupor. She pulled away with a jerk, shocked at her own thoughts. He did not know her. He did not even know her true name.

· · ·

SHE HAD RESPONDED TO HIM AS MISS CAROLINE Graves, as a woman whose response to a duke was if not equal, at least of her standing. What had she been thinking? She hadn't been thinking. She wasn't Emily, had never been and never would be. He had only ever known her as Emily Baker, the maid of all ridiculous things. He did not know Caroline, Miss Caroline, she corrected in her mind. He might seem a decent enough man on the surface, at the level that she might have witnessed as the noble lady she had lost herself in the moment before, but she was still a prisoner and there was still a very real possibility that he and his father had no qualms with such seedy business dealings. Hadn't her own father given warning after warning about this family? She could not trust him. She cursed herself for having allowed her guard to slip.

She stepped hastily away.

"I'm sorry," he said quickly. "I shouldn't have done that."

"It's not your fault," she replied in haste. "You were thinking about someone understanding you and what it would feel like if Lady Lydia could see such things."

He furrowed his brow and shook his head. "I was not thinking of Lydia…"

He seemed ready to vehemently deny her words and then stopped himself. He assessed her discomfort. "Perhaps you are right," he said. His voice was husky as if he had been just as ready to give himself over to the pull of the moment as she had been. "I suppose I've always hoped that a lady would understand me so completely." He cleared his throat and turned looking out at the falling leaves again. "Perhaps one day she will," he said, but the words felt like a lie.

Caroline could not say whether he had thought about her claim to his motivations and decided that he did, in fact, agree or if he had merely told her what she needed to hear to ease the tension of the moment. Either way, she was grateful.

With a swift curtsy she excused herself from the room and was glad for the mindlessness of the hours of work ahead of her. She yearned for the distraction.

That had been too close. She had come far too close to letting him in when what she needed to be doing was keeping him firmly out. Or better yet, getting herself out of this blasted house. Caroline felt more desperate than ever to find her way home. Perhaps some part of her had wanted to stay for Robert, but she knew now, that was a fool's errand. She shook her head with incredulity at her tumbling thoughts. She had to escape.

Lizzy had called the house cursed and Caroline had laughed at her. Now, she was beginning to believe. Perhaps it was. In the past months there had been a turnover of seven maids. In a household this size, Caroline did not know any of them. Nonetheless, she did not believe they all took other employment; not when the household of a duke was a coveted job. She needed to get back to her own life.

CHAPTER 16

L ord Robert must have been as shaken by the encounter as Caroline because he was not in the study the following evening. She had decided that it would have made things all the more awkward if she did not maintain the ease of their friendship, had wanted to show him that despite the heated moment, nothing needed to change between them. It had taken the entire afternoon to steel her nerves. Now it seemed that the effort had been for naught.

Caroline had picked up her most recent book of interest when she found her mind unable to focus on the tale, thrilling as it may be. Her gaze wandered the room. It felt empty without one hulking presence to accompany the silence. How strange that she had first ventured to this place in search of isolation, but now found herself lonely and bereft.

"He is allowed to be busy," she muttered to herself as if her brain might listen if physically told that such a thing was perfectly within reason. Missing one evening here or there meant little in the grand scheme. It was not as if he owed her his time. It was not as if they had a standing appointment, or as if a maid even had the right to expect such a thing. No, he may have been called away on an important matter. He might have received an invitation to some ball or dinner. She was shocked to admit that she had nearly forgotten that such things existed having had her own hours overflowing with chores and mere survival. That was it, she decided, he must be at a ball with Lady Lydia and his brother. The thought sent a wave of pain through her, but she shoved it away. It was no wonder that the house had been over-quiet this evening, she told herself.

It was at this moment that her ashen eyes lit upon the duke's desk that sat nestled in the corner, facing the door and with a large arched window at its back.

A pile of his outgoing letters sat haphazardly in the center of the desk as if he had been too hurried to post them. She imagined that on the morrow he would scoop them all up without a thought and off they would go. Her heart leapt in her chest.

Nobody would dare to check the duke's letters, would they? Why hadn't she thought of this sooner? If Caroline happened to slip one of her own amongst his pile, she doubted anyone would be the wiser. She could get a note to her father and be free of this townhome by the end of the following week. Relief flooded through her at the thought.

She made her way over to the desk, pulling the curtains closed before she turned to the task at hand. Her heart beat in her chest so loud that she was afraid that Mrs. Reilly would come running and demand what in heaven's name is that pounding?

Her hand trembled as she grasped the quill pen, its vane still smooth as if it had only been used once or twice, else the duke was a very careful writer. She inspected the hollow shaft, a fresh cut. She unscrewed the bottle of ink and dipped the tip into its black depths. She noted the location of the blotting powder, procured herself a single piece of the duke's personal stationery, and began to write.

She had only meant to pen a line or two but the sense of assurance that this letter would go undiscovered made her bold. She told her father as much of the tale as could be managed in a few paragraphs. She expressed the importance of rescuing "Lady Kate" and added "the dear friend who departed with me that very day that I removed from Gravesend Manor." She told him that the house was not safe and that he should trust no one, not even the duke himself and certainly not his brother, Lord Edward.

She felt a pang of guilt as she wrote those words but found that they were necessary. It would be best for her father to barge in with the law and grab her up rather than send notice and there be a chance that she was squirreled away to some other location. She signed the letter with nothing more than C.G and set the words to dry.

She had been distracted in her folding of the letter and the lighting of the small candle that sat below the wax spoon.

When a hand grasped her wrist and spun her away from the desk, she had little time to take in anything save that which was at eye level, the wide chest of a man that loomed above her.

"What do you think you are doing?" the duke demanded. Caroline felt all of the color drain from her face. The door must have been left ajar for she had not heard him enter. Her wrist remained in his grasp in such a way that she was easily restrained but she noted that he was careful not to harm her.

"I…" she stammered. She shook her head. There was no excuse that a maid would have for going through his things, and yet, she wanted him to trust her. She willed it so.

Caroline straightened her back and stared up into his eyes, no sign of fear or subservience had a place in this moment. "I'm sending a letter," she declared with a level of authority that caught him off guard.

"With my stationery and seal?" he asked. She had hoped that he would be intrigued or perhaps bemused so that she might attempt to persuade him to allow it, but it seemed that he had erred firmly on the side of betrayal.

After evaluating all avenues, she realized that honesty was the only option, at least in part.

"Yes," she said. She willed herself to use every ounce of noble blood and training that had taught her how to bend others to her will without question. "I attempted to send a letter through the usual means and they were… returned." They were standing so close and she could sense that he had expected her to cower. He towered over her so that she had to crane her neck to look up at him, but she did not balk. She met his eyes. It was not the usual behavior of a maid, she knew, but she needed him to understand the severity of the situation. Furthermore, she needed him to not ask questions. "It's urgent, and I had hoped that your seal might get the letter to its recipient without delay... without inspection."

"Where are you sending it?" he asked. He leaned to look over her shoulder, the motion bringing them within a hairs-breadth of each other. Caroline was very nearly distracted by the deeply masculine scent of him, like a dark forest after a fresh rain. Instead, she reached her free hand behind her and grabbed the letter from the desk, tucking it behind her back before he could note her father's name penned in dainty letters.

"Please, I beg you, don't ask." This time when he looked down at her he would not have seen the confident stature of a moment before, but a friend begging him for his trust. Her eyes pleaded with him and her breath caught in her throat when she saw that he wanted to believe her. She thought she could kiss him if he did. She would be so grateful.

Yet, that look of trust only lasted for a moment. He was too battle-hardened by misfortune to believe her so readily.

"What are you up to?" he demanded, his eyes narrowing. "What sort of trickery are you playing at? I've known since my return that something has been off with the hands in this house. Too much has changed in the five years that I have been gone, too many new faces. I can't place my finger on it, but I find myself suspicious of the lot of them, but you…" his hand tightened on her arm. "You were the only one that I was certain that I could trust. You seemed different, smarter than the rest. Perhaps that is what should have tipped me off. Are you an enemy of my father? Or some insurgent spy poised to take down the aristocracy? Have you been playing me this whole time? Tell me what is going on. Tell me what nefarious letter you must be sending to need my name to keep it from inspection." He paused and looked down on her with fire in his eyes. "Tell me the truth." He grasped her shoulder and forced her to look at him.

His eyes were hard and cold and accusing. This was not the man she had befriended. This was the formidable duke who was so unfathomable.

She couldn't speak. She could not tell him the full truth. Her mouth felt dry as dust. Not for Marilee's sake and not for her own. He thought that she was part of the plot that caused his father's murder, and she could understand why he might think that. Still, some little voice inside of her screamed that it would be dangerous to involve him.

In this very moment, she felt that she trusted him. She trusted him deep down in her heart with a certainty that made her want to allow him to protect her. But the forces against her were too evil.

She could not trust him fully.

She could not bring him to that danger.

She did not know which it was, she only knew she could not tell him the truth. Not yet. Not when Marilee was in danger.

Not when such knowledge might get him killed as well.

"Please," she begged once more, "I cannot tell you what is in the letter, or where it is going. All I can say is that it is a matter of life and death. My life or death." She shook with the enormity of what she was asking. He had just professed, and with good reason, his hesitations. Here she was expecting him to aide her, to put his seal to the matter, and to do so without any of his questions being answered. She pressed the letter to his heart, the paper doing nothing to keep her from feeling the heat of him, his deep thudding heart-beat beneath her fingers and the sweet masculine scent of him. "I am asking you to trust me, to send this with your seal. And... I'm asking you not to read it."

She knew that this was a losing game. This moment would be the end of their budding friendship one way or another. If he refused to send the letter then he would be declaring that he thought her base and duplicitous. If he demanded to read it, he might also be revealing his own complicit role in the backwards ways of the London underworld. She did not want to believe that he could have been lying about his suspicion of the staff, about the fact that he had no knowledge of the goings on in his own house for the past five years, or even the past five months. She wanted to believe him more than anything. His statement had given her hope that changes were nigh, if not for her sake, then for that off all the women who might have come after. If his speech had been an act, then Caroline thought it fine enough to have earned him a place among the actors on Drury Lane.

If the reverse occurred, and he did provide his unconditional trust, she would stand to lose his forever. Her request could only mean that she was potentially deviant in nature or, perhaps the worse of the pair, that she did not fully trust him the way that he had trusted her, what did it say about her?

If he was suspicious of the house, if he ever found out about the link between these people and his father's death, he would never forgive her. He could have no way of suspecting that she might be acting out of self-preservation as well as an attempt to protect him from meeting the same swift end that hung over her head.

The request hung between them for a painfully long moment.

Ever so slowly his free hand came to rest over the one that still remain poised against his heart. "Is this what you want?" he asked in a tone so low that she thought she could have imagined the words. His gaze held the weight of understanding. He knew the wall that this deal would place between them. His eyes begged her to tell him all, but he did not voice the request again.

Caroline felt her heart breaking. She hadn't even realized how much she had come to value the duke's respect until she now faced the prospect of losing it. She nearly cried with the injustice of it. And yet, it was more than her own life that could be saved with this posting. Marilee, and maybe even other women as well. That had to be worth more than her own wishes, she told herself. It had to.

For the second time in their short acquaintance, he pressed his forehead against her own. The action, so endearing and unique to him, had her biting back a sob and nearly begging him to forget the letter altogether. But she knew that she could not do that. Her own survival depended upon it, as well as the others and she could not be a maid forever. Perhaps when all had come to light, he would forgive her. She could only hope.

The hand that had first accosted her wrist upon her discovery loosened and slid gently to cover hers, pulling it beside the other pair so that he was now clutching both of her hands to his breast. Her eyes fluttered closed, heart aching, and breath trembling at the gentle affection with which he held her. It was far too personal for their opposing stations. That he had even allowed it meant that in some way he cared. Again, she was crushed under the weight of the importance of the loss that she had not even expected to matter.

"Is this what you want?" he repeated. His breath hitched, as if he were holding it while awaiting her response.

"More than anything," she replied with a barely contained sob. The importance of her words rang true even as the hurt sprang to life between them.

Lord Robert lifted his head, gently released her hands, and stepped around her to approach the desk. It was only afterward that she noticed that with that movement he had secured the letter from her hand.

He leaned forward, spooned a pile of wax over the folded closure, and pressed the full weight of his seal into the binding. Without turning the letter upward where the addressee would be revealed, he slipped it into the middle of the pile of his own correspondence.

With nary a word he had given her everything that she had asked of him, and she had taken away everything in return.

Silence reigned between them, but this silence was not peaceful. It was oppressive and dark.

Caroline was unable to say the words of thanks that she knew she had ought to speak. She did not trust herself to speak over the lump that had taken residence in her throat. She nodded, tears already spilling from her eyes, as she turned and walked slowly from the room. She held her head as high as she could manage but as soon as she was clear of the doorway her shoulders slumped, her head sagged, and she knew that she would cry herself to sleep this night and perhaps for many more to come.

In the battle for her freedom, she had just won a great victory. And yet, something inside of her knew that she had simultaneously suffered the greatest of losses.

WITH EVERY PASSING HOUR CAROLINE WAITED FOR her rescue. She had nothing else to think of since the duke had left the house on business, she had been told. She had little doubt that he had in fact left to escape her, and she found that she didn't mind. Seeing the hurt on his face would have made her relive that moment over and over until nothing remained in her but an empty shell of regret. Oh, her heart still ached when she went to talk to him and realized that he was no longer in the study each evening, likely never would be again. She told herself that was just because she really didn't have anyone else, she cared to talk to in the house, except Lizzy who had been so busy with the surprise departure of two more of the scullery maids that they hadn't been able to get in more than a passing phrase each day. Mostly it drove her near to the point of insanity that she could not ask him when the post had gone out, and if he was certain that he hadn't dropped it and if he had received any response.

Each time she walked the main hall she stared at the door, willing it to burst open with the army of men that her father had rallied to retrieve his daughter. When she washed the windows, she looked out hoping to see her father's carriage would drive by and signaling that he had arrived in London.

She listened to every whisper and hint of gossip. Perhaps they had captured the Madam first so that they might root out Marilee and retrieve both females in a duel-edged attack. That did not seem likely, however, as someone would have warned the others in the criminal web. The servants did not seem nervous. Not even Mrs. Reilly seemed the least concerned that the rouse was up, that was if she were actually involved. Caroline still did not possess a lick of proof, but it seemed too implausible that any housekeeper worth her salt would accept the constant ebb and flow of workers without explanation.

By the third day, Caroline was becoming irritated. What was her father doing? Taking a leisurely carriage ride to London? He ought to be racing on horseback through the night to get to her. Where in the heavens was he?

At the end of the week Caroline was enraged. At first, she had thought her mind had just given over to paranoia, but now she was certain, the duke had not sent the letter. He couldn't have. That was the only explanation that made sense to explain why her father was not bursting down the door and demanding the return of his only child.

The betrayal cut deep. The duke had seemed so thoughtful and resolute in his actions that she had even believed that he would not make an attempt to spy the name on the front of the letter. She had believed him that honorable, had believed him without reservation and she had fallen for his act the way that he must have known that she would. Perhaps he had known who she was this whole time. Perhaps their friendship had been nothing more than a ruse to keep an eye on her lest she attempt just such a feat. She felt like an idiot. She felt like a fool. Good Lord, what had she done? What if he had taken her letter and handed it over to the madam, declaring that Marilee be punished? Caroline groaned when she thought of how daft he must have thought her when she had walked away believing that she could put her very life in his hands and that he would deliver the letter without question. She was a fool, and her foolishness may have just signed away her own life and Marilee's.

CHAPTER 17

Caroline was polishing the pianoforte in the music room when voices drifted to her from the open doors to the adjacent drawing. She had been so enraptured by the keys, running her fingers over the smooth ivory and willing herself not to allow the digits to pluck a little tune, that she had not noticed that anyone had entered in time to exit with discretion. The male and female voices were arguing. The doors to both rooms had been shut to the hall and they must have thought themselves alone. There was no way for her to escape without being seen. The music room opened into the drawing room and the door between the two rooms was open.

"We can make this work," the male voice said as his footsteps chased the lady across the room and closer to the doors that would reveal a frozen Caroline. She hoped that they would not come any closer. But at least, if they did, she would be able to hear more clearly.

"I cannot see how," the lady replied. Her tone snapped as if she wanted to sound firm but there was something in it, as if she were holding back a smile that made Caroline suspect that she was enjoying the pursuit.

"It's forever been you and I," the male argued. "We've always known we would make this work, hell or high water. It's not my fault that it has taken so long." There was a note of desperation in his voice. "I want you, Lydia."

There was a pregnant silence and a sigh.

Caroline felt her stomach fall to the floor. A part of her had suspected that the pair in question was Lord Robert and Lady Lydia, but another part of her had hoped that it had been a pair of servants arguing or perhaps even Lord Edward with one of his many lovers. This is where the duke must have been this past week... wooing Lady Blackwell. Caroline reminded herself that she did not care. She was cross with him, she recalled, and he had proven himself most false.

"And I thought I wanted you but fate is against us. It just never seems to align," Lady Blackwell seemed pleased to have the upper hand. "Besides, I have heard enough whispers about you and that maid…" Caroline bit back a gasp. She was not surprised that there would have been whispers, others had been bound to figure out where she had been going. Still, she had not expected such information to reach Lady Lydia, nor did she expect the lady to have sounded threatened, if only slightly, over a maid.

"It's nothing," he promised. "It's over. There is only you."

"Only ever me?" she demanded.

"You are the only one who has my heart. I swear it. From now until eternity." Caroline felt a pang at the words but reminded herself that it was only because she had experienced a deep loss of the friendship, she had thought that she had, a friendship that had turned out to be a lie. The pair deserved one another. They were two spiteful, manipulative wretches who deserved nothing more than to make each other miserable for the rest of their sorry lives. Perhaps that was a bit harsh, she amended. Hadn't she been trying to help him repair things with his betrothed even before they had fallen out of sorts? Why should she be so disappointed at his success?

"Oh, Darling," Lady Blackwell crooned.

There was a prolonged silence that left Caroline with widened eyes and what must have been an apple-red blush to her cheeks. A soft, feminine moan told her that her assumptions had been correct. The pair were sharing in what they thought was a private embrace, a kiss that had Lady Lydia sighing with pleasure. Caroline tried not to think about the fact that she had nearly kissed the duke herself. Would it really have been that earth-shattering? She suspected yes as the heat rose to her face anew. He was too insightful to not know how to please a woman. She shook such thoughts from her head, reminding herself that she was intruding upon a very private moment.

"Promise that it will be soon," Lady Lydia whimpered. Caroline could hear the pout upon her face. Yes, the female was getting exactly what she had long wanted.

"I'll handle it all as soon as I can," came the soothing reply. "But you must be patient; these things do take time."

"I've been patient my entire life," she groused. "I don't want to be patient any longer."

"Soon, then," he promised and again they fell into that telltale silence.

Caroline felt ill. She ought to be happy. She ought to be thrilled that the duke was finally getting the response from the lady that he had long desired. She did not know why she had thought that during those magical evenings in the study there had been something between them. She cursed herself for a fool again. Then she thanked the fates that she had been freed from the gentleman's influence before she had had the chance to develop any irreparable feelings. No, she thought, she was just fine now and listening to him coax a gentle mewling from Lady Lydia didn't bother her in the least. Not in the least, she repeated just for good measure.

"Oh, Edward," Lady Lydia sighed.

Caroline's mouth dropped open and before a sound could come out, she clapped a hand over the offending orifice. Her eyes felt as if they might bulge from her sockets as she did her best to control the utter shock that had taken over.

Lady Lydia and Lord Edward? Certainly, it could not be!

Yet, it made sense, she realized. Lord Edward had been here these long years comforting the lady and chaperoning her on his brother's behalf. Of course, Lydia, who seemed vain in every sense, preferred the beautiful brother to the one who had been permanently marred, even if he was the duke.

Caroline almost vowed to tell the duke what she had witnessed as soon as he returned from wherever it was that he had gone, but swiftly changed her mind. First, she was still cross. Petty as it may be, she was disinclined to tell him the truth when he had so expertly lied to her. Besides, hadn't she just overheard the lovers discussing that the matter would be handled soon. Lord Edward was going to tell his brother. Oughtn't he be given the opportunity to come out with it in a respectful manner so that his brother might understand that the pair had found the passionate love that Lady Lydia had been dreaming of all these years? Discovery second-hand was never the best route. Caroline resolved to stay out of it although that did little to lessen the shock that had rocked her when Lady Blackwell had not said the duke's given name, but instead his brother's.

She wondered how Lord Robert would take the news, but she hoped that she would be long gone before she had a chance to find out.

CHAPTER 18

The duke returned to the townhouse less than an hour later. He had narrowly missed Lady Lydia's departure. Caroline wondered how long the lovers had been meeting in secret without the duke being made aware. He would have thought it strange that she would so readily visit the house when she had been hesitant to accept the previous invitations to visit her betrothed.

Rumor among the staff members was that the duke had ridden to his Manchester estate to settle some important business dealings. Caroline wondered what could have been so urgent that he had had to travel in the inclement weather for the winter season was now fully upon them. Again, she began to suspect that he had reached for the excuse to be free of her and the hurt that she had caused. It was sad really, to possess the knowledge that he was very soon to be dealt another blow.

"Did you hear that his Grace had met with the Baron Wickham on his return journey?" Lizzy had whispered that evening while they had each lain in bed.

"I had not." Northwickshire! Father! Caroline thought as she sat upright with interest. She then placed a placid smile on her face, hoping that the maid would not suspect that she was overly interested.

"They arranged to meet near Wollington where his father and the men had been discovered."

"To what purpose?" Caroline asked. She had heard that her father had traveled to the scene of the crime and had been in close contact with the local constable who was spearheading the investigation. She had not heard, however, that any progress had been made on that front. She frowned at that.

"They have yet to find any sign that her Grace had been harmed," Lizzy leaned over the side of her bed with a conspiratorial whisper. Caroline could tell that her companion viewed the information as nothing more than titillating gossip. Sweet, innocent Lizzy, Caroline mused. She had no idea that she was speaking to her mistress. No idea that the lady of the house lay on a straw mat on the cold floor of their pitiful room. "It seems she might have been taken, although no one can think why. Apparently, she was somewhat of a recluse. She oughtn't to have had anyone after her and the highwaymen hadn't shown the duke any mercy for his position, so why would they have kept the duchess? Unless she were as beautiful as the rumors suggest." Lizzy shrugged as if it mattered not. "They've decided to offer a reward for information. The duke pledged half the fee himself, on behalf of his father."

"He did not!" Caroline exclaimed. She had known that a reward would come to be offered, was pleased that the time had finally come. This new development meant that she was one step closer to returning to the safety of her own home. Still, she had not expected that the duke would feel any obligation toward his father's new wife, a woman which he had never even made acquaintance. She felt sure that any amount that the baron and duke had been able to collect would appeal to her captors. Her father was wealthy, yes, but the duke was drowning in coin.

"He did," Lizzy nodded. "The lady's father is to join his Grace here in London, where they will take up the cause in unison."

Caroline could not help but allow hope to swell in her breast. Her father was coming here? She could not speak with the joy of it. Her heart seemed to fill her throat. At last, she asked if the baron was to reside in this house, holding her breath while she awaited the response. Please, she prayed, please let her father come to the duke's home. All he would need do was lay eyes upon her and she would be saved.

"Of course not!" Lizzy giggled, dashing Caroline's hopes. "He has his own townhome that they will be using as their base of operations. I overheard his Grace telling Mrs. Reilly that any summons from the baron that comes to the house must be given to him immediately, no matter the hour. They have no idea when they might have word, if there is any to be had at all."

Caroline pondered her friend's words in silence. This must mean that the thugs would be offering her up before long. It had to. She could almost taste the freedom that now lay only just out of reach.

"Do you think that the duchess is alive?" Lizzy asked out of the blue.

"I think so," Caroline nodded but gave no reason as to why.

"I do too," Lizzy said with a yawn. "Although I cannot imagine how. They'd stand to make a small fortune for her return if she was taken. If she is alive," Lizzy's voice was a mere whisper on the wind. "She must have had a frightful last few months."

Caroline rolled toward the wall as she heard Lizzy drift off into her slumber.

She did not know what to make of the news.

Was the duke really searching for her out of the goodness of his own heart? If so, then that would mean that he did not know who she was. Did not know that she was truly alive and beneath his own roof. Why then would he not have sent her letter? His reasoning escaped her and infuriated her at the same time. If he were naïve to the corruption then why would he have lied? Or, perhaps he knew to thwart her from a criminal sense, something entirely unrelated, but did not know her exact identity. Perhaps he was not aware that the untoward goings on in his own home were somehow related to the death of his father. Or, perhaps they weren't related at all except for the fact that the players involved had the misfortune of being one and the same. It was all so muddled in her mind that she could make neither head nor tail of it.

Or, she allowed the suspicious part of her mind to take over her thoughts as the darkness settled around her, perhaps he did know who she was and was using this offer as a ploy to keep the baron close and to head him off the trail. That would explain why they had chosen to base their search from her father's townhome. That would explain why he had lied about sending her letter. He was a smart enough man to wrest covert control of the situation from whatever angle, if he wished it. And to think that she had trusted him.

Her mind ached as it threw the reverse back into her thoughts, spinning and twisting and confusing herself as she still could not decide if the man was evil. Even if it did make sense that her father would want all communication to pass through his own hands, even if the duke was attempting to play a supportive role out of honor and duty, even if he thought that the quiet of the baron's house was safer than his own, a household that he professed not to trust, she still felt that every excuse in the world did not repair her anger against him. He had told her that he would send the letter and he had not. He had lied and fooled her under the guise of trust. He had prolonged her suffering, and her father's misery, when it all could have been sorted long ago.

Caroline had thought that Lord Edward's declaration to Lady Blackwell would have meant that he would leave her be, but she had been wrong. True, he was more discrete in his efforts, but he had not relented. Now, instead of making a show of seeking her out, he merely waited for the natural crossing of their paths to whisper compliments into her ear or to brush a hand over her feminine form. She had wanted to tell him that she knew about his affair with Lady Lydia, had overheard his promises, but had been too afraid to enrage him. If she had any hope that the threat would quell his desire then she might have. Instead, she could only hope that he revealed all to his brother in a timely fashion but the opportunity had yet to present itself. The elder had been out of the house more often than not and the brothers had had no reason to cross paths, let alone have a deep and life-altering discussion about who commanded the heart of one beautiful lady. Once Lord Edward was fully committed to Lady Blackwell, Caroline thought he might pull back on some of his dalliances. Until that time she was to bear the full brunt of his misplaced attentions.

She wanted to throttle him. She wanted to lash out and lay him bare for all to see what a despicable creature was hidden beneath his angelic features. Never in her life had she been treated thus by a male, and she was resolute that once the protection of her title was reinstated, she would break any man who behaved with such depravity.

"Come, come," he would whisper. "You cannot mean to say that you prefer my brother's company to mine." Yes, he had heard that she had been spending time in the study, but no longer. "How you could stomach his company for so long is beyond my comprehension. I am glad that you have seen reason and given up the shield. Yes, I know you were hiding from me, you minx." He would laugh as if her actions had merely increased his desire for her. He had taken the move as if she had wanted to play at the chase, as if she enjoyed it. "All of the Ton thinks Robert such an honorable and reasonable man, but he is odious… grotesque. He was merely bland before. Now… none of the gentler sex could ever bear that for more than a short while." He gave a repulsed shiver and gestured at his own swoon-worthy features. "Honestly, there is nothing to compare. I could filch any miss of any station from his company if I desired. All you have to do is take one long look at him and you will come running into my arms." He had winked and implied that her falling out with the duke must indicate that she was warming to him. Caroline assured him that it did not but he would not be swayed. A gentle pat to her backside told her that he had staked his claim whether she willed it or no.

She had been glad to learn that he would be away in the coming days; lest she would have had to strangle him. She surely would not have succumbed, even though she knew a noblewoman had little recourse, as she had been shown with her marriage to the elder duke. A maid had even less. She shuddered and vowed to stay out of his way.

CHAPTER 19

The duke had awoken on the morning following his return with a fever.

"I told his Grace that the ride to Heatherton Hall in that storm would catch him his death of cold," Mrs. Reilly had grumbled as she thrust a tray of crusty bread and steaming soup into Caroline's hands. "Make sure he eats this. He'll need his strength with the chill nights we've been having. You hurry on up; I'll have Matthew bring up another load of wood when he has returned from the butcher."

"Why me?" Caroline had asked. She had not meant to be rude. It was only that she was still in the middle of mopping the trails of ice and mud that had been brought in through the servant's entrance. The task was unending. As soon as she thought herself finished another delivery would be made or another servant would have returned from some errand and the floor would be ruined yet again. She had been mopping for days and still had a mountain of mending that awaited her nimble fingers. She did not have the time to spare to tend to the duke day and night.

"Why me?" Mrs. Reilly had mocked. "Your impertinence is astounding, Emily Baker. Did no one ever teach you not to question your betters?" Caroline had secretly thought that she had only few and far between encountered true superiors before, but that was not something that she could point out in this moment. "YOU will serve his Grace until he is removed from his sickbed. YOU will do nothing else until he has recovered. YOU will do everything I ask in silence and without question. You will do so because I have told you that is what you will do! Do I make myself clear?"

"Yes, ma'am," Caroline dipped her head and turned to take the tray up to the third-floor bedroom.

"If you want to know why I chose you over the others," Mrs. Reilly said to her retreating back, "it's because you are more trouble than you are worth." She ticked the following explanations off on her fingers. "James has gone with Lord Edward and cannot be called back to sit by a bedside when his time is better spent making use of his skills. You are well aware that he has been serving both of the gentlemen until we can procure another valet for his Grace and I haven't a man to spare at the moment. What about the maids, you wonder? Well, the others don't put salt in the sugar bowl. They know not to place the fish next to the soup at the dining table and they certainly don't slop precious buckets of hot water on the stairs when drawing a bath! Honestly, sometimes I wonder if it were possible for you to be any more backward."

Caroline merely turned, muttered her apology and continued up the stairs.

"If you can at the very least manage to feed his Grace and make him somewhat comfortable, I shall be forever in shock," the voice wafted up the stairs behind her. "Lord in the heavens, even a child can serve a sickbed. All I am asking for is some peace," the woman grunted to herself as she turned off at the second floor. "A few days without a catastrophe. Is that too much to ask?"

She was still complaining below when Caroline reached the third landing. It was true that she had done all of those things. They had been honest mistakes, and she did feel as if she had improved a significant amount since her arrival. Still, she had to admit that she made a terrible maid. If Mrs. Reilly had not been forced to take her on, or desperate to fill the position, then she would have been tossed out into the snow-covered streets weeks ago.

She arrived at the door to the duke's bedchamber just as the physician was making his exit.

"His fever has broken for now but he will need rest," she was informed. The older gentleman made a point to express that under no circumstances was his patient to leave the room until he was fully recovered. "I've cared for the family since the duke was a child," he explained. "I know he is far too like to pretend that all is well far before he is recovered. He needs rest and I don't care what else he claims needs to be done; it can wait." He then informed Caroline that he would be away for several days attending to the delivery of his seventh grandchild. He would check in with the duke upon his return in a week's time. Caroline listened carefully to his instructions as to the care that she was meant to provide. Mrs. Reilly had been right in the assumption that Caroline could manage a sickbed, not because it was so basic a task that even she could not make a mess of it, but because she had served at her mother's bedside for all those weeks that the lady had clung on to the edge of life. As the physician seemed to have little concern that duke's bout was to be treated by anything other than a few days of well-deserved rest, she did not fret over the matter. Instead, she took her tray within and was greeted by the sight of the duke peering out from a set of barely opened lids.

"I can see that you are awake," she said with a laugh that could not be helped.

"I was meant to be sleeping," he grumbled but sat up against the mound of pillows and wrinkled his nose at a vial that he had produced from beneath the covers. He placed it on the bedside table and pushed it as far away from his person as could be managed without it tumbling over the edge. "I was made to promise that I would take the tonic so that I would drift off before he could even exit the room."

"I see that you have not," she laughed. Leave it to this man to refuse care on the matter of taste. She set the tray across his lap and unstoppered the bottle, sniffing the murky concoction. Quickly she replaced the cork and covered her nose with the flap of her apron so that she might be rid of the odor.

"You see?" he laughed. She did and told him that she would not enforce the doctor's orders so long as he ate his meal and remained abed until he had been declared fit. Lord Robert did not seem to care for this offer, but when she reached for the tonic, he conceded with a hasty breath.

Caroline could see that his coloring was a bit pale but as the duke had been evaluated only a moment before she refrained from pressing the back of her hand against his forehead. All at once she was far too aware that he was wearing only his nightshirt and that they were in his bedchamber no less! She willed the heat away from her cheeks but knew that when the duke tucked into his meal with the focus of a madman, he had noted the blush. She was meant to be cross with him, she reminded herself, and here she was teasing, making deals and, God forsake her, blushing. She resolved that the best approach was to ignore him as best she could in the hope that he would in truth put himself to rest.

Caroline took up a chair on the far side of the room, checking first that the fire was well fed. She did not have anything to occupy her hands, or her mind, so she abandoned the chair and began to move about the room, tidying it as she went.

Although the duke ate in silence she could feel his eyes follow her path, noting her futile attempt to keep busy.

"You should pilfer a collection of books from the study," he suggested when the last of the soup had been spooned from the bowl. "There is a stack of letters that require my attention on the desk, if you would be so kind as to bring those as well? I have all else that I would need on the table there." He indicated the table near the window which held a package of stationary and all of the other accoutrements that would be required to craft and seal a letter.

"Doctor Portner said that you are not to spend your energy with matters of business," she scolded. She would choose an assortment of books for herself, however. Anything to keep herself distracted from the hours and hours that she would be required to spend in this room. She had bristled at his mention of letters. Oh, how the thought of him putting his own writings to post and discarding her one made her blood boil. He could write his damned letters when he was feeling better, she thought with indignation.

"I promised not to leave the bed," he countered. "It would hardly sap my strength to read and write." He looked like a mischievous little boy trying very hard to get his way and Caroline almost laughed aloud. "Besides," he added as his pièce de résistance, "if I am to be busy then I shall have less reason to pester you."

The wretch, she thought. He was wicked, and he knew it. The duke had noted that she would have rather have been anywhere else than his bedside and he would use that knowledge to get her to do his bidding. Still, she hemmed, it would keep his attentions elsewhere and perhaps she could get through this ordeal without having much to speak with him. The more they conversed the more she became worried that she would have it out with him about the letter and demand to know his reasoning. A small part of her, the secret part that was clinging to the hope that he was innocent to the horrors of his house, did not want to hear the truth on the chance that it would crush that last kernel of optimism.

She approached the bedside and took the tray with a glower.

"Thank you!" he called after her and she could·have kicked him for his attempt at cheerful banter.

Caroline delayed her return for as long as could be managed without finding herself on the receiving end of Mrs. Reilly's wrath. She took her merry time choosing a handful of novels for herself and retrieving his letters. She may or may not have flipped through the pile in search of anything that might have been sent by her father, perhaps the reply that she had been searching for? There had not been. She then filled a pitcher with cold water, wrapped a hunk of bread and cheese in a napkin to stymie her own hunger, and headed back up the stairs.

The duke had lost his playful tone by the time she made her reappearance.

"Leave them on the table for now," he said, his voice weak and his lips dry. She did as she was told, bringing only the pitcher of water to his bedside. She filled his cup, perched herself upon the edge of the bed and bade him to drink.

He took a few sips before handing it back. She pressed him to take more.

"I'm only tired," he sank back into the pillows. She noticed a slight sheen upon his brow. Pressing her hand to his forehead she felt that it was warm and clammy.

"Drink a little more," she crooned as she filled the nearby washbasin with fresh water and carried it over to the bedside. She soaked the accompanying cloth in the crisp liquid, rung out the excess, and pressed it to his forehead, worried. Hadn't he been teasing her only an hour earlier? Caroline continued to blot the skin of his face and his neck until he had fallen into a deep slumber. The poor man was exhausted, and it was no wonder the way he ran himself ragged. There was a bone-deep weariness about him as if he carried the weight of the world upon his broad shoulders and knew not how to fix it. She looked upon his features as they relaxed in sleep. She had a better view of his scars, what with the way the laces of his nightshirt and been pulled open in his discomfort. Again, she thought that beneath the scars he possessed an innocent appearance. Interesting, she thought. It was a wonder that his injuries could play such a role in one's perception. The jagged lines and sheer volume of damage gave the impression that he was harsh and beastlike. They had taken away all of the softness that would have shone otherwise, a softness that only appeared now in sleep. Despite the fact that she was still very angry with him, she determined that he deserved more from the people around him than he had been given. She resolved to give him the best care possible. She could do, at least, that much.

"You are far more ill than you let on, aren't you?" she whispered as she made one more pass along his jawline. His skin had cooled now, and he was sleeping soundly, so she added another log to the fire and settled into her chair to read and watch over him.

He did not awake until some hours later when Caroline had gone to retrieve his evening meal. The sound of the door closing upon her return must have startled him because he jolted upright, his hand reaching beneath his pillow for what she assumed was a knife or a pistol, but it came up empty. It took him another moment to place himself but when he saw her standing just inside the doorway, he sank back against the pillows and sighed.

"I see that you are feeling better," she observed for the color was back in his cheeks and his eyes were much more focused than they had been during the bout of fever.

"I am merely tired," he repeated what she had decided would be his mantra for the duration of the illness. May the Lord help her, she raised her eyes to the ceiling and huffed.

"When the fever surfaces again, you shall take the tonic," she said with her best schoolmarm voice.

Again, he wrinkled his nose. She hated that she found the action endearing, the boyish side that he never allowed others to see.

"Agreed?" she pressed. She twisted her body as if she were to refuse him the tray of food, letting him starve if he did not take the medicine.

"If it rears again," he hemmed, "and if you tell me why you keep looking at me as if I might need to be throttled, then I will take it."

Caroline bit her lip as she considered his offer. She was not ready to have it out with him just yet but she nodded. "I shall tell you why you ought to be throttled if the situation arises." She said the words as if it were a matter of certainty. He did need to be throttled, not that he might need to be. She was also hoping that the fevers had passed and she would not be required to fulfill that end of the bargain.

"That's not fair," he argued. "What if it never does? Oughtn't we to hope that I don't have a fever?"

"Then it is a conversation for another time."

"You ought to tell me now," he pressed with a singular raised eyebrow. "If you wait for the fever then it is unlikely that I will remember what you say, so really it cannot be a fair trade. If you were to tell me now while I have a clear mind then I might have a hope to fix it." He must have been a nightmare of a child, she realized. His mother must have been hard pressed to deny her son anything if he would use such logic to get his way. She really ought to let him starve.

Her eyes were narrowed as she considered her options. Really, what harm could there be? She could be ransomed any moment now, perhaps even before the duke recovered. If he revealed his duplicitous nature to her now, there was little he could do from his sickbed.

She set the tray across his lap and stepped away, eyeing him with scrutiny. He took an exaggerated bite, a pointed gesture to show that he was being a good patient and doing her bidding.

She rolled her eyes. "You are a nuisance," she muttered. She nearly laughed at how similar she sounded to the cantankerous Mrs. Reilly in that moment.

"Thank you," he replied as he dunked the bread into the broth. "Is that why you are angry with me?"

"No," she admitted. She headed over to the safety of her chair in the corner. Perhaps with the space of the room between them she could keep her confrontation from exploding into an all-out row. He continued to eat in silence but she could tell from his rapt attention that he was waiting. She whispered a small curse and decided to be out with it. "Why did you not send my letter?" she demanded.

His eyebrows raised in tandem, surprise written across his marred features.

"I did," he answered with a matter-of-fact tone. He took another bite, wholly un-phased by her accusation.

"You couldn't have," she argued. "I would have gotten a reply but I have not. I know for certain that..." she had almost said my father... "that it was not received."

"I sent it," he shrugged. Again, she had the thought that he was either incredibly honest or a remarkable liar. "Beyond that it had passed out of my control."

"I would have had a reply," she repeated as if that explanation were irrefutable. Her tone was perhaps harsher than she had intended but her anger had bubbled to the surface. Her father would have acted if he had gotten her letter. He would not have waited this long. Had that letter been sent, she would have been rescued by now.

"Is that really the reason you have been angry with me?" he bristled. "That damned letter? Lud, here I was trying to recall when I had somehow offended you or worried that our interactions had gotten you in trouble." His temper clouded over, but he kept it in check, everything about Lord Robert was always in check she realized. "Should not I be the one that is cross about the blasted letter? I know almost nothing about you save what you do in this house and the one time that I might have been able to learn something real about your life, you shut me out. You've only ever given me vague stories and hinted interests. I feel as if I know who you are, but I don't know anything about you." He ran a scarred hand over his face. "I should be insulted that after everything you could not even find it within yourself to trust me. When I had given you no indication otherwise."

All at once Caroline realized that he was still very hurt that she had withheld her trust and that he could have no way to comprehend why. For all he had known, they had formed a close sort of alliance, a friendship, but even then, she had declared him unworthy. He was, she realized, used to women declaring him so.

"You are mad at me because you think that I failed to send it?" he set the empty bowl aside and pushed the tray from his lap. "You needed my seal, and I gave you use of it," use of me, the words hung between them. "I gave you what you asked, and I asked nothing in return."

She wanted to believe him. She wanted to believe that he was truly that good. But if she did, then that would mean that she had mistreated him horribly, that she had withheld her trust, not once, but twice.

She had had her reasons. She still had her reasons.

The thought that she could have been the hand that dealt even more blows to the man who seemed to be unable to escape life's rampage terrified her. She refused to believe him, refused to believe that she could have been so wrong. So, instead of regret, she allowed her anger, her self-preservation, to rise in its place.

"It would have been easy enough for you to say that you would post it and then toss it in the fire as soon as I had left the room," she hissed. She needed to keep her voice down. Someone would come running if either of them yelled. "No one would know and you could easily say that it had been done."

"Of course, I could have," he put both hands to his temples as if his head were aching from the accusations that she had flung upon him. "I could have, but I did not. You asked me to trust you and I did." Again, the implication of his unspoken words hung between them. He had trusted. She had not.

"Well, I do not trust anyone. I cannot trust anyone. Not even you," she snapped, throwing her hands into the air and barely able to keep her voice from rising. Her lash stung; she could see it in his eyes. Her accusation had implied as much but saying the words aloud was much worse. She wanted to trust him. More than anything she wanted to trust him, but every time she felt that she did a niggling voice in her mind questioned if she should. It was better to err on the side of caution.

They sat in stony silence, the argument hanging heavy in the air as if the foul mood were a tangible thing. When Matthew appeared with fresh wood for the fire, he offered to take the dinner tray down to the kitchens and so Caroline had not even that excuse to leave the room.

The duke shuffled through his letters but even though his eyes stared at the pages Caroline did not think that he read. He was furious, but he knew better than to press the argument. After she was released, she might be able to make him see the sense of it but only then when he could hear her full tale, why secrecy was intrinsic to her survival. Her knowledge would bring to light many of the misdealings in his household and so perhaps in time they might have a conversation to that end. Beyond that, she could not say.

He had finally given up on reading and rolled to his side so that his back was to her. He must have drifted off because for some time she could hear nothing beyond the steadiness of his breath.

When it grew labored and full of rasp, she abandoned her perch. He had not woken but she could see that his pallor had returned and the hair at his temple had grown damp. The fever had returned tenfold. Caroline hurried forward and put her hands upon either side of his face. His skin was damp and clammy.

"Your Grace," she gave him a gentle shake. "Your Grace wake up."

He did not respond.

She tried again, shaking him harder this time. "Lord Robert," she said with urgency now. "Wake up. Lord Robert, come now! You must wake! Robert!"

She had said his name with such force that he startled but it did cause him to wake so she did not feel remorse. He was fortunate too because she had been very near to slapping him. Still, she ought not have spoken so informally but she thought he might over-look the slip. From the glaze of his eyes, she thought he was not even like to remember it. She breathed a sigh of relief and gingerly brushed his overlong locks away from his eyes. The dark tones made a stark contrast to the pallor that had lightened his skin to a near ghostly white. Even the crème tones of the bedding looked more vibrant than he.

"It is time for the tonic," she said, more to talk herself through her actions than to inform him of the require-ment. She gathered the vial from the nearby table and pulled its stopper before pressing the offering to his lips. The fact that he did not voice any resistance as she poured the liquid into his mouth was cause for grave concern. He was so weak. For a man that exuded overbearing strength and power in his usual state Caroline could hardly bear to see how difficult it was for him to even swallow or open his eyes. His breath came in rattling gasps and his limbs were over-come by tremors.

He was lying in the center of the bed so Caroline had had to crawl up beside him to wash the sweat from his brow. She knelt there, pressing the cloth against him, and murmured mindless comforts. She told him that he was going to be fine, that he was strong and had survived much worse. She promised that she was beside him and that she would take care of him. Her words meant nothing to his unhearing ears, but she hoped only that the tone of her voice might reach him. He was awake and yet he was not. She coaxed a few mouthfuls of water down his throat before he was overcome by another fit of coughing. Caroline hauled him into a seated position with all the strength that she could muster. He was so much larger than she and so weak that he had not the strength to do it himself. It was then that she realized that his nightshirt was soaked clean through, clinging to his well-defined muscles and revealing the true majesty of his form. It might have captured her interest if she had not been so worried for his life. The doctor had said it was only a slight ailment. That it would pass with nothing more than rest. Hadn't he told her that there was no cause for concern? Well, he had been wrong. Caroline was terrified, and the physician was too far away to be called. A glance out the window at the onslaught of snow that had begun to fall with a vengeance told her that another would take hours to be fetched. She tamped down on all distracting thoughts and instead focused only on pressing the cool cloth against the back of his neck as his body was wracked with fits and starts. She would have to get Matthew to bring fresh nightclothes and change him, she added that to her list of tasks. Perhaps bath and dry clothes would do the trick. Not until he was settled though, she decided. He was far too ill to be manhandled by the reedy servant at the moment.

"Deep breaths," she coached as he finally began to settle. "There you are. One more."

The duke had been leaning forward with his head hung low as she crouched protectively at his side. He blinked hard, squeezing the lids as if fighting for clarity of sight and thought.

"I have to tell you…" he muttered and then shook his head. The words were little more than a slur. Caroline had one hand at each of his shoulders as she kept him balanced in the upright position. His skin beneath her palms was on fire but, more than that, she felt a strange rippling texture where there might have been smooth muscles. Another scar then, she noted.

"Don't speak," she murmured, again pushing the hair from his face. "You must reserve your strength." She tucked it behind his ear as she might have her own and he seemed to lean into the comfort of the gesture.

"...have to know." His long slow breath was shallow but the determination in his voice was clear.

"Tell me what?" she prompted when he seemed to have drifted away. She needed to keep him focused. Talking nonsense was better than slipping back into unconsciousness. "What would you tell me?"

He mumbled something incoherent, only allowing her to catch the final word. 'Important.' He shivered as the fever rolled over him anew. She refreshed the cloth in the basin, freeing one hand by stretching an entire arm across his shoulders and allowing him to lean slightly against her. For a man without a spare pinch of fat upon his frame, he was so very heavy.

"Tell me," she pressed. The cloth circled his face and then his neck but the chill water had little effect. He caught it on the next pass, holding her delicate hand palm upward in his two dwarfing paws. He stared down into their hands as if there were answers to be found there. One thumb traced lazy circles in the center of her palm. She knew that he must be delirious but she did not pull away because the action seemed to help him focus and if she were being honest with herself, it felt nice.

"I sent it," he breathed with great effort. She had had to lean forward to hear him, but she was certain that is what he said.

"I know," she murmured in reply. And she did know. She had known it somewhere deep within but it had been easier to blame him than to wonder what could have kept her father from coming to her straight away. In this moment all of her anger from their earlier row had dissipated. It seemed petty now to hold a grudge for reasons that seemed no longer important.

"I did send the letter," he murmured with what little energy he had left. He seemed not to have heard her response because he continued to repeat his truth as if he must make her believe. "I promise. I did."

"I believe you," she said a bit louder this time. She flipped her hand so that theirs rested palm to palm and he curled his fingers to hold on. He then turned his face an inch or so in order to look sideways at Caroline. He was struggling hard; she could see it in the way his eyes had trouble focusing on her face. Again, he whispered his promise and for a third time she told him that she believed.

An ease took over and he released a deep sigh that seemed to lift the weight from his shoulders. She begged that he rest and not think on it any further. They could speak when he was recovered. He must recover. She willed it with every inch of her being. Of everything she had endured there was one thing of which she knew to be good, and that was the duke.

Even if he did find himself caught up in the wrong of this house, she knew that he would not allow it to continue once he was well and truly at the helm. If anyone could right the wrong in this house, it was he.

"Not supposed to… you know," he added when Caroline disentangled her hand and began wiping his brow once more.

"What?" Her breath hitched. Not supposed to help her? Not supposed to tell her the truth? What was he not supposed to do? She felt at once that the answer was important.

"I'm not supposed to…" She could shake him for the fact that getting answers was as simple as wrangling a bull but she knew that it was the fever talking. Yet again she called for clarification. One frail hand reached up to brush her cheek before it fell away. "Want you," he said with a tone that could break even the steeliest of hearts, "for myself."

His eyes rolled back and his full weight fell against her nearly knocking her back onto the bed. The tonic had taken hold. It was indeed as effective as he had been led to believe. She grunted as she pushed and shoved him into what she hoped was a comfortable position. She pulled the blankets up around his shoulders and even though she knew that she should not have, she pressed a hesitant kiss to his temple.

Despite what he had said there could be no future for them. It was a truth that they both knew, although for differing reasons. Still, she could not help but wish things had been different if fate had not been so cruel time and time again. She had come to cherish their friendship and was loath to know that it would soon come to an end. She had allowed herself that small affection as a memory that she could treasure, as some small token of this conversation that not even he would remember. When all was said and done, he would hate her even more for having kept her secrets. For the depth of trust that she had withheld that went far beyond that of the letter. What might he think when he discovered that she had been wed to his father? What might he think when he found out that she had been lying to him for months about who she really was, that everything, or mostly everything, that he knew about her was nothing more than a farce? She had lied so completely and thoroughly to him. He had no knowledge of how much she had not trusted him, but he would know. Once her father came, he would know, and he would hate her. Oh, he might understand her motivations but he would never trust her again. So, she had kissed his forehead to express her deep regret at the hurt that was yet to come and to thank him for caring when no one else had.

She checked once more that he was sleeping with ease and then she left the room in search of a few manservants who could bathe and dress him when he woke.

CHAPTER 20

Caroline could not stop his words from replaying over and over in her head. She could tell from the way that he had spoken that he knew that there could never be a future between a maid and a duke. His tone and the sadness that it held had said as much. He had already resigned himself to that fact and had never pushed her for more unlike his brother who had had no qualms about such dalliances. Caroline found that made her respect him all the more, that he would not ask a maid to take on such a risk when his position would protect him and hers would not. If it had not been for the fever Caroline doubted that he ever would have made the confession that could only hurt them both, and yet she was glad that he had. She was glad that she knew that he had cared even if it was to be fruitless.

But he had said such things at a time when he did not know that she was not a maid. He did not know that if it had not been for this muddled life, this messy situation that Caroline had found herself in, then there was no reason why a baron's daughter and a duke could not have made a pair. True, she was reaching, but they were both gentry, and they would have never met since she would have remained in Northwickshire, she reminded herself. Still, she found that his confession had wrecked something inside of her. Despite all of the anger and the fear that she had experienced these past weeks she could not deny that he had been a light in her darkness. He had been a friend when she had been alone in the world. It was true that she had wanted to hate him. If she were honest, she had gone out of her way to hate him on more than one occasion. Yet, he had risen to the challenge, and she found herself acknowledging that she did care for him. Not in that way, she amended. She did not think that she loved him. One could not afford romance when one's life was quite literally on the line. She only clung to him because even though she never showed him her trust, he was one of the only people in the house she could trust at all. She cared for him to be sure. She enjoyed his companionship and valued his brilliant mind. She already mourned the loss. At least let him live, she prayed. If they never spoke again, she would sleep at night knowing that he was at least alive and well. That much she could hope for. That much would be enough.

"It is not as if he said that he loved me," she found herself saying aloud when it seemed that her mind needed a firm talking to. He had said he wanted her. That could mean any number of things. Lord Edward wanted every female. Mrs. Reilly wanted a good maid. There were many ways that he could have meant that he wanted her. Except, she recalled, he had said that he had wanted her… for himself. What was she meant to do with such knowledge? She needed to put such thoughts from her mind. She shoved the thoughts away. The duke's feelings were the least of her concerns at the moment. In a day or two it would not matter either way. She would just have to pretend that their conversation had never happened. That was the only solution. He would have no recollection of it, she was sure, but telling herself to forget was going to be more difficult.

She was pondering that exact matter when she over-heard voices in the kitchen.

"Put a pinch more," Mrs. Reilly's voice could be heard along with that of the head chef. Caroline had never actually learned the man's name as he was resolute that he only be referred to by his title. "It worked better this last time."

Caroline peered covertly around the corner to see the portly man pouring a clear liquid into a bowl of soup. The housekeeper then placed that bowl on the duke's tray! She could not believe her eyes. She knew without a doubt that there was no tonic being added to his soup. She recognized the concoction. It was the same elixir that caused nausea with only a drop, but they were adding much more than a drop. They were poisoning the duke. She felt the truth of it deep in her bones.

"When that wench comes down to collect the tray tell her that he needs to drink all of the broth this time," Mrs. Reilly added. "This round should do it."

"You made sure that she was the only one to serve him?" the man asked again with a tone that said he doubted Mrs. Reilly's abilities. Caroline had never heard anyone talk down to the housekeeper.

"Do you think me a fool? Of course, I did," Mrs. Reilly snarled. "She said we need to make sure she knows that we could pin the entire thing on her if she ever opens her mouth about her time here." Caroline felt rage grow within her. Not only would they murder the duke but they would pin it on her? She knew exactly which she the pair were referring to. Caroline made a promise to herself in that moment that she would destroy this entire operation if it were the last thing she did.

The chef swore, low and foul. "What do you think the twit did that they need that kind of promise to keep her mouth shut?" Not what she did, Caroline thought, but who she was and all that she had seen. These ingrates were mere henchmen. She felt some relief that they were not fully aware of her position or else she might have received poison herself.

"I don't ask questions," Mrs. Reilly huffed. "We do our job and that's that."

Caroline barely had time to slip behind the door that led down to the cellar before Mrs. Reilly came stomping out of the kitchen and into the hall.

She waited ten minutes before abandoning her hiding place and retrieving the tray, which came with firm instructions regarding the broth. While she had been waiting, she had taken the time to mull over what she had learned. Unbeknownst to her she had been feeding the duke his poison. Looking back, she acknowledged that he had always taken a turn for the worst after a meal but she had never tied the two together as it had taken time for the potion to do its work. She felt like an idiot. Worse, she hated that he had suffered at her hands. She had thought she had been caring for him and she had been unknowingly aiding in an attempt to kill the man!

For the first time Caroline knew for certain that her husband's death had been no random accident. It was far too coincidental that the second duke should be eliminated now. She shuddered to think what her fate might have been if the marriage had been known at the time of the attack. She looked back upon the fateful evening of the robbery with fresh eyes. Not robbery, assassination. The carriage ought not to have been on that road. So how was it that the murderers had found them? She then recalled the overturned carts that had blocked the main way into the town, the safe route. Like a bell chiming in her mind, it all made sense. The carts had not collided by accident. Their carriage had been diverted with a neat ruse. The vagrants had known that the duke was impatient, that the carts had too few horses to be moved. They had offered the secondary pass as a solution, but in truth it had been nothing more than a trap. The highwaymen had lain in wait, in the darkness, on a road upon which they had no fear of discovery by a random passerby.

Caroline had another recollection from that night, a piece of the puzzle that she had never thought twice on, certain that it was irrelevant. Their attackers had asked if she were linked to the duke, not by acquaintance or happenstance. No, they had inquired specifically if either of the females might have had intimate relations with the man. She recalled them specifically asking if there was any chance that one might be carrying the duke's child. Her hand went unbidden to her stomach, and she felt ill all at once. Had she carried an heir it would have meant her death. Had there been any chance that the duke's line would continue through her they would have disposed of her without a thought, as they had her husband. Had her marriage been consummated, it would have been the ticket to her own demise. The duke had been hunted, and now his son was being poisoned. His line was being exterminated.

The duke had hinted on several occasions that he had many nameless, faceless enemies and she wondered who could want his entire line deleted. Perhaps now it made sense that he was so thoroughly obsessed with his heirs. Caroline wondered if Lord Edward were even safe at this moment. She could not say, nor was there anything that she could do for him at present. What she could control was the health of the present duke. She would be damned if she let one more bite of food that she had not filched herself, pass by his lips.

She wanted to hurl the soup at the wall but that would not do. Mrs. Reilly and her cronies needed to believe that it had been consumed. They needed to believe that the duke was on his deathbed so that she had time to make a plan.

Caroline carried the tray into the room just as she had for every other meal. She could hear the duke and the young servant, Matthew, in the adjoining room. Her cheeks reddened when she recalled that the large bathing basin resided only on the other side of the door.

"Get ahold of yourself," she scolded.

When the men appeared, they saw only the picture of feminine ease. Caroline was reading in her chair by the fire as if she had had no untoward thoughts about their business.

Matthew was attempting to help the duke to the bed, but he was having none of it. He walked for himself although she could see that the exertion cost him greatly. He had abandoned his nightclothes and chosen to wear britches and a linen shirt. It could not be considered fully dressed, but she wondered if he had decided to be slightly presentable on her behalf.

Rather than sink back into the bed he crossed the room and took up the chair opposite Caroline.

"I've brought your meal," she said in the hope that Matthew would report that all was as suspected. "Cook said that you should finish the broth for your strength." She made a show of bringing the tray over to the small table at the duke's side and setting it before him.

The duke thanked her and ripped off a piece of the bread, chewing slowly. When he picked up the spoon Caroline's heart leapt into her throat. She had just turned intending to tell Matthew that he could leave to please fetch more wood when the door clicked shut signaling his exit.

"Good heavens don't eat that!" she cried slapping the spoon out of the duke's hand. It went flying into the hearth with a clang.

"Beg pardon?" he said in shock. "You just told me…" He was looking at her as if she were a wild woman. At least his eyes were clear, and he seemed himself for the moment.

"I know what I said," she snapped in a low tone so that if by chance anyone were listening at the door, they would not hear. "You cannot eat another bite. It's been poisoned."

Lord Robert stared at her in disbelief. She held one finger to her lips and looked over her shoulder at the door. On silent footsteps she moved to the fire and fished the spoon out of the flame with a pair of large metal wood tongs. She then dropped the silver into the washbasin where it hissed to cool.

When she returned to his side, spoon in hand, she breathed a sigh of relief. He was shocked but did not argue with her declaration. With a wave of her hand, she gestured that he should remove his elbow from where it rested on the arm of the wing-backed chair. When the space was free, she perched herself upon it so that her back was toward his lap but their heads where close enough for a whispered conversation.

"I only just overheard Mrs. Reilly and the chef discussing the additive," she informed him. "They are both complicit but I cannot say who else in the house may know."

"Mrs. Reilly?" he pondered the potential. Then, to Caroline's utter relief he nodded. "Most of the staff are new since I left. She was brought in only a year ago I'm told and the chef only a few months."

"The only one I can vouch for is Lizzy," Caroline added. "I cannot be entirely sure but she seems innocent."

Again, he nodded. "Her family has been with us for generations. I would think her loyal." He made mention of Lizzy's mother at Heatherton Hall and how the old woman had always been very kind. He looked down at the bowl of soup at his side with amazement. "Is it really poisoned?"

Caroline offered a grave nod. "I saw them add it myself although they have no idea that I was spying."

"Then I am glad that you were," he moved as if to place a hand on her own in thanks but thought better of it and withdrew. No, he did not remember what he had said, she realized. He was back to being proper.

Caroline pulled the satchel that she had hidden beneath the curtain of his chair and placed it in his lap.

"Eat this instead," she instructed. "It isn't much, but it is safe. If we can get a few good meals in you, then you should be strong enough to take charge." She was worried that he would rush to action too soon, while he was still weak and susceptible to an attack.

He pulled out two small hand loaves, an apple, and a length of dried beef. He laughed. "This is more the sort of meal I am used to." She had forgotten that he had spent many months aboard ships that would have needed the basic, preserved foods. "What are we to do with that? They will know if it has not been eaten."

Caroline bit her lip and looked around the room. They could not pour it in the chamber pot for that would be discovered. Even if the maid who did so were not in league with the housekeeper, it would certainly make for a comment that might get back to someone who wished the duke dead.

While she thought she reached over and ripped a hunk of bread off for herself. Lord Robert seemed to suppress a smile, happy that she was comfortable enough to share his meal without asking. Still, she remained perched at his side. They ate in silence. The duke's vigor seemed to be coming back. She could not say if it was the food or merely the fact that he had always functioned best under pressure, but she was glad to see his determination take hold.

"Spoon it into the fire," he said after a few moments of staring into the flame deep in thought. "A little at a time will burn off and go undetected." He reached for the spoon in her lap and laughed again. The sound was still weak, but she was glad to hear it.

"I never thought I'd have a maid slap something out of my hand like that," he rumbled again. Or a Lady, Caroline thought to herself.

Instead, she shrugged and allowed herself an apologetic smile. "I acted impulsively. I did not expect it to go flying so," she admitted. "I suppose it was a bit much." Perhaps in her fear she had been too exuberant.

"You saved my life." He looked up at her with a solemn expression, all joking aside. "I shall be forever in your debt." She wondered if he would feel the same when he knew all. She supposed that would negate the debt when he realized that, despite saving his life, she was a liar. Not only that but she had been in situations with him that no Lady ought. In his bedchamber no less! Her reputation would be ruined. There was no doubt of that. She could not help the miserable groan that escaped her. Thinking she had responded to his words he put a warm hand on her forearm. "I mean it, Emily," he repeated. "I can never thank you enough."

Emily. Her gut rocked at the name. Emily, a silly lowly maid to whom he felt… what? Attraction on occasion, gratitude in this moment, and quite possibly irreversible betrayal in the future.

Caroline closed her eyes and decided that now was as good a moment as any. She could not stand for him to look at her as he was now, as if all the trust that he had ever given were deserved.

"There's more," she began, "so much more."

He must have read something on her face that the news was crushing because he shook his head.

"Not now," he breathed. "I think someone is trying to end our entire line. I'm worried about my brother being next." The fact that he cared for Lord Edward, despite their obvious dislike, was endearing. No matter what they were still brothers and someone, one of their father's enemies perhaps, was trying to kill them all.

Caroline opened her mouth to continue despite his command but his hand moved from her arm to her lips. The gesture silenced her.

"When I'm more recovered," he told her. "There will be time, but for now I need to rest. This is already so much. Please, just let's take this small victory for the moment."

She wrapped his hand in hers, drawing it away from her mouth and holding it against her heart. She nodded. "You'll get better and then we shall talk." She had forgotten that he was still so weak. He had seemed so strong in his resolve but she saw now that the effort had taken its toll. She withdrew from his side and gathered the tray of poisoned food. Then, seated before the fire with the tray at her side she began to add one spoonful at a time to the flame. The sizzle and pop of the fire spat as if it too detested the poison. When she had finished the task, she turned to see that the duke had fallen asleep in his chair. She brought a tasseled blanket over from the end of the bed and covered him with it. He would rest and then she would tell him the truth about his father's death, the truth about her.

CHAPTER 21

The duke awoke in the middle of the night to take another meal of bread and dried meat. Now that his body was receiving the sustenance it craved, he was ravenous. She watched as his strength slowly returned. Caroline reported to the house that he was in a downward spiral and that when the storm cleared, they ought to call for a doctor. Mrs. Reilly had wiped a tear from her eye and played the part of concern well. Caroline had wanted to slap the woman, but she too had a role to play. She brought fresh water and cloths for the sickbed and even asked Matthew to help the duke to change into his nightshirt once more. They had dampened his linen shirt and pants with water from the washbasin so that it might appear he had taken a bad bout of fever. Caroline had found the task unnerving. The duke had been able to soak the front of his attire himself but had required her aid for his backside. She had had to press the cloth up and down the length of his body. Never had she touched a man in so many places despite her best effort to remain indifferent to the necessary chore. His shirt had become nearly transparent across the wide breadth of his shoulders and the narrow curve of his waist. Through the fabric she had been able to see clearly the scars that she had suspected crossed the length of his back. She had not been able to resist the urge to trace her fingers along them. Her feather light touch had gone from his left shoulder to the base of his ribcage on the opposite side. He had shivered and then frozen when he had realized what she was doing.

"They don't bother you to touch?" he had asked with disbelief. He had not turned, perhaps unwilling to see what her face might hold.

"They bother me," she had answered, "though not in the way that you might think."

Only then had he turned. He searched her face for answers and the questions in his eyes had told her that he was unwilling to allow himself to hope that she was not repulsed by his form.

"I hate what they mean that you had to endure." He must have been nearly gutted, splayed open across the back. Cut across his face. She had heard of such injuries leaving men crippled. He had been very fortunate to have survived with only his scars to tell.

She ached at the thought that he must dread the moment that he revealed such scars to his future wife. Caroline refused to think of Lady Lydia in that role any longer as it was now clear that she preferred his brother. Though, the thought was likely still a burden to the duke. That the woman who could hardly look upon his face would have many more scars to contend with overall.

He took a steadying breath but said nothing. He only watched her eyes travel over all of his hurt. Caroline dared to reach up and touch the scar on his face for the third time in their acquaintance. His breath rose in trembles as she followed the path from his temple, pushing the hair out of the way as she had often done. She let her fingers trail down his cheek and over the firm line of his jaw. She felt her touch pass beside the pulse at his neck, thanking the heavens that it had not been an inch or two nearer that delicate heartbeat. Her journey stopped at the collar of his shirt. She pulled her hand away but her gaze lingered.

"How far does it go?" she whispered. She should not have asked. It was an inappropriate question, and he certainly did not owe her an explanation. Still, more times than not she had wondered and she might never have another chance to know.

He pulled the strings of the front of his shirt open to reveal several more inches of skin and the path of the line. It traveled over his collar bone and down to the muscular curve of his chest, stopping right above his heart.

Caroline did not dare to touch him this time. She had only nodded. He had remained statuesque under her gaze and she had realized that in his own way he had bared himself entirely to her.

By nightfall the duke had recovered enough to enact his plan. Caroline had waited for the house to go to sleep before slipping into the servants' quarters to wake Lizzy. The maid had been given quick instruction to slip out and wake the constable and his men so that they might take the house unawares.

If pressed, Lizzy was to say that she had been sent to retrieve the physician as the duke was not expected to make it through the night. This would certainly bring Mrs. Reilly and her companions no end of delight. The duke had remained in his room under the guise of illness while he crafted a series of letters that would go out the following morning. Caroline had told the duke that she did not know London well enough to fetch the law keepers, which was true, and so he had trusted her decision to allow Lizzy to carry the missive that had been penned and sealed only an hour before.

She had not told him that she would not be permitted to leave the house while the criminals were present. Although he had recovered enough for this task, he had still not asked her for additional information. Either, he was not yet well enough to take on more burdens or he was delaying the inevitable blow that they both knew she must deal.

Caroline had left his room to allow the duke the privacy to dress himself in preparation for the confrontation ahead. He must be outfitted in all of his lordly glory so as to make it clear that he was not ill but in fact more than capable of handling his own. She found herself pacing in the study as she counted the minutes until the house erupted into chaos around her.

When the thrice pounded knock at the front door occurred, she found herself biting her knuckle, her fists clenched white with anticipation. Soon it would all be over. She could tell her tale and Lord Robert could send the officers to interrogate the madam and recover Marilee. She prayed that it would not be too late for her dearest friend.

Swift boots headed up the stairs to where the duke would be waiting.

A few moments later shouts rang out as the servants were called out of their sleeping quarters. Caroline guessed that they would all be in the fourth-floor hall at this hour, save the butler who had answered the door.

She allowed herself to open the door and peer out into the silence of the main hall, a small smile of satisfaction creeping across her face. She could hear the commotion above. She stepped out into the hall and made her way toward the stairway that led down to the kitchen so that she might be sure that Mrs. Reilly or the chef did not slip out the back. Footsteps sounded behind her and as she turned, a blinding pain struck her head. Then all went dark.

CHAPTER 22

Caroline came to with a pounding headache. It took a long moment to realize that she was seated in the center of a dark room upon a rickety chair and her hands were bound to the arms of that self-same chair. There were voices shouting on the other side of a cracked door.

"This is insanity," a male voice raged. "Why on earth is she still alive?"

"We didn't think she was connected," another male pleaded. Caroline thought that she recognized the whining voice of one of her abductors, but it had been so long that she could not be sure. "She said he was just escorting her and that her father would pay a fine ransom."

"A ransom?" the first shouted even louder. "So this is about a ransom, your greedy whelp! And you didn't think to tell me? This could lead back to us. To me!" There was the sound of pacing and something shattering against the wall. "They were married. When that news came out about who was in that carriage you should have killed her then."

"I didn't know at first, honest," the miscreant begged. "We were too busy smuggling the duke's valuables out to India where they could be sold without identification. It wasn't easy. All the ports were being watched."

A voracious growl was all that came in response.

"Ames made a good point that if there were survivors then it would look more like an accident," a third voice offered. "Too many deaths would be suspicious. A ransom will distract from all that. What with your brother on his deathbed."

It was all that Caroline could do to smother her gasp. They did not know that she was awake, and she certainly did not want to draw attention toward her little room, but she had to get loose. She pulled on the bindings. The chair creaked, and she stilled.

"He should have died at sea." Lord Edward growled. "I waited five years for him to die on that ship. It should have been easy, but the French just couldn't do the job. I suppose that it would look too convenient for two deaths in the line above me, if I alone survived." Again, Caroline heard him pace, and another glass shattered. "But damn you why didn't you tell me she was in my own house."

It is not your house, Caroline thought with spite.

"We thought we had it handled," one began. "We didn't think she had any connection there. You didn't even recognize her. No one did, she hasn't been seen in London in years."

"When we killed the duke, your brother was supposed to already be dead, and you were supposed to be next in line," one of the hired thugs argued. "It was supposed to be done and easy. We didn't ask for all of this, and I don't kill ladies. It's bad luck." The men had a long debate over who should have known that the late duke had married and how that might have changed their plan for the attack.

"She won't talk," one of the men informed Lord Edward. "They'll pin Robert's murder on her if she does. Reilly said so. We could probably even say she killed your father. Didn't want to marry him and all. Took it out on the family."

It was a solid argument, Caroline thought. With no evidence either way she would likely go down for the crimes.

"Damn it all," Lord Edward groused. He took a deep breath. "You said the constable is there right now, that they have the whole house locked down."

"Yeah," came an annoyed grunt, "but we got her out first. She can't talk."

"Do you think that they suspect my connection?" he asked.

"No one will rat," came the assured reply. "You said that once you are duke that you'll take care of us and by God you better."

"I told you I will," Lord Edward snapped. He then asked if they thought that his brother might have his suspicions.

"No," came the young voice of the servant Matthew. Caroline's heart sank. He was so young that she had hoped that he hadn't been involved, it was clear that the duke had wished as much as well. "He sent me to warn you to watch your back, tell you he'd been poisoned. That's how I knew what was going down and Jack and I clocked her good and brought her here." That seemed to settle Lord Edward's rage for nothing else smashed for a few minutes.

"Sentimental fool," the duke's brother made a noise that indicated he had spat on the ground. "How did he get a letter out to the constable? I thought you were to monitor his letters?"

"I did," Matthew whimpered. "I threw out all contacts to the baron until after they met. I couldn't very well keep having post go missing before that. I don't know who he sent it by but it wasn't James or I." Caroline's heart sank. So he had sent the letter, but even the Duke's own mail had been monitored to a certain extent. James, the duke's part-time valet had to be involved as well. Was no one innocent?

"We'll keep her with my birds for a week or so and then offer the ransom," the Madam's feminine voice chimed in. "That way we have another point of leverage. We can always say she's been well had if she thinks anyone will believe her."

"You should have known better than to put her in my home, Mildred," Lord Edward growled again. A slap resounded, and the lady whimpered. "I expect you won't make that mistake again."

"We only knew her name," the Madam hissed. "No one knew that she had wed your father. Not until it was too late."

"Lud," Matthew guffawed. "What if she's with child?"

"She's not," Mildred snorted. "First, she'd be showing by now but the marriage wasn't consummated."

"How on earth would you know that?" Edward asked.

"When I heard the news that the Lady traveled with only her maid it didn't take much to determine which was which. I beat her maid within an inch of her life until she admitted that your father never touched her. I suppose that's one thing that's gone right."

Caroline's eyes filled with tears and they ran freely down her face. Poor Marilee. In the darkness of the musty room, she cried as silently as possible. She must look a wreck but she did not care, could not even wipe at her nose or face with her hands bound behind her. Anger and indignation welled within her. She would make each and every person involved pay. She did not care if they threated to send her to the gallows for murder. She did not care if they ruined her reputation. Nothing would keep her silent. If she had to take every single one of them down with her, she would. Lord Edward most of all. If doing so freed Marilee from her torment or saved the duke from further attempts on his life, then it would be worth even her own downfall.

"Lady Lydia better not hear a word of any of this mess," Lord Edward declared. In her fear Caroline had forgotten that the Lady Blackwell had entangled herself with this wretch of a man. She had thought that she had been betrothed to a monster when in reality she would have been far better off with Lord Robert. Instead, she had fallen in love with the real monster. A wolf, no, a devil in sheep's clothing. Caroline felt a pang of jealousy at the thought of Lady Lydia perhaps returning her devotion to the elder if ever all came to light. Certainly, Lord Edward feared as much.

The door swung open without warning and Caroline was suddenly cast in light. She squinted against the shocking brightness.

"Uh," Matthew's voice hemmed. "We've got a problem."

Lord Edward burst into the room to find Caroline well and clearly awake. "How much have you heard?" he demanded, grabbing her chin and forcing her to look up at him. Caroline bit back a cry as pain shot through her jaw at the rough grip. She would have bruises the shape of his fingers no doubt.

She only shook her head to indicate that she had not heard a thing.

"Liar," he dropped her chin but only to smack her with the back of his hand. "I bet you thought it entertaining when I showed interest in you," he snarled. "Thought it was funny that you are what… my mother now?"

Caroline only glared in reply.

"I always wondered why you acted like you were better than the other maids," he mused. "A real maid would have leapt into my bed at the first hint of an offer but, no, you were too good for that. Here I was thinking you preferred my brother but really you were just biding your time and having a good laugh at my expense. Who have you told?" He shouted the last bit so harshly that she flinched.

"No one," she breathed in truth.

"Another lie," he slapped her again.

"I knew your house was teeming with snakes," she shouted right back at him. "Why would I trust anyone that was put there by you?"

"Ah, so you aren't the usual dense female." He grinned. "That works to my advantage. Unfortunately, now you know far too much." He turned to the faces that had gathered in the doorway. Caroline was not surprised to see his valet among them. How thankful she was that he had not been present to serve the duke's sickbed and administer the poison. "Plans have changed. You'll have to kill her. The good news is, everyone thinks she was killed months ago. Weight her down and throw her in the Thames."

Lord Edward had stalked from the room after giving his firm order. An argument had ensued in his wake about who exactly he had meant to carry out the deed. Apparently, neither of the men wanted to soil their hands with the murder of a duchess. They would certainly get the drop for such an act if they were caught. After much heated discussion the decision had been made to leave two men to guard her while the Madam Mildred went to retrieve her man. Caroline could only assume that indicated her regular executioner. She had not heard the voice of the leader of the highwaymen this night, the one who had killed the late Duke without a thought. Caroline assumed it would be one and the same. He would have no compunction about killing a duchess. He had already killed the duke.

She felt ill.

CHAPTER 23

T he group dispersed leaving only two male voices muttering outside of her door. She determined that they had been the lowest ranking members as they had not seemed pleased with the task of being left behind. One was assuredly young Matthew and the other one of the abductors.

She began working in earnest on her bindings. Her wrists ached and had grown raw against the rough rope. It had been hastily tied but she could not get it loose. She tried the other hand, and realized that the wood of the chair itself had some give to it. Sitting in the damp air, the chair had warped and rotted. The wicker of the armrest was fraying in one spot and so she yanked at it in frustration. Her wrist began to bleed in earnest now, but she was able to loosen the arm of the chair. That gave her the leeway she needed, stretching the fibers just enough that she could slip one hand free. Using her other hand and her teeth, she managed to get her other hand loose.

She did not know what she would do now that she was free. She had no idea where she was or how much time had passed. She crouched in the center of the room and listened for anything that might give her a clue to her surroundings. The men were still grumbling somewhere to the right of the doorway. They had moved far enough away that she could hear the tone of their voices, but not their words.

The room had a musty damp smell to it as if it never properly dried out but that told her little about her location. It was empty save for the chair and her own person.

She had no idea how long she had been unconscious or how far they might have taken her, but since many of the faces that had made their appearances were based out of London, she thought it safe to suspect that she was still within reasonable distance of the city. Perhaps even still within its bounds. If only she would be so fortunate, she might have a hope of reaching a location that was safe.

She carried the rope with her, thinking it a better defense than her bare hands. At very least she might be able to wrap it around an attacker's neck and strangle them. The thought, even for her own self-preservation, sickened her. She doubted she would have the will or the strength. Her left wrist was throbbing something terrible and her head still ached.

She thought about slipping her shoes off to dampen her footfalls but it was winter and she would need her shoes if she were to outrun her captors and survive in the snow. Instead, she took painstakingly slow steps, careful to test each floorboard before setting her weight upon it, testing it to see if it might creak.

Through the sliver of light at the door she could make out nothing more than stacks of crates strewn about. A warehouse, perhaps? She was in some sort of storage facility to be sure. She could feel the cold creeping in from the larger room. The chill breeze gave her hope that there was an exterior door nearby that was open or at very least unlocked.

The two men were bathed in the light of three lanterns. Their stark forms sat at a table and they appeared to be passing a bottle of some amber liquid between them. She heard Matthew hiss at the burn of the drink and the older man roared with laughter.

Caroline inched the door open, praying that the hinges were well oiled. If she stayed low, she could remain hidden behind the nearest crate, yet that would mean she had to open the door wide enough to crawl through rather than slip sideways. The risk was one she would have to take in order to remain out of view. The door was miraculously silent as she pulled it open. She crept forward until she was crouching on the other side and safely behind the crate. She considered inching the door closed again but was afraid that any more movement would draw the attention of the men.

To her left stood an open door from which the breeze was coming. That then was her exit. She would have to make a run for it as there was nothing between her crate and that door. She would be in open view of the men for no less than ten strides. She steeled herself, knowing that she must begin, but too afraid to make the dash. She would have no second chance.

"What's that?" Matthew's voice said with a jolt.

"The door's open!" the other man shouted and Caroline heard a chair slam to the floor as the men stood up.

She had leapt at the same time, racing for all that she was worth. She had grown up in the country and was strong. Weeks of hard labor had made her even stronger.

She passed through the doorframe just as a shot rang out and embedded itself in the wood beside her head. She did not even pause to look at it. She bolted through the door, made a hard left and ran straight down a hallway that opened into the darkness of the evening snowstorm. Shouts and curses followed her. Another shot, then another, rang after her but she would not stop running. She barreled out onto the docks of a London wharf. She knew the Thames when she saw it. Knew that wide river that bordered so much of London's cityscape. Although she did not think it was frozen, she could not be sure. She did know falling into the icy river would be death. Hadn't that been what Edward had said? Throw her body into the Thames? Nonetheless, she was running directly toward it. She could not turn back toward the shore for that would lead her straight into the arms of her assailants. She wove between the crates and barrels that littered the dock hearing one bullet and then another fly after her. There was a pause as the men reloaded and she bolted.

She remembered her father saying that pistols were wholly unreliable, but she never thought she would bless that fact.

At one point she knew that they had lost sight of her because the next shot was off toward the other side of the dock. Still, the men knew that she had reached a dead end and there was only one way off the dock that did not lead straight into their arms.

She could not leap into the Thames. The ice was new and would still be thin. She would either crash through the ice and be caught beneath it, or die from the cold of a frozen dress in the winter night. She found herself crouching at the end of the dock amidst a line of barrels teeth chattering. She contemplated whether the risk was worth it. She was going to die either way, better by her own hands.

A thought struck her. It just might work.

She heaved her full weight against one of the barrels. It barely budged. She heaved again. The voices were getting closer now. The barrel slid against the icy deck and tumbled over the edge and with a mighty crash sunk into the murky depths of the Thames.

"She leapt!" Matthew exclaimed with horror.

Caroline sank away from the edge of the dock and squeezed herself into the tiny space between two enormous crates. They would either believe the ruse or find her here to be shot.

"Did she come up?" the other man asked as they both looked into the dark icy water.

"No," Matthew gaped. "Should we go down to be sure?"

"Have you gone mad?" the elder replied with what must have been a slap to the back of the head because Matthew yowled. "The ice is cracked now. We'd be more like to go in ourselves if we go down there. If she hasn't come up yet she won't come up now." They stood watching the ice for several more minutes while Caroline held her breath. "No doubt her dress took her straight to the bottom," Matthew mused.

"Weight her down and throw her in the Thames," said the other bloke. "Just like the master said."

"What are we going to tell the others?" There was terror in Matthew's voice. Fear of punishments far worse than death hung over his head.

"We tell them we shot her and dumped her overboard. They'll be pleased that there won't be a body to bury. Come springtime there will be nothing left to find."

Matthew gave a hesitant agreement before asking if they could return to the warmth of the warehouse.

"We'll even tell them you took the shot," the older man laughed, throwing an arm over the younger man's shoulder. "Your pa will be proud of that."

Caroline now understood why the young man had become swept up in such a devious crown. His father must have been one of the many thugs working for Lord Edward, perhaps even the one who killed the old duke.

Their voices retreated, but Caroline knew that she ought to wait awhile before picking her way toward the shore. She could not wait too long however because the others could return any moment and they may not be so willing to believe the tale without further investigation. Besides, it was freezing and her teeth were already chattering. She would not be safe until she had reached her father's townhouse.

Her legs began to ache from the crouching, one more so than the other. She reached down to rub the offending muscles and nearly shrieked with pain. Thankfully, she had the foresight to bite down on her knuckles instead. The hand that had brushed her calf had come away wet. Even in the darkness she could see the inky color that had covered her palm. Blood.

Caroline took a steadying breath and pulled the hem of her skirt up to reveal a wound that had passed straight through the meat of her lower leg. She had been shot. How she had not noticed, or how she had kept on running, could only be considered a miracle. She supposed to she had been too cold and too afraid to think of anything else but now that she was aware of the wound the pain reared its ugly face. She was glad then that she had brought the rope with her. It lay a few yards away near the place where she had pushed the barrel into the river. She scrambled forward, clutched the length of it, and began to tie it off beneath her knee. She pulled as tightly as she could but knew she would require better care. She had seen enough injuries with her father's tenants to know that limb wounds could bleed something terrible if they weren't tied off, but she couldn't leave it unattended. The wound would need to be stitched. She was not relishing the thought, but it was better than the alternative.

Slowly she began to make her way off the dock. Time was now even more of a luxury and she feared that a trail of blood might lead her enemies straight to her. For the first time she was grateful that it was snowing. She didn't have a cloak but she would suffer the chill if it meant that the fresh flakes would cover her bloody footprints.

It was not until she came out on Fulham Road that she had her bearings. She took the curve of Brompton, staying in the shadows and out of rings of light provided by the lit lamps. Straight ahead she knew was Hyde Park. If she cut across the wedge to the east of the Serpentine and toward Park Lane, then it was only a matter of a few streets to get to her father's townhome near Grosvenor and Davies. She willed herself to move faster as the snow accumulated around her frozen feet. Cutting through the park would save her precious time but it was also a deeper trudge. Still Caroline soldiered on. Her leg was nearly numb now. She needed to rest. Park Lane was just ahead. Then she could sit on a stoop for a few moments to rest.

Her mind was weary and her only thought had been to get to her father, when she realized that the view was familiar. She was looking out at the same trees and lampposts that she had viewed from the duke's windows. One of these Park Lane homes was his.

Caroline changed her plan without hesitation. She needed to rest. She was frozen and her leg sorely needed tending. She may have caught her death. Those were not her only reasons, however. The duke did not know about his brother's duplicitous nature. He did not know that his own brother had ordered the death of their father, had arranged for the duke to be poisoned. When Caroline had overheard Lady Lydia ask the gentleman to do something, Caroline had assumed that Lord Edward would speak with his brother about the matter, not eliminate him as a potential problem. She assumed that Lady Blackwell would be horrified to hear the depths her lover would have gone to procure her hand as well as his own esteemed title. With a groan Caroline realized that the duke did not know about Matthew either. Poor sweet Matthew, she had thought. No, poor terrible Matthew.

Caroline stood beneath one window after another until she found the one that she suspected was the duke's study. There were no lights on in the house. Were there even any servants within to answer the door? Caroline would have walked around to the back entrance but her leg was doing a poor job of supporting her weight. Now that she had made the decision to stop here, she thought she probably could not have made it to her father's house. She was so exhausted.

She nearly crawled up the steps, and she sat against the frame, heaving great breaths from the effort, as she tried the door. It was locked. She hammered her fist into the wood.

There was no answer.

She banged again. Nothing.

She closed her eyes and started to cry.

CHAPTER 24

S he would die here on this stoop, she thought. Just as she had been about to give up entirely, the latch on the door clicked and it opened no more than a crack.

Old Mr. Jenkins, the crippled coachman who was used for local driving, peered out into the might. He released a low string of curses that she had never heard uttered in her life.

"Miss Lizzy!" the man shouted without decorum. "Miss Lizzy come at once!"

There was a scrambling and a clanging in the hallway as Lizzy came flying down the stairs. Caroline had never seen servants behave in such a way, and she might have thought it comical if she had not been in so very much pain.

"Emily!" Lizzy screamed. "Good heavens we've been worried sick! I thought his Grace was going to throttle the entire household when we couldn't find you. They carted the lot of them away to be questioned. Where have you been? Lud, is that blood? I think I'm going to be sick."

"Stop your jabbering and go get his Grace," the coachman grumbled. "I canna' lift her with my leg and there's only the two of us left after that mess."

Lizzy turned and ran.

Mr. Jenkins did his best to get his arms up under Caroline's own and drag her into the hall. It took both of their best effort, but they got her inside enough to shut the door against the blowing storm.

By the time the door was shut, the maid and the duke were racing back down the hall. Lizzy was still talking a mile a minute.

"She was on the stoop. There's blood everywhere. We had the doors locked like you said but we heard the banging. I don't know if Jenkins was supposed to open it, but I'm glad that he did." The maid skidded to a halt. "Oh my, I still think I may be sick." Caroline had never heard the maid speak so much. It was clear that she was overwhelmed. The duke, on the other hand, was deadly silent.

"Boil water and get fresh linens, Lizzy," he ordered when they finally came to stand above her. "Jenkins, heat some food. Anything warm. Can you do that?" The old man nodded.

"Lizzy can bring it up," the duke continued. "Get yourself a brandy while you are at it."

"Thank you, your Grace," the old man ambled off.

The duke shooed Lizzy off and then crouched beside where Caroline was leaning against a potted fern.

"Will it hurt too much if I move you?" he asked. His voice was both incredibly tender and assertive. She recalled that he had likely dealt with hundreds of wounded men in his time, himself not included.

She shook her head. "It's only my leg." She rested her hand upon the place below her knee so that he might know that the wound was not higher. Without hesitation he scooped her up and turned toward the staircase. Caroline leaned into the warmth of him. She had never felt so cold in her life and she wanted to bury herself in him. She settled for wrapping her arms around his neck and resting her cheek upon his shoulder instead. Her teeth were chattering.

He did not speak until they entered his room. Caroline could tell from the firm set of his shoulders that he was angry but his concern seemed to be keeping the temper in check. No, she corrected, he always kept his temper in check even when it boiled right below the surface.

He walked straight over to the bed, threw back the covers, and set her down with nary a jar to her aching wound. He then ripped the covers from the bed and deposited them over her upper half.

"I'll have to inspect the wound."

Caroline's instinct had her pulling her legs toward herself and under the blankets but the action had her yelping with pain. She'd never allowed a gentleman to see her legs. It was indecent!

"Come now," he allowed the break in his stern demeanor to reveal a small quirk of one half of his mouth. "You've seen practically all of me."

"Not all of you!" she argued before she could take it back. Her blush elicited a brow-raised look that said he would dare amend that fault if she did not allow him her leg. Slowly, she inched the limb toward him. Just the one.

He flipped the hem of her skirt up without preamble, all business. She did not know whether to be shocked that he had not eased her into it or grateful that he was approaching the tender flesh with all of the impartiality of a physician.

"Good of you to have tied it off," he noted. "I'll have to remove the strap. It cannot be on too long."

Caroline nodded, and he released the knot just as Lizzy burst into the room. The maid took one look at the pair, her eyes going wide in horror as she glanced down at the bed. She gingerly set the tray with the kettle and linens on the table just within the door before turning around and retching in the hall. The duke shook his head and walked over to retrieve the tray, instructing the maid that she could leave the next delivery in the hall rather than come inside the room. The last thing that Caroline heard before the door closed were Lizzy's promises to have the hall cleaned and another delivery as soon as the water could be set to boil. Caroline was again surprised by the duke's unflinching response. She supposed it was a common thing for onlookers to become sick at the sight of blood. Caroline had simply refused to look at her wound in the light. She did not want to know. Instead, she had focused solely on the duke.

He set to work cleaning the wound all the while talking to distract her. Caroline gritted her teeth but answered as best she could.

"Mrs. Reilly told the constable that you took off so that you wouldn't be caught as the leader of their horrible plan." His voice was unaffected as if he waited her confirmation or denial but nothing more.

"I did not!" She shrieked when he squeezed the hot water over the wound.

"You are fortunate that it went straight through," he observed. "You did not do which? Leave or command their band of malefactors?"

"I did neither," she said through clenched teeth. Her eyes glared darts at him for even suggesting that he believed anything that Mrs. Reilly had said.

"I did not think so," he nodded and sponged the blood from around the hole as he attempted to get a better look.

"Is that why you were mad?" she asked, her breath hissing out of her at the sting.

He gave her a look that said that he was mad for any number of reasons this evening. "I was furious at first that it might be true," he admitted, "but when you show up on my doorstep with a bullet wound, I would say that was fair confirmation that you aren't the enemy."

"Thank you," Caroline mumbled.

"But good heavens, Emily, what happened?" A knock sounded at the door indicating the arrival of the next tray. He returned with another kettle and a piping-hot meat pie. He set the old tray outside the door and came back to his work. Caroline brought her arms forth from the blankets and accepted the pie into her still trembling hands.

She did not know where to begin.

"I did not leave. I was taken," she said while blowing onto the pastry. "And I was not a part of their group, I was their unwilling hostage." He nodded. "And my name isn't Emily."

He pinched the bridge of his nose and bade her to explain. He did not even seem all that ruffled when she had mentioned the bit about her name, or perhaps he had not heard her because at the same moment he had been digging through the chest at the end of his bed and come up with what looked very much to her like a sewing kit.

"No. No. No!" she repeated as she tried to inch away from him but only came up against the headboard.

He only shrugged and began threading a needle.

"Why did they take you?" he asked. He was so calm it was irritating her. She wondered if he were merely asking questions to keep her busy and not listening at all. He was so focused on her wound that she wanted nothing more than to rattle him, to keep that sharp needle away from her tender flesh.

"Did you hear me?" she cried.

"I did," he replied.

"My name isn't Emily," she repeated. "It's Miss Caroline Graves. Or, I suppose it's Bennington now, but I never had a chance to use that so it hasn't stuck."

When she said his own last name, the needle had dropped from his hand and onto the floor at his feet. So, he had been listening. He stared at her without moving. Without breathing, it seemed.

"That is no joking matter," he said in a mere whisper.

"Then it's a good thing that I am not joking," she replied meeting his gaze without hesitation.

He bent down to retrieve the needle, disappearing out of her view for longer than she thought was necessary. She would give him the moment to collect himself but she would not pretend any longer.

When he stood he did not meet her gaze.

"I told you that there was much more to tell," she set the meat pie aside. She was too anxious to eat at the moment. "Are you ready now?"

He steeled himself, glanced up, and presented his challenge. "Are you ready now?" he countered, needle in hand. She understood the trade. He would stitch both sides of the wound while she wove her tale. She supposed that the distraction would help her through the pain but this was not how she had imagined the conversation going. Maybe he too needed the distraction. Maybe having his hands busy would help to soften the blow.

She nodded, and it all began to spill out.

She told him of the byway and how it had delayed his father's journey north for a fortnight at Gravesend Manor.

She hissed as the needle pierced her flesh.

"Try to be still," he said gently.

She nodded. She told of her tempestuous engagement, although she left out the part about her father's duel. Perhaps one day she might tell him, if he ever spoke to her again after this.

She poured all of the aching details of the highway murders into the air between them. She had not told anyone, had not realized how much it had needed to be said. She found he was nodding along with her when there were parts that only she could have known, like that the duke had been shot through the heart and his valet through the eye or that they had taken a diverted path because of the hay carts that had collided. She told him of her suspicions that it had been a trap from the outset.

This caught his attention, and he paused in his stitching.

"Why would you think that?" he wondered.

"I did not at first," she admitted.

He bent again to his work, and she gasped when he pulled the wound closed at its widest point. She laid a hand on his arm. "Stop a moment," Caroline panted.

"I am almost finished," he said, and she looked at the neat stitches and the still gaping hole. She sucked in her breath.

"Don't you faint," he said.

"I am not the fainting sort," she retorted, sucking in a deep breath. "Finish it then."

He nodded and made another stitch and she hissed, a tear escaping her eye.

"Finish telling me the tale," he urged trying to distract her, but she could not think. She squeezed her eyes shut and groaned.

"You thought it was just an accident with the hay carts."

"Yes," she agreed. "I thought it mere accident. But you shall see as I go that it began to make more sense with time."

She told of the ruse to save Marilee, their capture and arrival at the brothel. She told everything that she knew about the London whorehouse and its Madam Mildred. She explained the threats and her coming to work in his home. She told him of the horrible things that happened to the women who came and went. She felt tears begin to flow as she spoke of her fears, her worry that she could not trust a single soul or that she might never see her father again when they had parted on such bad terms. She told him of finding her first letter in her bed, a clear message.

She gave a small cry as he knotted off the final stitch and snipped the thread. "All done," he said, and she sighed with relief as he held a cool cloth against her leg. Still the throbbing pain was still acute.

"So, you tried again," he filled in the next part for her, "with a letter, except that you weren't sure if you could trust me. This is, after all, my house and my staff. My responsibility."

She nodded. "I am so very sorry about that part."

He did not reply but seemed lost in his own thoughts. He went back to work bathing her wound with cool water.

"Why did you befriend me, if you could not trust me?" he said

She hesitated. "It all began as a way to escape your brother," she hung her head as she realized just how terrible it sounded aloud. "I know that the pair of you did not get on and you had said that I could use the room. It was the only place that he would not search me out. I didn't mean to befriend you. That just… happened."

He inhaled one long breath. "My brother has a," he pondered his choice of words, "reputation with maids. With women in general. Did he ever…?"

She shook her head. "He was forward, and far too willing with his touches, but he never harmed me."

"He is not used to being told no," he grumbled. "Father spoiled him."

"I do not disagree with you."

He looked up at her with horror. "If he had known you were a lady…" his voice trailed off.

"He ought not to have treated me any different whether lady or maid," she remarked. "You never took advantage." The unspoken words hung between them. Lord Robert had not done as his brother, although he had had several opportunities.

He bowed his head, thankful for the respect that had laced her words. "Lydia always said that it was because I wasn't romantic enough."

Caroline scoffed. "Lady Lydia wouldn't know romance if it kicked her in the teeth." They were both surprised at her defensive remark and he paused in his nursing her leg, both realizing the compromising situation they were in, but he did not remove the cool cloth. She stared into his dark unfathomable eyes, and he into hers.

Caroline had felt romance quite literally rolling off of the duke on several occasions. It was only that he held himself back unless he was certain. If he ever gave himself over to those urges, then good luck to whatever woman was fortunate enough to stand in their wake. Caroline felt her cheeks redden at the thought and pressed onward before he could notice.

"There is something that you should know," she confessed in the hope of turning her mind from such thoughts. She told him of what she had witnessed between his brother and his betrothed. She prepared herself for the crush of the blow, for the anger that might come her way for having borne the bad news but he only nodded once more.

"I had my suspicions." He revealed that although he had often wondered if Lydia preferred his brother, it had never made sense to him that she would make the trade official. "She always seemed to want the title more than anything else."

Caroline's mouth dropped open in understanding. Of course, Lord Edward would have known that his lover wanted to be a duchess more than anything. He would have murdered his entire family to secure the title for them both. "She would have had the title," Caroline admitted.

"I suppose they could have carried on an affair," he agreed without comprehension of her true meaning. "Although I doubt Ed would have played seconds for long."

"He wouldn't have played seconds at all," she murmured.

Lord Robert looked up at Caroline with an expression that tried to wrest every meaning from her words. "What are you saying?"

Caroline looked into the face of this man who was so trusting, who gave trust where it was not warranted. How could she tell him his brother betrayed him? How could she not? Her voice dropped to a whisper as if that would soften the blow. "I'm saying that Lord Edward is behind it all. I didn't know until tonight, but now there can be no doubt. It was his men who did this," she gestured at her leg. "He was going to have me killed when he found out who I was and how much I knew. I only barely escaped."

He closed his eyes in pain, but he nodded. "Go on," he said. He went back to gently bathing her wound although Caroline thought that all of the blood was washed away by now. Still the cool water was soothing, as was his touch.

And so the last of the story came forth. Caroline tied up all of the loose ends. She told the harrowing tale of her evening. She repeated every word that she could remember and listed all of the names and misdeeds that she could provide. She told of her escape, her trek across the snow-covered streets, and every bit of her agony until she had arrived upon his doorstep bloodied and frozen to the core.

"Everything else you know," she concluded. "I still do not know what happened to my maid, but I'd do anything to find her and my father must be worried sick." She covered her face with her hands. Now that he was done with the stitches, he was watching her with rapt attention. "I've been so worried that you will hate me for all of the secrets but I had to keep them."

Gentle hands pulled hers away from her face.

"Why would I hate you?" he asked, confused.

"You've only ever asked for my trust and I never gave it," she sobbed. "If I would have shown even a little then this all might have ended weeks ago. Instead, I was stubborn and so willing to believe that you knew something. I made you out to be the villain when you've never been anything but kind."

"Emily," he pressed his lips together and started over from the mistake. "Lady…Miss Graves… I mean, Benning…"

"Caroline. Just call me Caroline, please," she pulled her hands back up to her face. She prepared herself to receive all of his anger and judgement. She deserved it. Hadn't she treated him just like everyone else? Like he was a monster.

"Caroline," he began. She felt the bed move as he sat down beside her. She was a mess and yet he did not shy away. "I understand every reason you had to keep your secrets. If the situation had been reversed, I would have done the same." He laughed. "In truth, I probably would have done worse and willing poisoned every potential captor. I owe my life to the fact that you didn't."

She gave a small laugh through her sniffles. He would have. He would have taken the whole house down like a ship at sea.

"Caroline."

She liked it when he said her name.

"I wish you might have told me sooner if only so that I could have protected you or returned you to the safety of your father." He tugged at a loose lock of hair, tempting her to come out of her hiding but she was not yet ready. She should have told him sooner she thought. "I can't regret that you did not, however."

Her hands dropped a few inches so that she could look at him with shock.

"I wish that I could have protected you, especially from this," he gestured at her leg that was now pressed against his hip. "I wish a great many things but I fear that if I had known then I would have acted sooner, and we would both be dead. You didn't know about my brother's connection until this evening. He would have simply kept trying to kill me in new ways and likely you too just for what you know. I hate that you suffered more for it but now we know our enemy. He did not expect me to find out. Now I won't fall for the ruse again."

"You don't hate me for the lies?" she dropped her hands to her lap. Caroline could not keep the hope from welling in her voice. "I told so many lies."

"Did you, though?" he laughed. "Other than your name and how you had come to be here you weren't all that different than I imagine you might be in your own life."

"Well, I wasn't a maid," she countered.

His laughter rang even louder. "You were never a convincing maid to begin with!"

"What do you mean?" she cried in confusion. She thought she had played it off quite better than she had expected.

"You speak too well and you are a nuisance in the house," he chuckled. "I had it in my head that you were some demoted lady's maid or a merchant's daughter who had been educated before the fortune was lost. At least you might have had a wealthy bene-factress that trained you up before you fell. I never once considered that you had been born to servitude."

She harrumphed.

"You're cross that I did not believe you to be low-born?" he grinned.

"No, I am cross that you said I was a nuisance in the house!" she argued, crossing her arms over her breast like a petulant child. Perhaps he was not mad at her, but insulting was not much better.

He raised his eyebrows but said nothing. His expression clearly dared her to deny the accusation.

"I nursed you well!" she decided for her best argument.

"Well yes. Besides the poisoning part," he grumbled but grinned when she swatted at his arm. When she laughed alongside him, he released the breath that he had been holding. He scooted closer and his hands came to settle on her upper arms. The slight squeeze of his hands implored her to believe his words.

"Caroline, I cannot begin to think why you expected me to hate you when I can't find it in myself to be anything but overjoyed. It's better than I could have ever hoped for."

Her confusion must have been written deep in the furrow of her brow. Hadn't he implied several times that her lack of trust was unforgivable?

He pulled her slightly forward, leaning in so that their foreheads met and her eyes fluttered closed. They had been here before, she realized but not like this. Never as themselves. That was when she realized his meaning. The barriers between them had crumbled. She had always known that the limits were only a ruse, but this was the first he had ever come to hope that there might be a potential for something more.

"Are you really Miss Caroline Graves?" he breathed against her. She liked the use of her maiden name. That was who she really was. She had never felt like the late duke's wife. Had never wanted to be the Duchess of Manchester. He believed her story and yet this was something different. He needed to hear the confirmation not for his mind but for his heart.

"I am she," she whispered in reply and brought her hands up to cup his elbows, drawing him closer yet.

He released a contented sigh and his mouth descended upon hers. The kiss was tentative at first, giving Caroline the chance to draw away if she willed it. She did not. Instead, she melted into him the way that she had longed to when he had carried her in his arms. He was warm and gentle, yet so firm against her that she could not help but cling to him.

Just as she had imagined, although she would never admit to how many times she had done so; he gave himself over completely to his passion holding nothing back. She received it with a vigor to match his own until they were both breathless with wanting. His arms wrapped around her, crushing her against him. Her hands roamed up his arms, over his neck, until she was cupping his face in her hands. She held him and let all of her love flow into him. For she did love him, she realized.

Her thumbs stroked his cheeks, not caring that one was smooth and one was scarred. It did not matter. They were a part of him and she loved all of it, all of him. He shivered beneath her touch, reveling in the knowledge that she was not repulsed by him, that she had seen all of his ruin and still wanted him.

He murmured her name against her lips and Caroline was consumed by the sound of it. The duke, on the other hand stilled. He pulled back, a look of shock and horror on his face.

"You're a lady," he gasped, "and you've been in my bedchamber… for days."

She could not suppress a giggle. "Yes," she understood his concern. "Perhaps that is a bit that we ought to leave out of our retelling of the tale."

He pressed his forehead to hers once again, stole one last kiss from her smiling lips, and extricated himself while he still could.

"I'll speak with Lizzy," she said. "I think she would be willing to protect my reputation." The duke nodded but his eyes still roamed over Caroline as if he might come back to join her in the bed if she would but give the word. She laughed again. "Go fetch her before you get us both into trouble."

"I'll have Jenkins bring round the rig," he added. "It's not yet sunrise but I think we should get you to your father straight away." And out of his bedchamber, Caroline thought to herself.

CHAPTER 25

When Lizzy entered the room, she did so with hesitant steps as if checking first that there was no offensive blood in sight.

"His Grace said that you wanted to speak with me," the maid looked around the room as if expecting Caroline to start bleeding upon sight.

Caroline laughed and gestured to the chair opposite where the duke had placed her. He had carried her from the bed before departing so that she might have the conversation with the maid away from the ruined bedsheets. They had thrown a blanket over the wreckage.

Caroline took her time to tell the tale once more. Lizzy's eyes were wide with wonder the entire time, but she did not interrupt.

"A lady," she mused at the end. Then her jaw dropped with realization and she leapt from her chair and sank into a curtsy. "Oh my, your Grace," she corrected herself.

"I don't think of myself that way," Caroline clarified. "We were only married a matter of days and, as I said, the marriage was never consummated."

Lizzy groaned. "You slept on the palette on the floor. You should have asked for the bed."

Caroline shook her head and reached out to place a friendly hand upon the only other servant she had come to trust in the house. She explained the predicament.

"I can say that I tended to his Grace," the maid offered before Caroline had gotten that far. "No one need ever know." She made a locking motion over her lips.

"I know that it's a lot to ask," Caroline said.

"Not at all," Lizzy replied. Then, she bit her lip. "Is it true that you vouched for me to his Grace?"

Caroline nodded. "Of course. I could see straight away that you weren't involved. But you understand why I could not tell you. It would have been far too dangerous, for you as well."

Lizzy brushed off the concern. "It was only that the duke had all of the servants who had held positions less than ten years taken away for questioning. That left only Jenkins who had come to the house with his mother well before his Grace was even born. He even sent word for the same at Heatherton Hall although that will only eliminate a handful of the staff. Then, he said that I could stay, because you had vouched for me. I've only been here a short while. My mother... she would have been so distraught."

"Your mother should be proud," Caroline replied in earnest. "You have proven yourself both hardworking and loyal. She's the head housekeeper at the country home, is she not?"

Lizzy nodded.

"Then you shall have had excellent training and a knowledgeable mentor," Caroline grinned.

"I... I don't understand?" the maid stammered.

"His Grace is going to need someone that he can trust to run this household and you've proven yourself more than willing to keep our secret as well," Caroline explained. "As a reward he has asked that I offer the position of head housekeeper, if you wish it. Though, I will admit that the task will be cumbersome until we can gather new trusted servants beneath you."

Lizzy's mouth dropped open. "Do you really mean it? I mean, I'm so young."

Caroline nodded. Unbidden Lizzy flung herself into Caroline's arms. She would have welcomed the gesture more had the act not jarred her tender leg and caused her to gasp.

"Oh, my Lady… your Grace," Lizzy leapt back. "My lady. I'm sorry. I hurt you."

"It's alright," Caroline said between gritted teeth.

Lizzy gave a respectable nod, straightened her back, and collected herself. She was already preparing for her new role, Caroline noted with a grin. "I will not fail you."

"Serve him well," Caroline replied.

"But aren't you staying as well?"

"I told you," Caroline shrugged, "I don't consider my time as duchess to have been a valid marriage. It will be dissolved."

"I didn't mean…" Lizzy blushed and glanced toward the door. "I thought that maybe you and…"

Caroline understood the notion. Perhaps the affection between herself and the duke had not gone unnoticed by the keen-eyed maid.

"I don't know," Caroline admitted. "There is too much else to sort out first."

Lizzy nodded, curtsied once more, and excused herself.

Shortly afterward the duke returned to carry Miss Caroline down the stairs and into the waiting carriage. He was pleased with the news that Lizzy would keep their secret and also that she would accept the position as his trusted housekeeper even though she was young for the job.

"What else did she have to say?" he asked when they had begun to roll the short distance to her father's house.

"Nothing," she lied. She was not going to tell him that the maid had wondered if Caroline herself would become a permanent fixture in the household. The truth was that Caroline had begun to wonder the same thing herself.

The Baron Wickham was running a sparse household of only a butler, valet, housekeeper and a handful of maids. He had been used to the townhome being closed for the winter and had only compiled the barest of needs as he had searched for his missing daughter.

Caroline paced circles, limping on her wounded leg in the parlor that she had not set foot in in six long years.

"It's going to be fine," Lord Robert crooned as his hand drifted a soothing pattern down her back. The touch had felt so natural that she had allowed herself a deep breath as she leaned into him. "Please sit down. Your wound will be bleeding again."

She sat and knotted her hands on her lap.

"Your father was worried sick."

"We ended so poorly," she worried. "I said that I never wanted to speak to him again."

"Things are different now. None of that matters."

"I glowered at him at my wedding," she groaned.

He breathed a huff of laughter. "I can imagine that."

Hurried footsteps sounded in the hall and they drew apart.

The doors burst open with such force that they slammed back against the walls to reveal the harried baron wearing a striped banyan and slippers.

He entered the room with two swift steps and then froze. Caroline feared at once that he was furious. She had not seen her father move about with anything but slow, dreary moping for years. She tensed.

Then he was upon her. He enveloped his daughter in his arms and pulled her against his shaking form. He was sobbing and speaking all manner of incoherent apologies. His hands ran over her face as if he did not believe her to be real, needed to feel for himself that she was not some ghost who had been brought here to haunt him.

He turned to the duke with Caroline still tucked against his side and clapped Lord Robert on the shoulder.

"You did it!" the Baron beamed. "You brought her back to me unharmed."

"I wouldn't say that," the duke hemmed.

Caroline was struggling to stand under her father's embrace. He had flung her around so that her leg was aching to give out beneath her. The pacing had been more than she ought to have done, but she had not been able to sit still.

The baron pulled back, holding Caroline away from him with both hands and scanning her visage.

"It's only a gunshot," she said with a grimace.

"A what?" the baron gasped. Caroline explained her injury and in the barest of terms credited the duke for her repair. The baron slapped the duke on the back once more, nearly causing him to pitch forward. "So long as she is home. I have you to thank for that."

Lord Robert pinched the bridge of his nose and Caroline had to suppress her laughter. She knew exactly what he was thinking. It would take the pair days to get the tale out with the chaotic manner in which her father was behaving. She could not even find it within herself to be bothered. He was elated. He was pleased to see her. She had hoped, had prayed, but had prepared herself for the same steely reserve with which she had been handled for ages past.

"Caroline," her father turned to her once more and pierced her with a determined stare. "I am so sorry."

"It doesn't matter," she shook her head.

"It does matter," the baron replied. "If you don't want to marry, I shall abide by your wishes. I swear it. You never have to marry again. I swear it now. You can grow old with me in Northwickshire and I'll never say a word otherwise."

Caroline felt the duke's gaze upon her but she fought the urge to glance up at him. The gesture would be far too telling and she was afraid of what she might see written on Lord Robert's face. He had kissed her with abandon, yes, but he had never claimed to love her. He had never spoken of marriage or anything of the sort. Hadn't she learned from the example of Lord Edward that lust meant little more than nothing to a gentleman?

"Papa," she led her father to the settee so that she might get some reprieve. "We have much to say and you must allow us out with it." She glanced up at the duke and bade him to begin. It was her tale, but she had already told it twice and she was weary. He would be able to craft a concise version that would allow her father all of the necessary details without any of the frills.

The duke took up his posting opposite the father and daughter and began to speak in his deep, soothing voice.

Caroline had fallen asleep sometime in the middle of the tale, but the men had continued on for hours talking and planning without her. She had been brought a tonic for her pain and the concoction had lulled her into a deep slumber that she had not even realized had been sorely needed. The duke must have carried her unconscious form up to her bed for when she woke the following morning, she was still in her servants' clothes but tucked into the delicate pink blankets of her own four-poster bed.

It was strange to find herself in this room so many years later. So many eager conversations with her mother had been shared well after her father had thought that she had gone to sleep. Caroline had dreamed of a different future in this room. She had dreamed of things that she had long tucked away and told herself that she no longer yearned for—things like a husband or children of her own. She would have thought that after her frightening exposure to the outside world these past weeks she would be hesitant to want any attachments. She had not thought she wanted children. She had no experience with children, being an only child herself. And yet, she found that there was a kernel of want that had grown within her. A light in her darkness.

She dared to face the thought for the first time. Only a short while ago she had been married with the promise of children and she had dreaded the prospect. What had changed?

The duke had altered her outlook, she realized. Robert.

His father had been odious. She had rebelled against the idea of subjecting herself to that life, of bringing a child around a man who might only craft him into a tool to be used. How his eldest son had survived such an upbringing only spoke further to his character, to the strength of his own person and will.

She realized that Lord Robert had proven to her time and again that he was a kind and compassionate man. He would protect and defend his family without resorting to cruelty. He was smart and driven in his goals but not manipulative or scheming. He had treated Caroline like a person of value even when he had thought her nothing, but a servant. He had respected her words and opinions; saw more in her than what most gentlemen allowed for in the capabilities of women. He would be a good husband, she had realized, and perhaps an even better father. In his singular person, he had the capacity to undo generations of terrible habits. His time away from his family had taught him that, she realized. He had rather faced the horrors of warfare than the hate and anger of his own father and brother. He must have stayed away after recognizing the poison that seemed to leach from their every word and action; figuratively and then in reality.

Caroline moved carefully about the room with a secret smile upon her face. The duke had kissed her, and with such passion! That had to be a good sign.

She realized that the gowns that hung in the wardrobe were from when she had possessed a much smaller frame, before her womanly form had filled in. She crossed the hall to her mother's dressing room and was unsurprised that it remained untouched, like a memorial that her father had kept to the memory. She ran her fingers over the horsehair brush with the jeweled handle. A small bottle of perfume sat beside its cap as if it had only been used a moment before.

Caroline squeezed the bulb and directed the spray at her throat. A deep inhale and the distinctive scent of her mother surrounded her.

She opened the wardrobe and found the gowns that she had once run awestruck fingers over. Her mother had been a woman of definitive taste. She had been known as one of the most remarkably dressed women in London in her time. The gowns, although outdated, were still so elegant in their making and style that they would never go out of fashion. Caroline chose a dark green brocade with gleaming silver snowflakes stitched into the fabric. It was perfect for the season. Now that she had regained her freedom, she was determined to decorate every inch of her father's home. They had not made the effort in years but no more. She would celebrate.

Perhaps she might even convince the duke to outfit his home as well, Caroline mused. The gentleman could use a spot of cheer in his life. She would surround him with it she promised herself.

Since her father had only brought the barest of staff, Caroline pinned her own hair back in a simple knot at her nape. She checked her features in the mirror, pinching her cheeks for a spot of color, and made her slow passage down the stairs. Her leg still ached but she could bear it.

She had expected to find the gentlemen in the parlor but was dismayed to learn that they had gone out. She might have overslept, but she had not thought that reason enough to have left her alone in the townhouse. The butler, a middle-aged man who she had recognized but had been obliged to ask his name, had informed her that they had gone out on important business.

"I will have one of the maids come sit with you when they return from the market," Belton had promised.

Caroline wondered where the men could have gone off too. She worried that they would make an attempt to confront Lord Edward without the officers of the law and be overwhelmed or worse by his cronies.

No, she told herself with a firm shake of her head, the duke would never take such a risk. She had to trust that he would think well before he made a move. He was not a man of haste. His experience with battle would have taught him that there was a time to hold and a time to strike.

Caroline would have liked a cup of tea to settle her nerves but both maids had gone out and the house-keeper was upstairs fussing over the fact that Caroline had been sleeping in a room that had not been prepared to be occupied. Caroline had not cared if the linens were fresh. The fact that they had been maintaining her room at all these past years had been shocking enough. Perhaps her father had harbored the secret hope that she would have chosen to join him in London on one of his visits.

Caroline felt a surge of remorse at the thought. She had loathed her father for pulling away after her mother's death. Caroline wondered if she had done the same in some way. Perhaps she had stopped giving him chances to prove that he still cared. Perhaps she had walled herself off from any connection so that she might not suffer the same pain of loss ever again. She had felt so much anger whenever he had struggled to look upon her that if he had tried to show affection, would she have been receptive?

No, she realized. She had steeled herself in return. She had been so guarded against her father's withdrawal that she had closed herself off to him, and the world around her. She had loved him just as she had loved her mother and some part of her must have thought that the loss of her only remaining parent would have been unbearable. She had fortified her heart against all hurts. Only Marilee had managed to slip through her defenses.

She prayed that her maid could be found. Marilee had to survive the ordeal. Caroline would not consider any alternative.

CHAPTER 26

A knock sounded on the parlor door and Caroline turned away from the piano. She had been plucking the keys in a pensive rhythm that had matched her clouded thoughts although it had not been any true tune.

"You have a visitor, my lady," the butler had informed her. "Shall I send her away?"

Caroline furrowed her brow but nodded so that she might receive the visit. Had the duke returned? Was he not with her father? It was several minutes before the door opened again.

Lady Blackwell stepped through the door with a weary sigh.

"I am sorry to intrude," she said by way of greeting. "I only just heard the news and came straight away to express my shock and horror at your ordeal."

The lady rushed over to where Caroline was reclined on the couch with her injured leg elevated on a pillow. Lady Lydia knelt beside Caroline and took her hand. Had the news already broke in London this morning? Had her father and the duke been so busy in the morning hours while she had slept?

"Had I known I would never have been so awful," the dark-haired beauty whimpered. "I might have helped you. We could have been like sisters, you and I, both promised to men that we did not love." Caroline bristled at the notion that Lady Lydia had found the duke unlovable but then reminded herself that she ought to be grateful for that fact. It alone had opened the door for their own affections to grow.

Caroline considered the fact that the lady could have been acting out of jealousy. She had heard of Lord Edward's interest in what she had thought was a maid and looked upon it as an insult. Caroline wondered if she had also heard of the growing friendship between that same maid and her betrothed. She supposed that it was reason enough to have been horrible.

Caroline released a slow breath and looked upon the worried features before her. Lady Blackwell was as pristine in her attire as ever but there was a tension in her frame that made Miss Caroline feel for the shock that she must have endured.

"It is no matter," she replied. "All is forgiven."

"Thank you," Lady Lydia bowed her head and pressed her lips to Caroline's knuckles. "When Lord Edward was arrested this morning, I could hardly believe it. Then the whispers started that you had been recovered and that you could lay his entire story bare, a true nightmare." Lady Blackwell sniffled and looked up at Caroline with tear-filled eyes. "To think that you have suffered so. I cannot bear it. I had thought..." she paused. "I had thought that he was good, you know?"

Caroline pressed a calming hand to her guest's shoulder. She had never cared for Lady Blackwell but she could see now that the female had been wronged. She had put her trust in the wrong gentleman. She had been fooled by Lord Edward just as so many had been led into his web of duplicity.

"It will all be set to rights very soon," Caroline promised. She felt a pang of worry that Lady Blackwell might present a hindrance between Caroline and the Duke. He was a man of honor after all. He had made his offer to Lady Blackwell years before and if she asked that he upheld his end of the promise Caroline was not certain that he could refuse. She tried to quell the ache in her heart. Lady Blackwell was not to blame for the fact that Caroline had fallen in love with the duke.

"It certainly will," Lady Blackwell's voice had transformed to cold ice in the matter of an instant. Caroline felt something hard pressing against her ribs and looked down to see the reticule pistol in Lady Lydia's hand.

Caroline's mouth fell agape but she could not make words. She glanced toward the door, wondering if help would arrive in time if she screamed.

"No one is coming," Lady Lydia grinned. "The butler told me that the maids were out and so I had my man lock him in a closet. If anyone else appears, my men have orders to kill." Of course, she would not have come for the visit without her thugs, Caroline realized. Caroline hoped that the housekeeper did not wander down to this level else she too would be taken.

"You'll pay for this," Caroline said through gritted teeth.

"You must be an imbecile to think that your story could take down one as renowned as my Edward," Lady Blackwell spat. "Fortunately, without your side to tell, he shall be released in a matter of days."

Caroline forced her breathing to slow. She needed to think. She needed to have a clear mind so that she could understand what was happening. Lady Lydia had come here to kill her, she realized, to silence her tale and free Lord Edward from the accusation. They were both well aware that well-positioned gentlemen rarely stood trial for their crimes. A conviction would take more than hearsay. It would take a witness. It would require Caroline alive and possibly even more than that.

"Lord Robert will avenge me," Caroline replied with a cool tone that she could not recognize. The steady words did not match the erratic beating of her pulse.

"Lord Robert will be disposed of one way or another," Lady Lydia snarled. "He ought to have done the world a favor and died at sea."

Caroline's fist made contact with Lady Blackwell's face before she had finished the sentence.

"Get up," Lady Lydia demanded as she pressed the back of her free hand to the lip that was already swelling.

"No," Caroline protested. If she were to be killed, it would be done here, where there could be evidence to follow and the memory that Lady Blackwell had made her visit. She would not be carted off to one of hundreds of warehouses on the edge of the Thames as she had been before.

Lady Blackwell grasped Caroline by her arm and hauled her with brute force to her feet. The elder female was so much taller and stronger than Caroline's moderate frame.

"You will obey me," Lydia growled. "You may think that you are the duchess, but that title is mine. By one brother or the next I will not be thwarted. If I have to marry Robert and kill him in our bed, I will have it done. Edward and I will share our victory." Her hand had curled into the hair at the back of Caroline's head and forced Caroline's neck to crane back so that she might look up into the angry gaze above. "We have worked too long for this end for some nobody to come ruin us now."

Caroline cried out, the jerking motion against her neck had shifted all of her weight to her injured leg. She understood with full clarity. Caroline was in Lady Blackwell's way from several angles. She could send Lord Edward to the gallows and force Lady Blackwell to marry a man that she loathed, or Caroline and the duke could die and Lady Blackwell and Lord Edward could see their plot to completion.

Caroline cursed herself for an idiot for not having seen that Lady Lydia had been involved from the start. She had underestimated her adversary. She had wanted to believe that the female had been deceived and innocent. She had thought that Lady Lydia had only been searching for love, for the passion that she had told the duke that she had so desired. Lady Lydia had wanted more than that. She had wanted the title, the wealth, the prestige. She wanted all of the accoutrements of being duchess without the scarred gentleman that came along with the title. She had waited five long years for the prize that she had deemed her due. She wanted it all and the beautiful Lord Edward at her side. Lord Edward had not been saying that Lady Lydia was unaware of their misdealing; only that he did not want her to know about the chaos that had been caused by keeping Caroline alive.

"You have been a thorn in my side ever since you arrived at that house," Lady Blackwell shoved the gun with more force against Caroline's ribcage. "First, Edward lusted after you. He would have never given up without having you. He said that he would, but I knew better." The disgust in her voice was evident, but not at the gentleman, only for the fact that Caroline had presented a temptation. Could Lady Blackwell truly blame Caroline for Lord Edward's inability to calm his own lustful fantasies? "Then we came to learn who you really were. I told him to kill you but he was still so blinded by the idea that you could be turned to his will over time. He should have put a bullet to your head at any time, but he didn't. I won't make that same mistake." Lady Lydia moved the gun from Caroline's waist until it pressed cold against her temple. The grip on her arm still bit against her skin and she wondered if blood were being drawn from Lady Blackwell's sharpened nails. "Do you have any last words?" Lady Lydia crooned. "I could tell Ed that you cried out for him in your last moments. That would pique his fancy. I could play it up for months at the least."

Caroline wanted to rage against her. She wanted to spew obscenities against the beastly Lord Edward and the Lady herself. That he would be aroused by the idea that Caroline might have wanted him was repulsive. That Lady Blackwell would use that tale to whip him into an amorous frenzy was worse.

She did not take even a moment to form a reply. Instead, she stomped her foot, crushing her heel into Lady Blackwell's toes while throwing her shoulder into her captor's midsection at the same time. The movement shot screaming pain through her injured leg, but there was no help for it.

Lady Lydia grunted and the sharp retort of the gunshot echoed through the room. The bullet had flung wide of Caroline's body and shattered the window that led out to the road. Caroline flung herself atop her opponent. Although the shot was spent, they grappled for the gun, rolling and wrestling as they did their best, each to overpower the other. Their gowns were a hindrance, getting caught up between their legs and tripping them as they scrambled over the Oriental rug.

Lady Blackwell shrieked with rage and turned away for what Caroline had thought would be just long enough to gain the upper hand. Rather than make her move, Caroline had been pierced with an unbearable burning in her calf. She screamed. Her vision blackened and her scream echoed through the house. No one was coming, she reminded herself. With great effort she forced her mind back into consciousness. Lady Blackwell gripped Caroline's wounds once more and dug her fingers between the stitches, ripping attempting to rip the wound open. Again, Caroline screamed. She realized that her skirt must have risen up and exposed the injury. That was what had drawn her opponent's expression. Lady Blackwell had taken advantage of the gunshot wound and used Caroline's agony to position herself above her prey.

Lady Blackwell was sitting with one knee at either side of Caroline's waist. Her hand was bleeding profusely, but a moment later, Caroline was looking down the barrel of the small gun. She completely forgot about her bloody leg as she felt a heat rush over her skin. This was the end. She had never known it with such certainty. Even when she had been tied up at the docks and told that she would be killed she had not felt this impending sense of dread. Lady Blackwell brought her second hand to join the other in its grip of the weapon. She steadied herself and took aim.

The gun clicked empty at the same moment that Lady Lydia was pulled without mercy from her perch above Miss Caroline.

Caroline's eyes had been closed tight against the impact that never came.

She opened her eyes and released a shaky breath just in time to see the duke quite literally throw Lady Blackwell at the wall of men who were standing in the doorframe. They subdued the female and dragged her from the room.

Caroline's wide, frightened eyes settled upon the duke who stood above where she lay sprawled on the floor. He had come for her, she realized. He had saved her. She raised her arms to reach for him when she felt another body land across her own and drive the air from her lungs.

A mess of curly hair covered her face and the sound of sobbing came from beneath the unruly pile.

"Oh, my lady," the trembling voice cried. "I thought I might never see you again."

"Marilee!" Caroline squealed. She grasped at the shoulders that were crushing her and pushed the form away enough to look into the face of her beloved maid. "Oh Lud, Marilee," she gasped, "I was so worried."

Marilee hugged her mistress anew and then pulled back to begin checking that Miss Caroline was unharmed. "Oh Lud," she cried out as she realized Caroline's leg was sticky with blood.

"I'm fine," Caroline protested. Caroline cupped the face of her dear friend and pleaded with her eyes for the truth. "They told me that you had been beaten to within an inch of your life," Caroline revealed. "How is it that you are here and seeming well?"

Marilee's eyes darted toward a man who stood upon shifting feet in the doorway beside Caroline's father. Her expression was apologetic as if she had not wished the man to hear such details about her demise. The gesture told Caroline that Marilee had indeed suffered greatly.

A violent scream sounded from the hall where Lady Blackwell was still being made to be restrained.

"My darling friend," Caroline sat upright and brushed a loving hand over Marilee's hair. "I wish I could have protected you."

"Don't be foolish," Marilee replied. "It was my honor to protect you." She wrapped her arms around Caroline's shoulders. "You are my dearest friend," the maid whispered into her ear, "I would have died before I betrayed you." Caroline shook her head against such a thought but Marilee continued on, no longer keeping her voice for only their ears. "As soon as your father recognized me in Lady Blackwell's house, I knew that I was saved."

Caroline glanced up from Marilee's shoulder and into her father's loving gaze. She softened her expression, the full value of her gratitude laid bare. The baron smiled in return and nodded.

"Your duke burst in with such force I thought that for certain it was to be my end," Marilee explained. "But when he said that he was looking for the Lady, one of the other maids said that she had gone to pay her respects to the Duchess of Manchester. I lost my mind," she admitted. "I knew that Lady Blackwell was a demon and to think that you had been freed... only to..." She shook her head. "She could only wish you harm."

Caroline did not comment upon the fact that Marilee had referred to Lord Robert as her duke but she allowed the words to blossom in her heart. A small smile began to grow on her lips even though she realized that she was exhausted and her calf was bleeding.

"You don't have any proof!" Lady Blackwell shrieked from the hall. "Unhand me! She's the one that you want. She tried to poison the duke! Oh Robert, you must believe me."

Caroline huffed with annoyance at the implication. The questioning looks with which she had been met faded away when it became clear from their expressions that neither she nor the duke would support such a claim.

"We do have proof," Marilee muttered. Her eyes darted between Miss Caroline and Lord Robert.

"Our word may not be enough," Caroline breathed with resignation. Lord Edward and Lady Blackwell may still walk free. Their reputations may be tarnished and their fortunes withdrawn, but it was rare that any of their standing might be charged in full.

"Lady Blackwell has Bella," Marilee whispered. "Lord Bennington," meaning Lord Edward, "gifted her the mare as an early wedding present." Caroline noted that Lord Robert did not even flinch at the implication. "He did not seem to have any knowledge that the mare was tied to our abduction."

Caroline could hardly believe her ears. "Oh," she breathed. Her prized horse was still alive, still nearby. She had expected the valued stead to have been sold or shipped to some far-off land. She recalled that the thugs had done their best to smuggle off what items could have been identified as belonging to the late duke. The horse had been hers and hers alone. There would have been no record or word that he possessed such a fine piece of horseflesh. The bill of sale had been in Caroline's name.

The animal amounted to prime evidence of property transfer from the act of robbery. Even if Lord Edward attempted to say that he had purchased the beast without information of its ownership history it would only add to the connections in Caroline's own story. There were too many coincidences for Lord Edward and Lady Blackwell to explain away. With Caroline placed in one home and both Bella and Marilee in the other it would amount to the final nails in the otherwise sealed coffin.

"Take her to the tower and throw her in with the others," the baron declared with a note of authority that Caroline had not heard in ages. The tower of London was where they kept the most hardened of criminals. Was that truly where they were taking her? Caroline wondered, but she could not help but breathe a sigh of relief that the guard had taken the criminals to a secure lockup. If she never saw any of them again, she would be glad. With Bella as proof of their wrongdoing, this would be no easy matter for the criminals to wheedle out of now.

"I will end you!" Lady Lydia's voice came one last time before the sound of the front door closed in the distance. She must have realized that she was well and truly caught. Her shouts of profanity could be heard even from the street. As the carriage rolled away, Lady Lydia's cries carried off into the distance.

It was only then that Caroline realized that she was still sprawled out on the floor with Marilee flung out beside her and her calf had dripped blood on the carpet. The maid scrambled to her feet and offered Miss Caroline a hand. Caroline reached up to accept the aid, but the duke had already bent down and picked her up from beneath her arms and set her quite firmly upon her own two feet.

When he made a move to step away, to follow her father and the other men that were exiting the room, Miss Caroline placed a hand upon his forearm to stop him. She needed the duke nearby. His presence at her side had bolstered her strength she found that she could not bear the thought of him leaving. Besides, her leg was aching something fierce and still dripping blood from Lydia's mistreatment of her.

Marilee's eyes had once again met with the quiet gentleman who stood at the edge of the room. Caroline nodded and gave her maid permission to go to the man. When she had, Caroline noted that he had placed his hand upon the small of Marilee's back in a supportive and possessive gesture.

The baron lingered within the doorway, staring at his daughter and the duke. With a solemn nod to the duke her father too made his exit. "I think I should find the doctor," he said shutting the doors behind him although there were servants who could go for the physician. Caroline wondered at the fact that he had so easily left them alone. It seemed that the duke and the baron had come to some understanding of one another during their acquaintance, a mutual respect.

"What happened?" she turned to face Lord Robert with a thousand questions in her eyes. "How did you come to be here just in time?"

The duke took her hand and noticed her abused calf. "This will have to be stitched again," he said as he drew her toward the couch so that she could sit. Caroline gave a small groan, but truly, it was a small price to pay. After all, she was alive, and with the duke. He wrapped her leg with his handkerchief with infinite care. "Put pressure right there," he said, and she nodded, holding the wound. They sat side by side, as he began to explain how he had come to be her rescuer.

"Mr. Crowley is a solicitor," he said in an even tone that began to calm the unease within her. "We were together at Eton and he is an old friend." He explained that he had tasked the man with looking into his brother's affairs. "Nothing seemed out of sorts until he informed me in strict confidence that he was in the process of enforcing substantial debts against Lady Blackwell's father. He had wanted me to know the truth of her financial situation since we were promised to be wed." Through their conversations, and the revelation that Lady Blackwell had been having an affair with Lord Edward, it soon became apparent that the money that Lord Edward had been attempting to hide had been funneled through Lady Blackwell's accounts.

She had been paying her debts in large sums through undisclosed sources.

"The women that they were selling?" Caroline gasped.

The duke nodded. "That and the items sold from a series of robberies of several noblemen."

"There have been more murders?" she asked in shock.

"Not that we are aware of at this moment," he revealed. "Or, at least none that we can pin on the group, save my father and his men."

"That still does not explain how you arrived that the precise moment of my need."

"I'm getting there." He tucked a stray lock of hair behind her ear and Caroline found herself pressing her face against his palm. "Your father, Mr. Crowley, and I met the guard at Lord Blackwell's house only to find that his daughter was out. Your maid happened to pass by in the hall and your father recognized her at once." Caroline learned that the quiet man beside her father had been that very same Mr. Crowley. In his visits to the Blackwell home to collect the debts he had come to be close enough with Marilee that his suspicions had been raised, although the maid had been just as tight-lipped as Caroline herself. They had pressed the staff with questions and it had not taken long to discover where Lady Blackwell had gone. Under the threat of the law, her own lady's maid had revealed that Lady Lydia had learned of Lord Edward's arrest and in a frenzied state gone to pay a visit to the newly recovered Duchess of Manchester. "Your maid told us that she had taken a pistol in her reticule and it was all that we could do to get here in time."

"You certainly did," Caroline reveled at their good fortune.

"It is all unraveling," he informed her. "The servants are talking. My brother's misdeeds go back several years and stretch well across the city. We were able to discover which rookery you had been taken to, and they were able to bring Madam Mildred in as well. So many of the ladies in her house were drugged and unwilling."

Caroline closed her eyes against the horror of such thoughts. Was any woman willing to settle for such a life? She wondered. She did not think so, but she did not protest. She felt infinitely tired now that all the excitement had passed, and she leaned against the duke's very solid and warm shoulder as he told the tale.

He took a deep breath and continued on. "My brother and Lydia had made many promises for when they had taken over the title, my title, but now that their companions could see that was never to happen, they all turned against one another."

CHAPTER 27

Caroline listened with her head drooping. She blinked up at the duke. The evidence was astounding. There would be no way that Lord Edward and Lady Lydia could escape the gallows, or at the very least transportation.

"Then we are safe?" she whispered, afraid to allow herself to hope.

"We're safe," he nodded and allowed himself a small smile. "You're safe. I won't let anything else happen to you."

His words were a boon to her heart. All that she had ever wanted was for this nightmare to be over. She had thought that the battle would be long and likely ineffective. With the network of criminals all racing to lay the blame on one another the entire system was about to come crashing down. To add to her ease, Marilee had been recovered and seemed to have found a protector of her own. Caroline could hardly have asked for a better end.

She had been lost in her wonder so much so that she had not even noticed the duke looking down upon her with an overflowing of pain in his eyes.

"What is it?" she asked.

His hands tightened around her arm and his eyes searched her face as if he were unable to believe that she was sitting here beside him. "I did not think we would make it back in time," he admitted with a trembling breath. "We heard the gunshot from the road and I was certain that you were dead."

"I was certain that I was dead as well," she whispered. "In that last moment, when you pulled her off of me, I thought I had died. I did not understand until I opened my eyes and you were there."

"I might have been a bit rough with her," he said with a grimace.

Caroline scoffed. She did not care how rough he had treated Lady Lydia. He could have thrown her attacker out the window, and Caroline would not have cared.

"She chose that life, and you saved my life," Caroline said. As she spoke, she watched the relief pour over his features.

"I was worried that you would be afraid of me," he said as he looked down upon their hands. Caroline released her grip and moved to cup his chin so that he would be forced to look into her eyes.

"I could never be afraid of you," she promised. "I was only grateful. You saved me."

"Then we are even," he offered with a shrug. "For you most certainly saved me."

Caroline grinned up at him. "I suppose I can accept that," she teased. "I would hate to have one up on you for the rest of our lives."

He stilled as he processed her words. "Do you mean that?"

Caroline bit her lip. "I mean—"

She had never meant to have been the first to have mentioned a desire for a future with the duke. It was not seemly. Wasn't a man supposed to make such statements? She knew that, but she supposed she had never been a conventional woman. It would not do to change now. She could only be honest, since their relationship had started with so many lies. Now, she would tell the unbridled truth.

"With every fiber of my being," she admitted after deciding that the cat was well out of the bag and there was no point in playing the shy maid.

The duke's face broke out into a beatific grin, and he wrapped his arms around her without fair warning. Caroline squealed with delight when he pulled her onto his lap. He kissed her with all the claiming of a brand and she returned his favor. They languished in one another for a long while, hands and mouths exploring and claiming for their own.

When the duke finally came up for air Caroline found herself laughing against him with what little breath she had recovered. "What?" she asked. He was looking at her as if he had never seen her before. His fingers trailed along the embroidery at her knee, the fine fabric and elegant cut unlike anything he had ever seen her wear. He must have only just recognized the change. "This is very fine," he said.

"This is what I usually look like," she informed him.

"I like it," he replied in a voice far too throaty to be the result of anything but the deepest desire. Caroline basked in the praise. She had never cared what others thought of her looks, but she found the fact that the duke thought her appealing to be the most potent drug of all.

"Thank you," she grinned. "Does that mean you'll keep it?" By it, she had meant her, but he knew that. The duke had yet to make an offer but Caroline felt that it was safe to assume that he wanted to. The gentleman was far too used to being rejected, she thought. It could take him ages to work up the nerve to ask her the question, and she wasn't willing to wait.

"Keep it?" he repeated.

"Yes," she said. "Keep me."

"Can I keep you?" he murmured, his eyes full of hope and wonder.

Caroline pursed her lips to one side and tilted her head. "I simply don't know," she hemmed. "I would have to be asked, you know. That is generally how these things play out, or so I am told."

"I've already asked your father," he blurted in such a way that he seemed to have shocked even himself.

Caroline's mouth fell open. She had enjoyed teasing him but she had not expected that.

He went down on one knee in front of her. "I love you, Caroline," he professed when it seemed she was unable to speak. "I don't know if you want me; if you feel the same, but I must speak, and speak now. I can wait for a proper courtship, but I want you to know my intentions. I've wanted you for a long time. I don't know when it first began because I spent ages trying to convince myself that it could never be. Even if I was allowed some dispensation to marry a maid, I could not have children with you, not if you were a commoner, but now—" His face broke into a beatific smile.

Children, Caroline thought. Of course, children. He would want an heir. The thought made her blush and a heat settled in the pit of her stomach.

"When you told me who you really were," he continued, "it was only then that I began to hope." His eyes were breaking something in her soul. It was as if he were begging to be loved but unable to believe that she would even consider such a thing. "I've thought I lost you so many times now that I cannot imagine another moment not knowing if there might be any chance that you could feel the same." He raked one hand through his hair, mussing it and a manner that she found most appealing. It was a nervous habit she realized but endearing all the same. "I know that you care for me in some way or else you wouldn't kiss me the way that you do, and I told your father that you might need time but I'm willing to wait if that's what you need to be certain." He was rambling in his nervous state, but Caroline could not bring herself to stop him. The sound of his voice was like music. Her heart had ached to hear every word that was now spilling from his mouth. "I don't know if you could ever love me, but all that I am asking is that you'll consider it."

"I do love you," she broke in when she could no longer bear his need to argue his case. "I don't need any convincing, and I don't need time. I've loved you for…" she searched her memory for the moment, "I don't know how long either because I too had told myself that it could never be. After all, I was married to your father, if only in name."

"Oh, he began, brushing off the thought with a nonchalant hand.

"And I lied to you," she said softly.

"You had no choice," he forgave her.

"It was only when you knew who I was and did not hate me for my deceit that I began to hope as well."

The duke released a shaky breath as if he feared that a sound might shatter the dream in which they were living.

Caroline reached out to take his chin with both hands, as always unbothered by the scar that was now so natural beneath her palm. She had her own scars now.

He leaned close and their lips met in a searing kiss. All of the passion they had stored up in the past months seemed to bubble forth like a tsunami. She kissed him. Once, twice, and when they heat of that encounter threatened to overcome them both, she pulled away breathless.

"I love you, Robert Bennington," she said so that there could be no confusion, "and I want nothing more than to be your wife."

The duke kissed her softly then without another word. He required nothing more to show Caroline the true depth of his feeling. She could feel his smile against her mouth and felt a deep satisfaction that she had been the one to make him happy. Caroline threw her arms around his neck and pulled him close, reveling in the scent of him and murmuring her love to him over and over. If she had to tell him ten times a day so that he would always believe, that was a task she was willing to complete.

A long while later they were still holding one another close as they made their plans for the future. The duke had vowed to sell his townhome on Park Lane and buy another. As Lizzy had mentioned when she had implied that the house had been cursed, he felt that the current location carried too many bad memories. Caroline liked the idea of making a new location their own. He had also told her all about Heatherton Hall. His father and his brother had taken little pleasure in the country setting. He and his mother had been the only ones who had enjoyed spending time at the estate nearly equidistant between Northwick and the smaller village of Wollington. Caroline thought that it sounded like a small paradise.

"I have to ask," he said when her fingers had drifted beneath the collar of his shirt to wander along his skin. "Are you certain that my scars do not bother you?" he inquired.

She hated that he felt the need to ask but understood his reasons. Had not Lady Lydia promised to love him and then been repulsed when the thought of living with his disfigurement had become a reality?

"Not in the least," she had replied in earnest. Her fingers drifted behind his neck and kneaded the knotted muscles there. He closed his eyes and sighed with pleasure. "Besides, I now have two new scars of my own." She raised the offending leg out in front of them and pointed her toe. The gesture was meant to remind him of the entrance and exit of the bullet wound on her calf that was now well hidden beneath her gown and stockings.

"New?" he wondered as he settled his hand below her knee and massaged the ache that he must have known was in her leg. He stayed well clear of the wound but soothed the muscles that had been forced to compensate for her injury. "Are you telling me that there are old scars as well?"

"One," she admitted.

"Oh?" His hand was distracting her. She had closed her eyes to enjoy the relief, but the sound had brought her back to their conversation.

"It is approximately the size of my palm," she said, holding her hand out before him so that he might gauge the circumference. "I acquired it in a riding accident when I was seven years old. I was thrown by a horse named Mayhem and landed upon a jagged rock." The duke halted in his ministrations and Caroline bobbed her knee to remind him to continue. He did as he was bid, and she continued her story. "The flesh was peeled back on three sides and although they tried to lay it flat and allow it to heal back together the edges still formed a large curve. My mother used to say that Mayhem had marked with the shoe of a horse.

"Mayhem," the duke laughed despite her harrowing tale, "a fitting name for such a horse, I am sure." Caroline's tone had revealed that she was unbothered by the ordeal and so he had not seen fit to coddle. She appreciated his response.

"Not really," she grinned. "He was mild mannered most of the time, but reared something fierce whenever he spied a snake."

"I see." Caroline's betrothed looked up at her with a devilish grin. "And may I be so bold as to ask where this scar is located?"

"No, you may not." She emphasized each word in her pert reply.

The duke exclaimed with mock outrage. "But My Lady, you have seen most of mine," he teased.

She blushed most profusely and he chuckled.

Caroline could not deny that she was aware of the locations of most of the duke's scarring. Her flesh heated with the memory of when she had allowed herself to trail her fingers across the wide expanse of his back. She had also followed the long scar that made a dive down into the collar of his shirt. She did not know how Lady Lydia had been repulsed by it. Caroline ran her fingers over that same location now. If anything, the mark was like an arrow beckoning her to explore what was beneath the fabric that covered his magnificent form.

The duke seemed to read where her thoughts had gone because his voice was husky when he said he would look forward to finding out where her own scar was located.

Caroline pulled her hand away from its devilish explorations. Her only response to his question was a sideways glance that very clearly indicated that he would have to wait to discover its location for himself.

"Oh, you are wicked," he growled as he wrapped his arms around her and pulled her more firmly against him. His lips met hers with a promise—a promise of his love and protection, a promise of the future that they would build together, and also a promise in response to her challenge. She might not yet tell him where her own scar was hidden, but he had every intention of finding out.

EPILOGUE

A year later, Lady Caroline Bennington, the Duchess in every sense of the word, had just finished tying the last of the red velvet bows that held the trail of pine boughs to the banister of the main staircase in Heatherton Hall. Her father would arrive in the morning and so would no less than twenty other guests that she had been aching to meet. The duke's men, most with wives and children, were coming to congratulate their friend on his nuptials. Some had been long delayed by the war, and the duke wanted to celebrate with those who recently returned from their service to the Crown. Although Caroline and Robert had exchanged vows over six months prior much of their public celebrations had been put on hold until after the sentencing of his brother and the others involved in the string of crimes that had brought Caroline and the duke together. No less than thirty-seven women had been granted their freedom with more being recovered every day. That process however had not kept them from having their own personal celebrations, she thought with a private grin. Still, she had been relieved to know that none of the criminals, those that had been allowed to keep their lives, would ever set foot on English soil again.

"What is that smile?" The duke asked with a cheery expression of his own. He came up behind his wife, wrapped his arms about her slender waist, and kissed her upon the cheek.

"I was only thinking how happy I have been these months," she replied and turned in his arms to greet him more fully. The duke sighed contentedly pressed a kiss to her lips.

"Crowley found us a townhouse," he revealed between kisses. "Marilee has already inspected it and said that you will find it just as you like."

Caroline hummed against him. She was hopeful that her maid would find her own happy ending, or perhaps she already had. Caroline was now in search of a reliable lady's maid but was glad that her dear friend could be a doting wife to a respectable man.

"Then I know I shall love it," she replied. "Marilee has impeccable taste. Make an offer."

"Don't you want to see it for yourself?" he laughed. "We could go in a month, after the new year."

Caroline looked up into her husband's eyes and shook her head. "I don't think I should be traveling in the winter," she replied.

"Why not?" he asked. "The roads from here to London are well maintained. We ought to see the house before we make an offer."

"I do not think that I will be travelling for some time," she said as she placed her hand upon her still flat stomach. "I want to stay in the country for the birth of our child."

The duke whooped with joy and pulled Caroline straight off her feet as he spun her about in the hall. His raucous cheers brought the staff out from every corner of the house. Even Lizzy, who had proven a quick study under the watchful gaze of her mother's tutelage, made her appearance. The future house-keeper cheered and promised that she would prepare the new townhouse with everything that the duchess would possibly need for herself and the baby.

Caroline threw her head back and laughed at the purity of the joy that surrounded her. Never had she suspected that life could be this wonderful. This time last year she had not known whether she would live to see another day. Now, she was preparing to bring another life into the world and she knew beyond a doubt that this child would be protected and, more than anything, well-loved.

CONTINUE READING FOR A SNEAK PEEK OF...

The Mayfair Maid
Spinsters of the North, book 2
by Isabella Thorne

**She's been kidnapped. He's hiding his true identity.
Can Love really conquer all?**

Miss Marilee Pelletier is a confirmed spinster. After all, lady's maids do not marry. They do not have romance in their lives except vicariously through their ladies. Marilee loves her mistress, Miss Caroline… and her work.

Until she is kidnapped by the people who murdered a duke, people who don't care about her well-being.

Marilee is separated from her friends and family… Locked down under house arrest… And treated as a slave rather than a person. Marilee wonders if there can be a happily ever after for her. When all she loves has been left behind. Can love really conquer all?

To cover his debts, Mr. Nikolas Harding threw in with some very bad people. Now, he can't get out. He finds himself attracted to the lovely new maid, Miss Marilee

Pellitier, but what does he have to offer her? He can't even give her his true name. Mr. Nikolas Harding has an alias, Mr. Nikolas Crawley.

Marilee moved about the room and lit the lamps, glancing at the man from under her lashes. Honestly, it was like this entire house lacked any sort of decency. Next, she crouched in front of the dying embers and prodded the fire back to life before adding a bit of kindling for good measure. If nothing else, Lady Lydia would appreciate the warmth of the room whenever she finally made her appearance. If she made an appearance.

The tea arrived just as Marilee completed her tasks. She stood next to the fire, glancing at it occasionally to be sure it stayed lit. Ella offered a pitying glance at the solicitor before she made a silent exit.

"Mr. Crawley," Marilee made a sweeping gesture toward the tray. He stopped in his tracks and looked down at the offering with his mouth drawn in a tight line. Then, he turned to Marilee.

Marilee felt somewhat embarrassed and heat flooded her cheeks. This was the same young man who had happened upon her whilst spying through a door. She felt the blood rise in her cheeks when he recognized her.

"You again!" he laughed.

"So, it would appear," she murmured.

"Spying again?" he asked.

"Of course not, and I wasn't spying!" she argued before she could collect herself. "Not the first time, nor now," she said as she crossed her arms.

He seemed to accept her admission but the small quirk in his grin revealed that if given the chance he might tease her for that moment further. Marilee knew she ought to be mortified but there was something in his ease, something kindred, that settled her into enjoying the jest. Smiles were rare enough in this house.

"If I *had* been spying," she continued, "I would have been sure not to make the same mistake twice."

"Trip over an ash bucket?" he laughed. "I do not see one nearby. You are quite safe."

"That," she agreed, "Or be seen at all."

"Oh? Then, you are here with purpose?" he wondered aloud, to which Marilee simply shrugged.

What was she meant to say? That Lady Lydia had the full intention of wasting his time simply for spite? That she had no idea why she had been sent down here or what she was to do to occupy a stranger for an hour or more while the lady played her games?

"The lady told me to come," she said, knowing how unusual this was.

He raised an eyebrow. "Did she say how long?" he asked without preamble. Oh, he was smart, she thought. Smart and handsome if she dared to admit. He had light brown hair and watchful warm chestnut eyes that at once told her, if his words had not, that he did not miss much.

"Would you like some tea?" she continued as if she had not heard.

"How long am I to wait this time?" he asked again somewhat testily.

Marilee bit her lower lip and wondered if it would be prudent to lie. His eyebrows raised as he awaited her reply, assessing her. She sighed.

"An hour at least, I am sure," she finally admitted. "But…"

"I didn't hear it from you," he interjected with a nod, and turned back to the tea tray.

Very smart, she thought. Then, as if appeased by the fact that she had shown him enough respect to be honest, he moved to sit and pour two cups of tea. Marilee remained by the fireside and watched him. Marilee had not expected two cups when she had asked the other maid for tea. The tear was for guests.

"Come," he declared and pushed a cup and saucer toward her. "You might as well sit. I am guessing you have been tasked with the burden of my company."

She glanced toward the door, wondering how Peggy was getting on without her and how late they would have to work to keep the pace.

"If you leave now, Lady Lydia will not receive the full pleasure of her slight," he said with a deep chuckle. "Anyway, I'm sure tea and biscuits are not your usual fare. Sit with me and enjoy them." He patted a seat beside him, but she had no intention of sitting so close to a man while unchaperoned, even if in this house chaperones seemed to be in short supply.

She noted his smile. He was amused! At her? At Lady Lydia? Any man in their right mind would be furious at Lady Lydia's posturing, but Mr. Crawley seemed to have expected it and decided to thwart the lady by appearing to enjoy himself. Marilee suppressed a grin. No wonder Lady Lydia did not like the man, he surely seemed unaffected by the lady's charms and maneuvering. She would not take kindly to anyone who did not fall easily into her pocket.

Even though he had patted the settee next to him, Marilee chose a perch across from him and as far away as was possible. She thought it was prudent since the man's very gaze seemed to rob her of sense and make her heart beat extraordinarily fast. She watched him over the rim of her cup while he picked at the biscuits on the tray and sipped his own cup of tea.

"My name is Nikolas," he mentioned in such an offhand way, so lacking formality, that Marilee nearly spat out her tea at the unorthodox introduction. On the other hand, there was no one about to introduce them.

"And yours?" he asked.

"Err." She stumbled over the question, and stuttered, nearly offering the man her true name. She evaluated him in that moment. She felt she could trust him, but really, could she? He watched her without guile. With purpose, she collected herself Finally, she said one word, "Kate."

"Well, Kate," he laughed to himself, "Lady Lydia would do better to saddle me with that crass old butler next time if she wants to punish me. You aren't so terrible."

Marilee raised her eyebrows in shock. It was not much by way of a compliment, but it was amusing just the same. She gave a short laugh despite herself, but stifled it immediately. "So nice to know that my countenance is likened to Smyth's. I'll try to be more forbidding next time," she promised.

He chuckled heartily.

She did not know if there would be a next time, but she found the thought pleasing. She hoped there would be a next time.

Would you like to be notified when my next novel is published?

Click Here to Join my VIP Readers!

The Lady to Match a Rogue ~ Faith

Nettlefold Chronicles

Not Quite a Lady; Not Quite a Knight

Stitched in Love

Other Novels by Isabella Thorne

The Mad Heiress and the Duke ~ Miss Georgette Quinby

The Duke's Wicked Wager ~ Lady Evelyn Evering

Short Stories by Isabella Thorne

Love Springs Anew

The Mad Heiress' Cousin and the Hunt

Mischief, Mayhem and Murder: A Marquess of Evermont

Mistletoe and Masquerade ~ 2-in-1 Short Story Collection

Colonial Cressida and the Secret Duke ~ A Short Story

Would you like to be notified of new releases, and special updates from Isabella?

Sign up for my VIP Reader List!
Receive Weekly Regency Romance Top Picks
and an EXCLUSIVE FREE STORY

Click Here to Join Isabella Thorne's VIP Readers

WANT EVEN MORE REGENCY ROMANCE...

Follow Isabella Thorne on BookBub
or
Visit my Amazon Author Page

www.isabellathorne.com

Please Like Isabella Thorne on Facebook
https://www.facebook.com/isabellathorneauthor/